An
Unexpected Gift

by

Katherine Grey

This is a work of fiction. Names, characters, places, and incidents are either the product of the author's imagination or are used fictitiously, and any resemblance to actual persons living or dead, business establishments, events, or locales, is entirely coincidental.

An Unexpected Gift

Cover Art by *Rae Monet, Inc. Design*

The Wild Rose Press, Inc.
PO Box 708
Adams Basin, NY 14410-0708
Visit us at www.thewildrosepress.com

Publishing History
First English Tea Rose Edition, 2013
Print ISBN 978-1-61217-688-8
Digital ISBN 978-1-61217-689-5

Published in the United States of America

Olivia backed up until she hit the edge of the desk. Afraid to take her gaze from him, she reached for some type of weapon. From what the Bow Street Runner had told her, Lazarus could be dangerous. She just never expected him to hurt her.

Her fingers closed over a paperweight shaped like an apple. It was small but heavy, being fashioned from sterling silver. Could she use it to cosh him over the head if necessary?

As though he had read her thoughts, he grabbed her hand and forced the trinket from her grasp with ease. He turned it over in his hand, tossed it up in the air, and caught it. "You weren't thinking to hit me in the brain box with this, were you, Olivia?"

"Don't be ridiculous." She hoped the tremor in her voice didn't give away her fear. Leaning back to put as much space between them as possible, she cleared her throat, gathered her courage, and continued on as any good soldier would. "I do believe I haven't given you leave to use my Christian name."

"Surely after seeing me without a shirt, not to mention having your hands all over my body, we are beyond formality at this point." He tossed the paperweight onto the desk, his eyes alight with laughter.

"My hands..." she sputtered. He made it sound as though they had been intimate when nothing could be further from the truth. She'd cared for his injury, nothing more. "You are no gentleman to say such things."

His smile disappeared, and his gaze turned serious. "I've never claimed to be one. It is best you remember that."

Praise for Katherine Grey

Also by Katherine Grey:
Impetuous
The Muse
available from The Wild Rose Press, Inc.

~*~

IMPETUOUS
"I found it a very refreshing read! Great for regency lovers. It will definitely make you a fan of Katherine Grey."

~Romancing the Book

~*~

THE MUSE
"If you are looking for a quick, sweet historical; this would be a good choice…"

~ Night Owl Reviews

~*~

Note: Lazarus (the hero) in *An Unexpected Gift* is a major secondary character in her short story *The Muse*, released as part of the *Love Letters* series.

Dedication

To my mother,
who made do with so little so I could have so much
and who taught me that anything is possible
if you put your mind to it.
I love you, Mom.

Chapter One

"Are you certain they asked for Sir Phillip?" Olivia St. Germaine stopped mid-stride at the sight of the two men in the foyer. They seemed on the verge of an argument, the sound of harsh whispers filling the air.

"Yes, they were most insistent." Jennings, the family butler, looked ill at ease.

Olivia studied the men as they stood unaware. Both were dressed well enough, but not in the latest fashion. The shorter of the two wore brown from head to toe with the exception of black gloves. The other was dressed all in black. Though he blended in with the shadowy area near the front door, he commanded her attention.

As though sensing her presence, their conversation came to an abrupt halt, and the man dressed in brown stepped forward. "We need ta see St. Germaine."

"My brother is not at home, and I am not certain when he will return to London. If you would like to leave your cards..." She let the sentence trail away, hoping they would do as she suggested. Something about the two men unnerved her more than she cared to admit.

"I willna be put off." The man in brown scanned the hall, then the staircase. "Stop hidin' behind the skirts of a woman, ya coward," he shouted. "I've come to collect yer debt." His voice boomed off the high ceiling.

Incensed, Olivia strode closer. "My brother is no coward. And I am no liar. He is not in residence. I suggest you take your leave."

"Lazarus doesna take orders from anyone."

The man's companion put a hand on his shoulder and tried to steer him toward the door.

"Then, Mr. Lazarus, perhaps you should heed your friend." Olivia noted the Scottish burr running through his words. She eyed him with speculation.

Did their presence have anything to do with Phillip's recent journey to the Highlands and his sudden decision to leave London without a word to her where he was going? The Lord himself knew Phillip St. Germaine had his vices, but they weren't the sort to cause a man to flee the city. Not when he often claimed it was the boredom of country life that caused one to age, not the passing of years. What kind of debt could he have possibly incurred in Scotland that would bring men such as these to their home?

"I am Lazarus," the other man said.

Olivia looked at him, noting the sheen of perspiration on his brow, his labored breathing, the way he held himself. He was injured. She knew the signs. Knew what to look for, much to her regret.

He stared back at her, his eyes a deep black and clouded with pain. His gaze was mesmerizing. For long moments, she stared at him. Olivia blinked, took a strangely shaky breath, and broke the spell he'd cast over her. All of her instincts clamoured for her to get them out of the house.

"Jennings, please show these gentlemen out." She turned on her heel and headed back to the library.

"Stop!"

She ignored the shout and kept walking. The sound of a gunshot filled the foyer. Her heart in her throat, she turned around. Bits of plaster filled the air, drifting down like tiny snowflakes to settle on the floor. She looked upward, her nose wrinkling at the familiar scent of gunpowder. The once pristine ceiling was now marred by a bullet hole.

The gunman tossed the spent pistol aside. It clattered across the marble floor, stopping inches from where Jennings stood, frozen with fear, his mouth open.

Withdrawing another gun from his coat, the stranger pointed it at Olivia.

She stared at it. The light from the chandelier overhead gleamed on the metal barrel. She glanced at the man known as Lazarus. He watched her, his expression unreadable. A trembling started deep within her stomach and spread outward until she was certain they could hear the vibrations of her bones if they but listened.

Gathering her courage, she cleared her throat. "If you mean to ransom me, you've chosen the wrong victim. I hold no titles. If you know my brother as you claim, you should be aware that he is a mere knight, given the honour due to his service to the crown. We have no great wealth."

Lazarus grabbed the gunman's wrist. "St. Germaine isn't here. He would have come running at the sound of the shot." He closed his eyes for a moment and took a deep breath. "We need to leave. Now," he said, his voice strained.

The gunman gazed at him in silent communication, his lips compressed into a thin line. After a moment, he nodded. "Verra well."

"We apologize..." Lazarus swallowed, gave a slight shake of his head as his hand crept up to his side. "...for the interruption."

Olivia dipped her head in acceptance, eager to see them leave.

Lazarus turned toward the door, his gait unsteady. He took another step and fell to his knees. A low groan escaped his lips. He laid a hand on the marble floor, his breathing harsh.

She rushed forward, habits of old coming to the fore without conscious thought.

The gunman stepped in front of him, his pistol aimed at her. "Stay where you be."

"He is injured."

"He is nae injured."

Putting both hands on the floor, Lazarus tried to rise without success. The hand that had clutched his side was covered in blood. Drops of crimson fell from under his coat onto the marble tiles in a steady stream.

"I can help him," she said.

"You know the healin' arts?" the gunman asked, his skepticism evident.

"I wouldn't call it an art. My brother spent a great number of years on the battlefield caring for wounded soldiers. I assisted him at times when those who were injured outnumbered the surgeons available." She glanced at Lazarus. His face was slick with sweat, his eyes closed against the pain. "Let me help him."

"Do you...know how to...care for a bullet...wound?" he panted.

"Yes. One tends to see a great many bullet wounds in battlefield hospitals." She tried not to think of it. At times it had seemed so hopeless. So many had needed attending. It felt as though she had tried to hold back a wall of blood and severed limbs with nothing more than a kind word and a single bandage.

Squeezing her eyes shut, she pressed her fingers to her forehead in an attempt to rub the images away. She shouldn't have offered to tend his wound. She couldn't help him. What if he died? She didn't think she could bear the loss of another person she believed she could help, but in the end had only prolonged his pain before death took him.

Forcing the memories back down into the darkness, she took a deep breath and let it out slowly. With a nonchalance she was far from feeling, she stepped closer to the gunman. "If you will not let me help him, then at least let me have my coach brought around. You may take it where ever you wish, but he needs aid and quickly."

The gunman watched her for a long moment. "Help him."

Olivia released a breath and turned to Jennings. "Hurry, we must get him to Sir Phillip's infirmary."

The butler didn't move. It was almost as though he'd turned to stone.

"Jennings!"

He jumped and rushed to her side. Between the two men, they carried the injured man to the small room off to the side of the stairs and laid him on the cot her brother used when examining patients.

She tried not to think about the last time she'd been in the room. It had been two long years and yet, not nearly long enough. Her brother had been disappointed by her decision, but he never let her know it by word or deed. She turned to Jennings. "Have Bridget bring hot water and bandages."

"There be one more thing, mate," the gunman said, addressing the butler. "If you or anyone else sends for the Watch…" He pressed the muzzle of the pistol against her chest, and Olivia froze. "…she'll be dead afore they get here."

Jennings gave a slow, careful nod, then hurried from the room.

"I need to get my medical case," Olivia said, working hard to keep her voice from quivering.

The gunman released her. "Do nae dawdle, or I will be comin' for ye."

She went straight to her room and the battered chest pushed against the far wall. Sinking to her knees, she reached for the latch, then hesitated. Could she bear to open it and let all the memories she'd locked inside escape? She'd packed them away along with everything else related to that part of her life. A life that haunted her still.

Knowing there was no other alternative, she opened the lid and lifted out her medical kit. Her fingers trembled at the touch of the cool leather case. She wanted to shove it back inside and slam the lid closed, but she couldn't. A wounded man needed her help, and she could delay no longer without risking the wrath of his companion.

She pulled a plain blue dress that buttoned up the front from the bottom of the trunk and quickly changed out of her gown. Rolling the sleeves to her elbows, she took a deep breath and held it, then picked up the medical kit and left the room.

She stopped in the doorway of the infirmary.

Bridget had laid a stack of clean cotton cloths on the bedside table along with a basin of hot water. She crossed the room and filled another basin sitting on the credenza.

As though sensing her presence, she met Olivia's gaze, concern in her eyes. Bridget, more than anyone else, knew what tonight would cost her. With a nod of understanding, the maid carried the empty pitcher from the room followed by Jennings.

The gunman crossed the room, grabbed Olivia by the arm, and dragged her into the hall.

Taken by surprise, she didn't have time to fight him before he came to a halt and called after Bridget and Jennings. "Turn around."

They froze for a moment, Jennings's shoulders hunching to his ears, then turned as one to face the gunman. Bridget tried to hide her anxiety, but it was there in her gaze. Olivia, too, was afraid of what the gunman would do next. Jennings looked like an oversized frightened rabbit, his nose twitching in fear. He would be no help in a confrontation. She would have to bide her time and hope for the best.

"Remember my warnin'. Any sign of the Watch or a Bow Street Runner and she'll nae see the dawn."

The two servants stared in horror as he dragged her back into the room. Once inside, he released her and moved back to stand guard over his companion.

Olivia rubbed her arm, knowing she would have a bruise in the morning. She used the gesture to play for time. She had to get rid of the jittery feeling that threatened her usual iron self-control. If she fell apart now, she could place the entire household in danger.

Assuming a confident air, she strode toward the

bed and set her medical case on the table. Her patient lay on his back, his hand pressed against his side. His gaze tracked her movements with a determination she couldn't help but admire. Most men would have lost consciousness long ago.

The gunman stood near the head of the bed, watchful and alert. His pistol had disappeared, but she knew he held it close.

She opened the cabinet in the corner of the room and removed a spoon and a small brown bottle. "I'm going to give you laudanum. It will allow me to tend you without causing you pain."

Lazarus held up his hand in an effort to ward her off. "No."

"I don't want to cause you unnecessary distress while I'm tending to your wound."

"No laudanum. I need my wits about me."

"But—"

"Do as he says," the gunman ordered.

Olivia set the bottle and spoon on the table with more force than necessary. Both men seemed determined to make the already difficult task ahead of her even more so. She took a deep breath and closed her eyes, needing a moment to calm her nerves and steady her hands.

"What are ye doin'?"

She opened her eyes. "Praying," she answered, though if it was for the man lying before her or herself, she wasn't certain.

Without another word, she unfastened his shirt and pulled it away from the wound. Her attention was drawn to the small hole at his side, a few inches below his ribs. It wasn't large, no bigger than the circumference of her finger. She picked up one of the bandages Bridget had left and pressed it against his side in an effort to staunch the flow of blood.

White lines of pain bracketed his mouth, but he didn't utter a sound. Olivia felt the unexplainable urge to brush the ink-black hair from his forehead, to tell him it would be all right. Realizing he watched her the way a cat stalks a mouse, she gave him a weak smile, hoping he hadn't been able to discern her thoughts, and looked down at her hands.

She lifted the wad of cloth, relieved to see the bleeding had slowed. Dropping it into the pail by the bed, she leaned forward to better examine the wound.

Tiny fibers sat at the edge of the circular hole. They would have to be removed first. She couldn't take the chance of one of them causing an infection. Picking up a clean pad, she swallowed, hating the thought of the pain she would cause when she extracted the bullet. Olivia took a pair of forceps from the medical kit.

One by one she removed the tiny pieces of linen. Wiping away the welling of blood, she probed the bullet hole to see if the lead ball sat close to the surface. Lazarus flinched, his breath hissing through his teeth.

"Would you help me move him onto his side?" She glanced up at his protector.

The gunman moved to the side of the bed and helped her roll the patient over.

The back of his shirt was blood soaked. Pulling the material upward, she found what she was looking for. A similar wound, though larger in size.

"The ball passed through his body." She looked over her shoulder at the gunman. "I don't think there is any internal damage."

He nodded.

Olivia thought she saw a hint of relief in his eyes before his expression became unreadable once more. She picked up her scissors and cut off Lazarus' shirt.

Using hot water the maid had left earlier, she washed away the blood, taking care to clean both wounds without causing him undue pain. She set the basin aside, then reached for her medical case.

Withdrawing the necessary items for stitching the wound, she threaded the needle and set to work. A short time later, she tied the last stitch and snipped the needle free. She picked up a clean linen square, set it against the wound, and bandaged his side.

Rising, she touched a hand to her back where the muscles protested the bent position she'd held so long. She allowed herself to look at Lazarus' face for the first time since she began pulling the stitches through his skin. His eyes were closed, and his breathing less labored.

She released a pent-up breath and turned away. The warmth of his hand grazing her own drew her attention.

He slid his fingers over the back of her hand. "You did well."

The unintentional caress burned her skin like a brand. She stepped back from his touch and nodded. Turning away, she brought her hand to her chest. She rubbed at the burning sensation, uncertain if she was trying to preserve the feeling or wipe it away.

Olivia cleared her throat in an effort to regain her equilibrium and addressed the gunman. "You will need to watch for signs of infection. If he feels hot to the touch, develops a fever, or if either of his wounds become red or inflamed or starts to ooze, you must get him to a doctor immediately." She listed the symptoms of infection by rote.

She picked up a pile of cloth squares and moved to the basin on the credenza. "You should try to keep him abed for the next few days. He lost quite a bit of blood, and his body will need time to recover."

"We'll be stayin' the night here," the gunman said.

Olivia turned around.

"We need a place—"

"That is unknown to your enemies," she finished.

"You'll be well paid for yer silence."

"I don't want your money. I want only your word that you will not harm me or my servants."

"I have nae reason to harm anyone if you do as I say. I sought out yer brother because of his medical skills. 'Tis well known he will help anyone who can pay, and without stickin' his nose in."

She frowned. What was he implying? Phillip was a respected member of society. Surely, this man was mistaken. Olivia didn't question him further. She was too tired, too overwhelmed by the night's events.

Turning back to the washbasin, she looked down at the dried blood crusted around her nails. Smothering a cry, she thrust her hands into the water. The clear liquid turned a cloudy red. She began to tremble, her breath coming faster as she scrubbed at her skin. The cries of dying soldiers echoed in her ears.

The sight of a cloth thrust in front of her brought her back to the present. She took the towel with shaking fingers.

Fighting for control, she inhaled through her nose and held her breath for a few seconds, then released it slowly. She had been horrified by the aftermath of a fierce battle and its casualties when Phillip had first suggested she try the breathing technique. Certain it wouldn't help, she had done it only to please him at first. Now she practiced it whenever she felt overwhelmed.

"Are ye feelin' a wee bit like Lady Macbeth?"

Olivia paused in drying her hands and met the gunman's brown gaze. Was that a flicker of compassion in his eyes? "Pardon me?"

He gestured to the basin of bloody water. "The way you were washin' yer hands. Practically rubbin' the skin off when they was already clean."

She looked down at her fingers. No sign of the crimson stains that had covered them before remained. Perhaps she and Lady Macbeth had a great deal in common. Both of them slowly going mad with guilt. Folding the cotton towel in half, she set it next to the basin. "I find cleanliness to be the best way to fight infection."

The gunman nodded, but she had the feeling he didn't believe her.

Lazarus gave a low groan, and she hurried to the bed, thankful for the first time in her life for the sound of a man in pain.

He tried to push up on his elbow.

She set a gentle hand on his arm. "You must lie still."

"Fingers," he whispered.

"Fingers? You were shot in the side." She examined first one hand then the other. Callused with a few scars scattered across the backs and knuckles, they were strong, hard-working hands, not the soft, almost feminine hands of the gentlemen of the aristocracy.

There was no sign of injury. Olivia frowned. Was he delirious with fever already? She touched his forehead, relieved to find it cool.

"Fingers," Lazarus said again, his voice insistent.

The gunman moved into his view. "I'm here."

"Your name is Fingers?" Olivia asked.

"Aye."

"His name is not important." Lazarus pushed himself into a sitting position. He swung his legs over the side of the bed, his face pale and drawn. "We need to leave. It's not safe here."

Fingers pointed at the window. "'Tis safer here than out there."

Gathering the instruments she'd used, Olivia crossed the room to the door, hoping the two men were distracted enough for her to escape.

Fingers seized her arm and pulled her away from the door. "You canna leave this room."

"Why not?" She pulled free. "I tended your friend as you demanded."

"Because you are St. Germaine's sister." Lazarus stood. His lips were compressed into a thin line of pain.

Olivia frowned. "I don't understand."

"St. Germaine will do anything for a few coins. How do we know you are not like him?"

Why did they continue to refer to Phillip in such unflattering terms? Was it possible they were confusing him with another? "My brother is a good and honest man who cares for nothing but to help others."

"While he helps himself to their purses," Fingers muttered.

"I will not let you malign his character in such a way," she snapped, her temper getting the best of her.

"There have been many times my brother aided others without any sort of compensation. If he cared only for money, why did he spend so many years on the battlefield trying to save those who were injured? If he was interested in becoming wealthy, he would have spent those years catering to the members of the *Ton* who indulge in the excesses of food and drink, then insist on the attentions of a physician."

Lazarus watched her for a moment, his dark gaze unsettling. "Such naiveté is unusual in one your age."

Olivia inhaled sharply, stung by his comment. At four and twenty, she knew she was firmly on the shelf, but she was hardly in her dotage. "I am far from naïve. I learned the harsh realities of life at the age of sixteen."

"How do we know you willna send for the Watch the moment you leave this room?" Fingers asked.

"I didn't do it before when I went to fetch my case so why would I do something so stupid now? You have a pistol. You've threatened me and my staff. Do you think I would risk my life or Bridget's or Jennings's?" She bit off the rest of her sentence. She didn't want to push him into using the gun he carried. A man who handled a pistol as he did used it often. And without remorse.

"You are rather forthright, aren't you," Lazarus said. It was a statement, not a question. "Sit down," he ordered.

She didn't move. She should do as he said, but some willful part of her, the part that hated losing control, refused to let them see how unnerved she was.

Fingers pulled the gun from his coat pocket and pointed at her. "Sit. Down."

Olivia sat.

While the two men conferred in quiet tones she couldn't quite hear, Fingers' gaze never left her. She searched for the compassion she thought she saw earlier. It was nowhere to be found. The brown color of his eyes had seemed warm then, now they reminded her of hard polished stones. She shivered and looked away.

Her gaze landed on the clock at the far end of the credenza. She watched the hands move slowly forward. It seemed to say, "Get help. Get help. Get help," with each second it ticked off.

A small opening in the curtains at the window drew her attention. She could see a glimpse of the night sky. It was dark and cloudy, with no moon in sight. She hoped she would live to see the morning.

The men came to an agreement of some sort. Lazarus turned toward her while Fingers walked to the door. She glanced between the two, her nerves jumping the way a stone skips over water.

"Thank you for tending my injury." Lazarus pulled his bloody coat on with slow, careful movements, fastened it closed over his bare chest, then gathered up the remnants of his shirt.

"You're welcome," Olivia said, once again feeling the strange sense of magnetism between them. It reminded her of the tension one felt just before the first shot of an ensuing battle.

Sensing a presence, she turned to find Fingers standing behind her just to the right of the chair. Something wasn't right. She started to rise.

"Sit a moment longer." Lazarus crossed to stand in front of her. "I have one more thing to say, and then we will take our leave."

Glancing over her shoulder at the other man, she

sank back onto the cushioned seat.

"I'd like to offer my sincerest apologies," Lazarus said, drawing her attention.

"For forcing me to help you or for speaking ill of my brother?"

"Both." His eyes held a touch of remorse before his gaze flicked away then back. "And for this."

Olivia felt the blow to the back of her head, felt herself falling forward, hands catching her, then nothing as a black void rushed upward to claim her.

Chapter Two

"Are you certain you feel up to this excursion?"

Olivia stopped rubbing her temple and forced a smile. "Of course." She shifted her straw chip bonnet a few inches. "I was just adjusting my hat."

Lady Amanda Riverton, one of the *Ton's* premier hostesses, raised her eyebrows, her disbelief clearly evident. "We are supposed to be shopping, yet you have purchased nothing."

Shrugging, Olivia tried to think of an excuse to cover her preoccupation. "I...I haven't seen anything I liked."

Amanda's brow hiked even higher. "You have found nothing you've liked? We've visited four of the best modistes on Bond Street. Lord Riverton will have apoplexy when he receives the bills for my purchases today." The younger woman eyed her with suspicion. "Now, tell me the true reason you are pretending to enjoy this outing."

Olivia glanced away. Was she so transparent? "I have a bit of a headache." It was one the reasons for her inattention, given the lump she carried on the back of her head, but not the main reason.

"Hmm." Amanda halted in the middle of the crowded thoroughfare. "And what else is giving you the megrims?"

Olivia sighed, knowing her friend wouldn't give up

until she knew everything. "I'm worried about a man."

Amanda grasped her by the arm. "Who is he? When did you meet him? Do not tell me it was that military officer at the Harrington Ball. I found him boorishly rude."

"Colonel Thompson? Good lord, no."

"Thank heavens for that. If it were he, I might have to find a new best friend." Amanda's smile took the sting from her words. "So, who is it? Not one of the young bucks around Town?"

Olivia started down the street. "I'm far too old for any young man to find me remotely interesting."

"Pish posh," Amanda said, slightly out of breath from her dash to catch up. "You make yourself sound like you're ready to lie in the grave. You are still a young woman."

"And firmly on the shelf. It has taken me a long time to come to terms with the fact that I shall never marry. I won't go back to pining for something that will not happen."

Olivia bit her lip. Truth be told, she still felt a stab in her heart whenever she thought about it. It was hard to accept. No marriage meant no children.

"I said the same thing and look at me."

"You were married before the end of your first Season. I don't think it qualifies as the same."

"True," Amanda conceded. "These last two years have flown by. I would never have believed time could pass so quickly back then. Are you certain you don't want to marry?"

"There's a great difference between not wanting to marry and there being no one who is willing to marry you." Olivia stepped to the side to allow a mother and child to pass.

Her gaze lingered on the two figures. It was senseless to be jealous of a complete stranger, yet she was. At one time she yearned for a child almost constantly, now it seemed to catch her unawares at the oddest times, like now when she should be enjoying Amanda's company.

"It bothers you much more than you admit."

Seeing her friend's too-knowing gaze, she forced a smile to her lips. "Perhaps. But I cannot stand people who wallow in self-pity." She linked her arm with Amanda's. "Let's see what Madame LaCoste has displayed in her shop window."

The other woman pulled free and came to an abrupt halt. "Madame LaCoste. You cannot be serious."

"Why not? She makes beautiful gowns."

"You haven't heard?"

Olivia gave a long-suffering sigh. "You know I can't abide gossip."

"This isn't gossip. It's the truth."

"What is it?" Olivia didn't really care to know; however, if she did not at least pretend an interest, Amanda would never let the subject go.

The younger woman moved closer, glanced at the other shoppers around them, then said in a loud whisper, "Madame LaCoste dresses Lord Hargrove's mistress."

Olivia burst out laughing. "Stop having me on. Hargrove is nearly five and seventy. I don't think he has a mistress nor, at his age, would he need one."

"It's the truth, I tell you."

Trying to hide her smile behind her hand, Olivia walked on.

"It is," Amanda said as she caught up.

"Even if it is, I shall not stop ordering my gowns from Madame. If no one purchased gowns from a modiste who clothed a mistress, there wouldn't be a single dressmaker in all of London."

"Must you always be so practical?"

Olivia shrugged. How did one respond to that? *I'm sorry; frivolity dies a swift death on the battlefield.* No, it was best not to respond at all.

Putting an arm around her shoulders, Amanda gave her a swift hug. "Do tell me about this man, and why you are so worried."

"He came to the house last evening looking for Sir Phillip."

"I thought he was in Scotland."

"He was. I'm not certain where he is now."

"Did you not tell this stranger that?"

"Yes, but—"

"Then why are you worried?"

"If you will stop asking me questions, I will tell you."

Amanda managed to look contrite for all of one minute. "Well?"

"The man, he'd been shot."

"Shot!" Amanda glanced around her. "Shot," she repeated in a whisper.

"Yes. He wanted Sir Phillip to help him."

"What did you do?"

"I helped him."

"You?"

"It is not as though I do not have experience with bullet wounds," Olivia said in a dry tone.

"Yes, but..."

"I didn't have a choice. Should I have sent him away?" Olivia kept the existence of the man called Fingers and his pistol to herself. No sense upsetting Amanda more than she already was.

"No, of course not. He is all right now?"

"I don't know, which is why I am worried. I wanted to make arrangements to see if he was healing properly in a few days' time, but..." Olivia hesitated. She didn't dare tell her friend she'd been knocked unconscious, nor did she want to tell her about the man and his companion's odd comments about her brother. "He left before I was able to do so."

"Have you tried to locate him? If he's injured, surely his friends are aware of it."

"I've tried asking if anyone had heard of him, but I get nothing but silence or strange looks when I mention his name."

"What's his name, perhaps I know of him."

"Lazarus."

Amanda laughed. "That would explain the strange looks you are getting. Has he risen from the grave?" she joked.

"I don't know about rising from it, but if he hadn't sought medical care when he did, he could have bled to death and found himself *in* the grave."

"I'm sure he is fine." Amanda pulled her along the thoroughfare. She stopped suddenly and looked back. "Did you see that bonnet?"

"Bonnet?" Olivia asked, completely lost from Amanda's quick change of conversation. She scanned the crowd but didn't see anyone wearing anything unusual.

"Yes. In the shop window."

"You purchased three new hats at the last milliner's shop."

"Not one like this. Besides one can never have too many bonnets." Amanda took a step back the way they came. "I just want to take another peek at it."

"I'll wait here as long as you're only going to just look." Olivia hoped her remark would discourage Amanda from going inside the shop. They had spent nearly two hours at the last milliner. She didn't think she could bear another two hours browsing through more hats when she could be spending her time looking for Lazarus.

"Very well." Amanda disappeared into the throng of shoppers, maids, and dandies visiting their tailors or viewing the latest fashions the haberdasheries had to offer.

As the crowd ebbed and flowed around her, Olivia caught a glimpse of Amanda, her tangerine and cream coloured gown making her easy to spot. A rather large gentleman stepped into Olivia's line of sight. She moved to the side, trying to see around him when someone pushed her from behind.

She fell forward, her hands outstretched to cushion her fall. A hand clamped around her arm and hauled her upward.

"Sorry, Mum. I was talkin' to me mates and didn't see ye afore it was too late."

The man, a boy really, stared at her as though taking her measure. His brown hair was in need of cutting. It hung in his eyes and brushed past the collar of his homespun wool coat. Olivia glanced at the rest of his clothing. A thin gray linen shirt she suspected had once been white, patched trousers, and scuffed shoes

22

that were in desperate need of replacing.

His grip was a little too tight, and he had yet to let go of her even though she was back on her feet. He proceeded to brush at her gown with his free hand. In that instant, Olivia knew exactly what he was doing. She tightened her grip on her reticule and leaned toward him.

"You'll steal no coins from me," she whispered.

His hand froze in mid-air.

"Yes, I know the tricks you play. Accidentally knock into a lady and then steal her purse all under the pretense of setting her to rights."

The boy grinned, his brown eyes twinkling with laughter. "'Tis true," he admitted, "but I ain't after yer blunt. I've a message fer ye."

"A message?" Who would have a message delivered to her in such a manner?

"Stop asking about Lazarus."

"And if I don't?"

His grip tightened, and she tried not to wince. He jerked her forward, no longer the charming rascal, his gaze menacing. "You've been warned."

He released her and melted back into the crowd. She lost sight of him almost immediately.

"Olivia, are you all right?"

She glanced at Amanda, barely registering her friend's concern. "Yes."

"Who was that?"

"I don't know." She stared at the place where she last saw the youth, but there was no sign of him.

"You don't know," Amanda exclaimed. "Did he accost you? I have heard the footpads were becoming bold, but I did not believe it."

"He took nothing from me. He thought I was someone he knew." Olivia patted Amanda's hand in a reassuring manner. "Do not worry anymore about it."

"If you are certain." Amanda looked around them, her gaze troubled. "I find I have lost the desire to continue our shopping. Shall we return to the carriage?"

"An excellent idea."

She bustled Olivia past the remaining shops and around the corner to Gunther's where she had instructed her coachman to wait. The two footmen gulped down the rest of their ices and jumped to open the carriage door as Amanda approached.

"Remember," she said as she passed them and entered the coach, "not a word to Riverton about Olivia and I shopping unaccompanied."

"Of course, my lady," the two men responded in unison.

She settled her skirts and looked up at Olivia. "Perhaps Riverton is right after all. It seems he does have a very good reason to insist a footman accompany me whenever I go out."

"Indeed he may." Olivia pushed the privacy curtain aside and stared out the window. Though she didn't want to admit it, she was still searching for the stranger who warned her against asking questions about Lazarus.

Had Lazarus sent him? Or the person who wanted him dead? And how was Phillip involved?

****

Olivia set the branch of candles on the small writing table near the fire and sighed. She'd stayed at Amanda's far longer than she had expected. She should have insisted on leaving instead of allowing her friend to cajole her into partaking of a late supper. Removing her hat, she crossed to the dressing table and pulled the pins from her hair, letting it tumble down around her shoulders. She massaged her scalp, then ran her fingers through the thick strands.

"Watching you do that could give a bloke ideas."

Olivia whirled around, her hand pressed against her chest. Her heart stuttered for a moment, then began racing like that of a runaway horse. She reached behind her and grabbed her hairbrush. As a weapon, it was the best she could do. She scanned the shadows for the intruder.

Lazarus lounged in her favorite reading spot, his feet crossed at the ankles while he rested his elbows on the arms of the chair. Situated as it was near the window, his dark clothing blended in with the shadows among deep blue drapery. He watched her over his linked fingers.

"Aren't you going to ask why I'm here?"

She didn't answer; the warning she'd received earlier replayed itself in her mind. Fear ran its fingertip down her spine.

"Shall I tell you then?" He stood with slow careful movements, then advanced on her until there was no more than a hair's breadth between them.

She took a step back and banged into the dressing table, setting the small collection of bottles jangling.

"Afraid?"

Olivia shook her head. "Of course not."

"You should be."

Uncertain, she posed the question uppermost in her mind. "What are you doing here?"

"Here in your house or here"—he gestured to the

room in general—"in your bedroom?"

Determined to quell the rising sense of panic and what it would lead to, she pushed past him. She brushed against his side, heard his sharp inhalation of pain, but kept moving, needing space between them. "If you don't leave, I shall have Jennings call the constable." She headed for the door.

"And how will you accomplish that?"

Olivia halted in mid-step.

"Yes, I know there are no servants in residence." He sauntered closer. "Did you play the benevolent mistress and give them the night off?"

Eager to keep him at a distance, she scooted around him and stood at the end of the bed. "What do you want?"

"What do you think I want?"

"Why don't we dispense with the games, and you just tell me?"

Lazarus closed the space between them in two strides. He pushed her backward onto the bed. Olivia bounced against the soft mattress. She dug her elbows into the thick counterpane in an effort to scramble backward away from him.

Grabbing her ankles, he pulled her toward him in one quick jerk. He leaned over her. His hand closed over her hip, freezing her in place. The warmth of his hand burned through her clothes to her skin.

Feeling truly terrified for the first time since he'd announced his presence, she searched his gaze for some kind of sign this was all a great joke. No, it was no game. His eyes were as hard and cold as glass. "What do you want?" she repeated, her voice a near whisper.

"Stop asking questions about me. Forget you ever

heard the name Lazarus."

His gaze roamed over her. It was a slow, thorough inspection, and she felt every second of it. It set off an unfamiliar fluttering in her stomach. She trembled, certain it was because he loomed over her in such a threatening manner and had nothing to do with the fact she felt the touch of his eyes like a caress.

He leaned closer, his face mere inches from hers. Their gazes caught, and Olivia found herself holding her breath. He muttered a curse and pushed away from the bed. "Remember this warning," he said, his voice harsh. "You'll not get another."

He crossed the room and disappeared into the shadowy hall. His footsteps echoed back to her as he moved down the stairs and out of the house.

Moving into a sitting position, Olivia hugged her knees to her chest. She breathed in through her nose in an effort to calm her nerves though she didn't know what upset her more—his sudden appearance in her room or the strange feelings he aroused in her. Nor did she want to examine the thought too closely. A dampness at her waist drew her attention.

She looked down at her gown. A circular scattering of crimson droplets stood out against the pale blue muslin where he leaned over her. Rising from the bed, she lifted the candelabra from the table. She crossed the room to the chair he used while he waited for her. Blood marred the cream fabric of the chair back.

He'd opened his wounds. Threats or no, she couldn't forget about him now. She had to seek him out. To know for herself he was taking proper care of his injuries. To know she hadn't failed again.

****

Olivia looked over the list of questions generated by her encounter with Lazarus. She glanced up as the Bow Street Runner entered the room and hoped she hadn't made a mistake. The man, dressed in a plain dark wool suit, looked as though he could have been a footpad himself. His nose had been broken in the past as it sat slightly off center, and a small scar in the shape of a semicircle sat near his temple.

She stood and gestured for him to take a seat in front of her desk. "Mr. Durant. Thank you for coming."

"Heard you wanted someone investigated." He sat down and pulled a small battered notebook from his pocket. He produced a stub of a pencil, licked the tip, and looked up at her, his expression inquiring.

"Yes." Olivia returned to her chair.

"Anything on this person you wanted to know in particular?"

"Whatever you can find out."

"A rival for a man's affections?"

She frowned. Why did men always assume women were willing to fight over them? "No. I'm interested in learning more about a man."

Durant's eyebrows rose. "What's his name?" he asked, though it was apparent he clearly wanted to ask something else.

"I'm afraid I don't know his name, only a moniker."

"That'll do."

She stared at the man, trying to gauge how much she should divulge about the Lazarus' appearance at her home. "Lazarus."

Durant burst out laughing. "You sent for a Bow Street Runner to find out about him?"

Olivia frowned again. "I fail to see the humour in the situation."

"Everyone knows about Lazarus." Durant shoved his pencil back into his pocket. "He leads the biggest band of criminals London has seen in many a year. Theft, smuggling. If it's illegal, he's got men involved in the process." He rubbed his jaw thoughtfully. "Except prostitution and the opium trade. Never heard anything connecting him to that."

"If what you say is true, why isn't he in Newgate or some such place?"

"That'd be the sticky part." Turning serious, Durant leaned forward in his chair. "You see, everyone knows Lazarus is a criminal, but we've never been able to actually tie him to anything."

"Why not?"

"His men are more loyal than most. They protect him, go to gaol themselves rather than turn him over to the magistrates."

"What does he do to inspire such loyalty?" She couldn't understand why a man would be willing to be sent to gaol or worse in the place of another.

Durant shrugged. "He is fiercely loyal himself. Will go to any measure to protect those he considers family."

Olivia asked the one question she wasn't certain she wanted an answer to. "Is he dangerous?"

"There's a number of rumours about him. Hard to know which ones to believe. None of them are fitting for a lady's ears."

"For example?"

Durant hesitated.

"Please do not worry about my delicate

sensibilities," she said in a dry tone. Heaven knew anything delicate about her sensibilities had long ago disappeared.

"It's said he once took a man's eyes just for looking at a woman under his protection."

She stared at the Runner in a mixture of horror and disbelief. "Is it true?"

He took a deep breath. "Can't say for certain."

"But?"

"But it wouldn't knock me off my feet if it were true. I've heard and seen the results of Lazarus' work whether we can prove he did it or not."

Olivia glanced at the window. Given her own recent experiences with the man, she was inclined to believe the rumours as well. But even now, after learning the type of man he was, she still felt compelled to find him. To ensure he had at least sought medical care after reopening his wounds. She *needed* to know she'd cared for them properly, that she'd done everything possible. And to find out why he had said those horrible things about her brother.

She took a deep breath. "If you know of a way to contact him, I'd be grateful to learn of it."

Durant stared at her as if she belonged in Bedlam. "I can't be giving a fine lady like yourself such information."

"Please." One more death that she could have prevented would be one more than she could bear. "It has to do with my brother, Sir Phillip." She linked her hands under the desk in an attempt to look frightened. "He's missing, you see."

"I'll look into your brother's disappearance," Durant said, digging out his pencil.

"No." Olivia almost shouted the word. "I need to meet with Lazarus. It was the one name Sir Phillip mentioned before he left." The lie rolled off her tongue with surprising ease.

"Ye won't be going alone if I tell you a place?"

She shook her head. "Oh, no. Lord Riverton will escort me. Have you heard of him? He is quite well known in the House of Lords. I imagine a number of footmen will be accompanying us as well."

"If you're certain?"

Pressing her advantage, she put a hand to her chest and did her best to look earnest. "Oh, very certain."

The Runner stared at her for a long moment, then bent his head and scribbled something in his notebook. He tore the page out and handed it to her. "Lazarus won't be there, but some of his men will be. You can make arrangements to see him through one of them."

Olivia read the address, folded the sheet in half, and set it on her desk. A sense of relief flooded over her.

Durant stood. "If you'll pardon me for saying it, I have a piece of advice. Don't do anything to draw his attention."

Olivia rose. "I'm afraid it's too late for that."

Chapter Three

Olivia stood outside the Lamb and the Lion. She checked the name of the alehouse against the note in her hand, then stared back the way she'd come. Maybe she shouldn't have insisted the footman remain with the carriage to help safeguard it against thieves. Who would safeguard her? Perhaps this hadn't been the best idea. She bit her lip and looked back at the building.

Raucous voices filtered out of the grime-encrusted windows and into the early evening dusk. The creaking sound of the wooden sign as it swung back and forth in the wind drew her gaze. She found the name of the tavern rather ironic. There probably wasn't a less peaceable place to be found in all of London.

Taking a deep breath, she pushed the door open and stepped inside. A wave of silence gathered and grew until it washed over her in its very stillness. Afraid to maintain eye contact with the men who stared at her with lust growing in their eyes, she focused on the man behind the counter, his meaty fist drying a tankard with a dirty rag. Surely, he would be willing to help.

"Miss St. Germaine."

Olivia turned toward the voice. Relief poured through her at the sight of the man called Fingers making his way through the crowd. As though sensing she was no longer vulnerable, the men turned back to their ale. Voices rose and fell as conversations resumed.

"What are you doin' here?" he asked in a low voice. He took her arm and angled her around so he faced the crowd.

"I need to see Lazarus."

"You shouldna come. This is nae place for someone like you. You coulda been robbed, or worse."

He seemed genuinely upset at her presence. She couldn't believe it. Not after the way they'd parted company four nights ago. Her fingers crept up to touch the lump she still carried.

"I'm sorry, but I need to see Lazarus. I was told this is the place where arrangements are made to see him." She glanced around as raised voices came from a group of men in the corner. "It's important."

Fingers dodged a flying tankard. "You shoulda sent a footman."

Olivia flinched as it crashed in a shower of ale against the wall. Shouts and laughter continued unabated. The liquid streamed down the wall to puddle on the floor. "Yes, I see that now."

She sighed and rubbed her temple. The yeasty smell of stale ale, unwashed bodies, and smoke, not to mention the noise, were combining to give her a headache. "Will you take me to him?"

"I canna do that, but I'll tell him you want to see him." He opened the door and gave her a gentle push. "Someone will bring you to him tomorrow."

"Tomorrow!" She dug her heels in. What if an infection had set in and had already done too much damage? It would be too late. "No. I need to see him tonight. Now."

Fingers opened his mouth to respond, but she cut

him off before he could utter a word. "If you won't take me, I will find him myself."

"Ye won't find him."

"Perhaps not, but I must try."

"It ain't safe fer a woman like yerself." He gestured to the men who watched her with hungry eyes.

She shivered and turned away from the lascivious gazes. "I realize that, but it is a chance I'm willing to take. The question is—are you willing to explain what may happen to me to Lazarus?"

Fingers took her arm and bundled her through the door. "He'll have my head for this, ya know."

"I'll tell him I didn't give you a choice."

"That ya didn't." He gave her a quick once over. "Stubborn woman," he muttered, then looked back over his shoulder. "Come on, then," he said and led the way into a nearby alley.

The smells of urine, vomit, and heaven knew what else assailed her as soon as she stepped into the alley. Taking shallow breaths, Olivia hurried after him, praying she could keep the contents of her stomach where they belonged.

The fetid air grew stronger, thicker. Unable to control the urge any longer, she gagged. Clamping a hand over her mouth, she rushed past Fingers to the end of the narrow street. She turned the corner and leaned against an abandoned storefront, breathing in the cleaner air.

He rounded the building a few minutes later, a small smile playing about his mouth.

"You did that on purpose," she accused.

"Did what?" He feigned innocence, but the laughter in his eyes gave him away.

"Chose to take me down that wretched alley instead of any of the others."

He put his hands in his pockets. "You asked me to take ye to Lazarus. Not how to get there. Funny sight you were." He laughed. "Would a wagered me last pound that ye wouldna made it out a there without gettin' sick."

"You almost won."

He looked up at the darkening sky. "We shouldna dawdle. There'll be rain afore too long."

She followed his gaze. Thick clouds gathered overhead, yet the wind was calm. She started to ask him how he knew when he took hold of her arm and pulled her across the street.

"Feel it in me bones," he said in answer to her unspoken question.

He led her through a maze of narrow streets, twisting alleys, and overgrown gardens. In a matter of minutes, she was completely lost. She would never be able to find her way back on her own. Sometime later, they stopped in front of a large warehouse.

She looked around but didn't recognize the area as part of the business district on the docks she was familiar with. "Where are we?"

"It's of nae importance to ye."

She scanned the dark windows, the peeling slate blue paint, and heavily locked door. "Are you certain he is here?"

"Aye." Fingers released three locks, one after the other, dropped the set of keys back into his pocket, then opened the door. He walked in and was swallowed by looming black shadows.

Pushing her uncertainty aside, Olivia followed him.

She needed to make sure Lazarus was all right, and she meant to do so. They walked down a long hall, stopping in front of a closed door. Light spilled from beneath it. Fingers gave a series of knocks and waited.

"Come," a voice called.

He turned the brass knob and opened the door blocking Olivia's view of the interior. "You be alone?"

"Yes. Why are you here? Did Wilkins fail to appear?"

Fingers stepped aside, leaving Olivia in the opening. "She insisted on seeing ye."

Her gaze focused on the man in front of her. The heavy oak desk he sat behind, the branch of candles sitting on the corner, it all faded away until there was only him.

He wore no waistcoat or frock coat, only a white linen shirt open at the neck with the sleeves rolled up to reveal sinewy forearms.

Relief that Fingers had actually brought her to Lazarus and that he seemed well coursed through her.

He looked from her to Fingers. His black gaze blazed with anger. She felt her stomach jolt.

He rose and walked around the end of the desk. "Wait for me outside."

With a nod, the other man moved to the door.

"Don't be angry with him. I insisted he bring me."

"I don't care," Lazarus shouted. "I told you to forget about me." He took a deep breath as though fighting for control. "You should have heeded my warning."

"I couldn't. You were bleeding. I had to find you." She heard the desperation in her voice and hoped he was too angry to notice. She couldn't, wouldn't explain why his life, any life, was so important to her.

He dismissed her concern with a wave of his hand and retook his seat. "I'm fine."

"May I check your wounds?" She produced a package of fresh bandages from the pocket of her cloak.

"Why?"

Of all the things she had expected him to say, "why" wasn't one of them. "When you broke into my home the other night, you were bleeding."

"Fingers and I knocked you unconscious when we left your home that first night. You've been warned, not once but twice, to forget we ever met, so why the continued concern?"

Because I can't handle the death of one more person on my hands. Of course, she couldn't say that, so she lied. "Blame it on the rules passed onto me by my brother—always provide follow-up care for any patient." It wasn't a true lie as he did tell her that when she first began caring for the wounded soldiers on her own.

Lazarus tapped a letter opener on his desk as he eyed her with speculation. The candle lamp cast a gleam on the blade with each tap, drawing her gaze. She realized it was not a letter opener at all, but a small dagger. Rubies decorated the hilt.

"That's an unusual knife," she said, searching for a way to ease the growing fear she had truly made a mistake in coming here.

"It has its uses." He tossed it onto the desk. "You expect me to believe you are here purely out of concern for my well-being?"

"What other reason would I have?"

"What indeed. You've been asking questions about

me even after I personally warned you against it."

"Only to find your direction." It was the truth, but he didn't seem to believe her.

He nodded as though making a decision of some sort and stood. "Very well. We shall strike a bargain, you and I."

"A bargain?" Olivia asked, wary.

"I will let you examine my wounds, then you will leave here, never come back, and cease asking questions about me."

She had no issue with his proposal. She planned on doing exactly that. She would do well to stay away from him. She had difficulties enough of her own without consorting with someone who threatened to bring more troubles down on her head. "Agreed."

He held out his hand to seal the agreement. She hesitated, then put her gloved one in his. His fingers closed around hers. He made no movement to shake her hand, just stared at her with an unreadable expression. Olivia found she could no more look away than she could break the connection of their hands. A strange current hummed between them.

Finally, he released her and stepped back. He rubbed the palm of his hand, then realized what he was doing and scowled. "We'll stand near the hearth so you may see better."

He lifted the lamp from the desk and crossed the room to the fireplace. He set it on the mantel and pulled his shirt from his trousers. He stood with his side facing her, his shirt pushed upward to reveal the neat bandage wrapped around his middle.

Olivia swallowed, hesitant to touch him.

He looked over his shoulder at her, his expression

questioning.

"Would you mind removing your shirt?" she asked, playing for time. "I'll be better able to examine you."

He watched her for a moment more, then unfastened the shirt, pulled it off, and tossed it onto the desk.

She moved closer and worked at the knot tying the bandage in place. She tried not to notice the muscles of his arms and chest, how her fingers itched to trace the scars he carried on his upper body, the way the firelight burnished his skin, the dark curling hair on his chest and the way it arrowed downward to disappear into his trousers. At last the knot came free, and she nearly wept in relief, only to feel the tension within her escalate as her body brushed against his with each unwinding of the cloth.

With the last turn, she gathered the material, clenched it in her hands to cease their shaking, then turned away to lay it on a nearby club chair. She released a shaky breath and turned back to Lazarus. She didn't understand what was wrong with her. She'd never reacted like this with any of the soldiers she'd cared for, and she'd seen many of them completely unclothed.

She dropped to her knees in front of him to better see the entry wound of the lead ball. Sensation pooled low in her belly as she inhaled the male scent of him. Forcing herself to concentrate, she probed the neat row of stitches for signs of infection. The heat of his skin warmed her fingertips, and her breath hitched in her throat.

His hand clasped her shoulder, his fingers convulsing with each touch of her hand on his skin. His breathing grew harsh.

She looked up at him. "Am I hurting you?"

He stared at her, his gaze heavy lidded. "In a way I'm certain you can't imagine." His voice was thick with emotion.

Olivia frowned. What on earth did he mean? Had he suffered internal bruising? The wound looked healthy enough. Had she been mistaken? No, the blood he'd left both on her chair and her gown when he surprised her in her bedchamber had not been products of her fevered imagination.

She started to speak when the door burst open, a boy looked at Lazarus, then at Olivia, still down on her knees in front of him.

"Oh, sorry," the lad squeaked and slammed the door shut.

Lazarus burst out laughing as what the youth thought they were doing dawned on Olivia. Her expression must have given away her dismay.

She jumped to her feet. "Aren't you going to go after him? Tell him I was just examining your wounds?"

"Why would I do that?" He grinned. "I do have a certain reputation to maintain."

"You're worried about how you are perceived?" Her entire body flushed with the heat of mortifying embarrassment. "I am humiliated."

He shrugged. "Should have thought of that before you came here. I doubt he'd believe me anyway."

"Why ever not?" She strode to the desk in a fit of pique and tore open the package of clean bandages.

She froze as she felt him behind her, so close she could feel the warmth of him through her gown. One hand splayed across her stomach and pulled her against him. "Because," he whispered in her ear, "he saw how much I want you." With his free hand, he tilted her head back, running his fingers along the line of her jaw.

Olivia fought the urge to lean back against him. To revel in the strength of his hands and body. To reach back, cup his head, and bring his mouth to hers.

His lips touched her neck, and she froze. What was she doing? She wrenched free of his caresses, upset over the emotions he aroused in her. He, a complete stranger whom she knew nothing about. She didn't know if she was more upset because of how he made her feel or the fact he had taken liberties with her person. "Don't ever touch me again."

"You wanted me to touch you, or you wouldn't have come here, wouldn't have sought out someone like me."

She lashed out, if only to put distance between them for deep in her heart, she was afraid what he said was true—she had wanted him to touch her and so much more. "You are vile and disgusting. I should have left you to bleed to death."

He stiffened. "You wouldn't have been the first to do so."

Lazarus stared at her a moment longer, his eyes like chips of ice. He crossed the room and opened the door. "Take Miss St. Germaine home," he said to someone out of sight. "And see that she doesn't come here again."

Turning away, he snatched his shirt from the desk and shoved his arms into the sleeves.

The boy who had accosted her on Bond Street moved into the room and stood near the door. "Miss."

She looked at the two men. "You sent him to warn me off."

Lazarus finished fastening his shirt and crossed his arms over his chest. "You were asking questions about me. Patrick was sent to frighten you into stopping."

"And if I continue to ask about you, what would Patrick do then?"

"Whatever was necessary."

Inhaling sharply at the implied threat, Olivia took a step back. She'd been worried about his health, and he stood threatening her with no more concern than if they were discussing the weather. Fingers was right; she shouldn't have gone to the Lamb and the Lion to seek Lazarus out. She should have forced herself to forget his very existence.

She glanced at Patrick. Remembering how he'd gone from a laughing young man to a menacing cutthroat in a manner of seconds, she didn't want to go anywhere with him. How could she be certain he still didn't mean to hurt her? "If Fingers could take me back to the tavern, my own coach is waiting for me there," she offered.

Lazarus shook his head. "He has other things to do."

"But he"—she gestured to Patrick—"is a stranger to me. You cannot expect me to ride with him alone."

"And Fingers is not?"

"I know he won't hurt me."

"Don't be so certain. He will do what I tell him."

"He could have taken me anywhere tonight, yet he brought me here, to you, as I asked."

"And he will answer for that." He motioned the young man forward with a quick movement of his hand.

"Miss St. Germaine is leaving *now*."

"I'm not going anywhere with him." She copied his stance, crossing her arms over her chest.

"You'll do as you're told," he snapped.

"I will not. I am not one of your minions to be ordered about."

"Fine. Then you go alone." He turned to Patrick. "Show her where the door is and make sure she leaves."

She stared at him in disbelief. He truly meant for her to find the way on her own? She would be lucky to make it out of the docks without her throat cut much less back to her carriage. "I thought you were a gentleman. You have proven me wrong twice this evening."

Lazarus' harsh bark of laughter filled the room. "I am no gentleman. Some say I am not even civilized." He held out his arms as though inviting her perusal. "Do I look like a gentleman?"

He wore black boots, not the fashionable Hessians the gentlemen of the *Ton* wore, but they seemed to be well made nonetheless, dark trousers, and a white linen shirt. His black hair was a little longer than the current fashion, but he could have easily passed for a member of the aristocracy enjoying a pleasant evening at home. She met his gaze with her own.

"Yes, you do," she said softly and walked to the door. She turned back, her hand on the door casing. "But you do not act like one," she whispered and left the room.

Chapter Four

Fingers pulled the collar of his coat tighter. He looked up. There wasn't a cloud in sight, and the moon shone brightly against the sky. Not a good night for what Lazarus had planned. He hoped a few clouds would blow in to cover the moon in time.

He took a pull of whiskey from his flask to chase away the bitter cold. It was early April, yet tonight it felt like the coldest winter night. He looked up and down the street. Patrick stood near the coach as it sat at the curb waiting for them. He took off his hat and slapped it against his leg twice before settling it back on his head.

At the sign of their pre-arranged signal, Fingers nodded to Muldoon, who leaned against the building, and sank deeper into the shadows and waited for their prey.

A few minutes later, he heard footsteps coming in his direction. He waited until the rich toff passed by, then pounced. He and Muldoon grabbed the man by his arms and bundled him toward the waiting coach.

"What the devil?" Lord Glenville tried to pull free, drag his feet, anything to stop the forward momentum, but Fingers kept them moving.

One hard shove between the shoulder blades sent his lordship careening into the coach. He landed on the floor with a thud, his shoulder bouncing off the opposite wall. Fingers followed him in, tossing a guinea to Muldoon for his trouble. As soon as Fingers pulled the door shut, the coach shot into motion.

Glenville scrambled to his knees and grabbed the bench seat to keep from being thrown sideways as the coach careened around a corner. Fingers smiled in the darkness. Patrick was the fastest coach driver in all of St. Giles. His lordship was in for quite a ride. "Take a seat, Guv'nor." Fingers lit the lamp nearest to him.

Glenville squinted against the sudden light. He slid onto the leather seat and faced his abductor. "What is this about? Do you know who I am?"

"Aye. The Earl of Glenville." Fingers spit on the floor in a show of disrespect. "Lazarus wants to see ye." He leaned back against the buttery leather seat.

"If this person wants to see me, he can call on me at the appropriate time. Now, I suggest you order the driver to take me back to White's before you find yourself in trouble with the law."

"Ooh, you be siccin' the Watch on us then?" Fingers rubbed his hands together with glee. It had been some time since he'd pitted his skills against the law. "Mayhap a Bow Street Runner, too?"

To prove their excursion wasn't a lark, he pulled his pistol from within the folds of his coat. "There isna gonna be a single thing *the law*"—he sneered the two words—"kin do. We're jus' going for a ride, two friends meeting another."

His lordship glanced from Finger's face to the gun.

Fingers cocked the pistol. He wanted the earl to have no doubts that he would shoot him without a moment's regret. He deserved anything that happened to him for the way he'd treated his wife, and if that

45

"anything" happened to be fatal, Fingers was certain the Lady Glenville wouldn't be shedding any tears.

Silence stretched between them, the tension growing with each passing mile. Fingers didn't allow either his gaze or the pistol to waver from his quarry. He hoped the intensity of his stare caused the earl to grow more and more uneasy. It served the bastard right.

"Where the blazes are you taking me?" Glenville demanded, finally finding his tongue, not to mention his courage.

The coach rolled to a stop just as Fingers opened his mouth to respond. The door opened from the outside. He gestured toward it with the gun. "Get out."

Glenville shook his head. "I don't think so. If you're going to shoot me, you'll do it here."

"I willna shoot ye. Yet. Now get out. Lazarus is waitin'."

"Tell him to come inside. We can talk in here just as well as we can out there."

"Nobody tells Lazarus what to do." Fingers looked toward the door, then tilted his head toward the earl.

Two hands reached into the coach and dragged the earl out. He landed in a heap at the side of the road.

Jumping to his feet, he advanced on Patrick. "What the bloody hell is going on here. I demand—"

"You aren't in much of a position to be demanding anything."

Glenville spun to the left, scanning the thick copse of trees.

A man dressed in black moved out of the shadows behind the earl. He nodded to Fingers and moved closer.

Glenville turned to face him. "You must be

Lazarus.

Will inclined his head. "I am he."

"And do you know the penalty for kidnapping a member of the peerage?"

"For there to be a kidnapping, a body must be missing. A letter from you stating you will be visiting friends but giving no specifics would negate any thoughts of foul play."

"My wife would wonder at my disappearance after a while."

Will raised his eyebrows. "Would she? I think not, given your treatment of her."

"Why have you dragged me all the way out here?" Glenville demanded.

"We need to talk, you and I."

"We couldn't have done that in town?"

Will looked around. "You know where we are?"

"A few miles outside of London."

He dipped his head in acknowledgement. "Three to be exact."

Glenville huffed a breath of frustration. "I don't care if we're a hundred miles from London."

"You might." Will clasped his hands behind his back and rocked back on his heels. "I wasn't pleased when I heard how you neglect your wife."

"You know nothing of my wife."

"I know a great deal. Her name is Kate. She is eighteen years of age. You've been married six months." He held up his hand as Glenville started to interrupt. "I was asked not to interfere, and I agreed. Until now."

"What the hell does that mean, 'until now'?" His lordship took a step forward.

Patrick and Fingers moved toward him. Will checked their movement with a slight gesture of his hand. "I agreed to..." He paused, searching for the right words.

"Stay out of my marriage," Glenville finished.

Will stared at him, hoping the hatred he felt showed in his eyes. "Allow you to live."

Glenville gave a harsh bark of laughter. "Is that the purpose of this meeting? To persuade me to bow to my wife's every whim by issuing meaningless threats?"

"You don't seem to know me very well. I suggest you remedy that. Keep in mind all rumours have a basis in fact."

The earl glanced at Fingers as he stood near the coach, still and silent. Transferring his attention back to Will, he stepped to the right.

Will quirked his lips into a slight smile. "You may prove to be a better adversary than I first thought, so I will tell you this. Provide for your wife's needs and all will be well. If you do not..." He let the sentence trail off.

"My wife has a home that is the envy of every woman of the *Ton*, food to eat, clothing. What more does she want? Money to waste on fripperies? I provide everything she needs."

"Do you?" Will glanced at Fingers and nodded.

The other man moved forward, pistol still in hand, and aimed at the earl's chest. "Take off your coat."

"And if I refuse?"

"Then Fingers will shoot you, and we will still take the coat," Will said in a conversational tone as though he was discussing nothing more important than the weather.

"Fingers?" Glenville asked.

"That'd be me." Fingers cocked the pistol. "The coat."

"Bloody hell." Glenville shrugged out of the heavy greatcoat. "I don't see the point in all this." He threw the coat at Patrick.

"You will." Will moved closer. "Now your frock coat and waistcoat."

Glenville shook his head. "I think not."

Will waved Patrick forward. "The earl needs some assistance."

"No, that kind of help I don't need." Glenville took off the garments and glared at Will. "You'll have to kill me because I'm removing no more of my clothes."

Will gave him a long look. "Are you aware your *wife* is without a proper wardrobe? That she is forced to go about in shoes that aren't fit for a ballroom much less the streets, but yet you have a heavy coat and a pair of shiny Hessians."

He moved toward the coach. "Let's be off. A tankard of ale and a warm fire awaits."

Patrick murmured his agreement, scooped the earl's discarded clothing from the frozen grass, and headed toward the coach. Only Fingers remained as he was.

"Thank God," Glenville breathed.

Will turned back. "Not you. You'll be walking back to London."

"Walking! Are you out of your bloody mind? You've left me in my shirtsleeves, and we're miles from town. You can't expect me to walk about without being properly attired in this weather."

Will felt his jaw harden. "I do. As you do your

wife."

"I didn't know she needed those things you mentioned," Glenville whined.

"You are her husband; it is your duty to know."

"If you leave me here, I'll see you and your cohorts in Newgate for this."

Will laughed. The high and mighty members of Society always thought the law would help them.

Fingers moved to his side. "Ye sure ya be wantin' ta do this? He's an earl."

"Perhaps you should listen to him," Glenville said.

"'Tis verra cold and three miles will be long." Fingers waved Patrick forward, Glenville's things still in his grasp.

Will stared at the earl for a long moment. "You're right."

He turned away and headed for the coach. "Take his boots."

****

"Mr. William Prescott to see you, milord."

Will stood behind the butler with tightly held patience. He didn't understand why the butler needed to announce him. Hargrove was expecting him after all.

"Good. Show him in."

He took a step forward as the butler moved to the side.

"Simmons," Hargrove called.

"Yes, milord?"

"Did Mr. Prescott arrive via the servants' entrance?"

"Yes, he did," Will said before the butler could respond.

"Thank you, Simmons. That will be all." The Earl

of Hargrove compressed his mouth into a thin line as Will moved into the room.

Taking stock of Hargrove, he was surprised to see the old man looked younger than when they first met months ago. His hair was still gray and thinning, but his eyes were no longer filled with sadness, but expectancy. Though still gaunt, Hargrove's frame had filled out, and the air of haunted misery no longer clung to him like a shroud.

The earl waited until Simmons closed the door, affording them privacy. "Did I not tell you to come to the front door? How am I, and whatever cachet my name still carries, going to give you respectability if you insist on using the servants' entrance."

"I've lived this long without respectability—"

"Only through the grace of God," Hargrove muttered.

"I won't start chasing after it now," Will finished, ignoring the earl's comment.

"You had better if we are to succeed. Without respectability and a sponsor, you'll never infiltrate the higher circles of society. That is what you want, isn't it?" Hargrove eyed him with speculation. "Or have you given up your search?"

"I'll never give up. Not until I find her."

"You believe your sister still lives then?"

Will nodded, unable to force words passed the feelings of guilt and failure constricting his throat.

"Good. We made a bargain, you and I, and I expect you to stand by your word."

"And I told you, I will not get involved in the marriages of the *Ton,* yet you still manage to involve me." He prowled the room. He took in the rich velvet drapery, the lush carpet beneath his feet, the books with their crisp leather bindings lining the walls of the library, the highly polished furniture.

He hated coming here. He felt out of place, as though he was a lad back in the streets begging every rich nabob that happened by for a coin. He'd accomplished much since then, but coming here...it all seemed to melt away. He was back to begging. Not for money this time, but for something much more important—information.

"Is it done then?" Hargrove asked, his voice quiet.

"Aye."

"The answer is 'yes,' not 'aye,'" Hargrove snapped. "You've spoken without a poor man's cant since I met you. Now is not the time to revert to it. If you are to infiltrate the *Ton*, you must look and sound as they do."

"Yes, my lord," Will said with a touch of belligerence as he sketched a mocking bow.

Hargrove sighed. "I apologize. That remark was unkind. I understand how important this is to you...and I owe you a great debt I can truly never repay."

Will waved away the apology. "You owe me nothing. I failed to save your daughter." Clenching his jaw, he forced the memory of Althea Hargrove's bruised and battered body away.

"You brought her home to me. I will always be grateful to you for that. I take a small measure of comfort in knowing she was at least laid to rest with a proper burial." The older man rubbed his forehead and subsided into an oxblood club chair near the fire. "Kate has left. She insisted on going back to the overstuffed mushroom. She feels Glenville will change now."

Will tried to control his laughter given the nature of their conversation, but failed miserably. He was still chuckling as he took a seat across from the earl. "You rich blokes certainly have a strange way of insulting each other. A mushroom?"

"What would you call him?" the earl asked, clearly intrigued with the seamier side of his friend's life.

Remembering what his mother and sister suffered at the hands of his stepfather, Will sobered. "An abusive bastard."

Hargrove nodded and gazed into the fire, his expression pensive.

"Is she aware of what was done?" Will asked.

"No. I told her I would take care of it." Hargrove turned toward him, his eyes full of questions. "What exactly did you do to him?"

Will quickly related his encounter with Glenville, how the earl was divested of his clothes and left to walk back to London.

Hargrove guffawed, wiping away tears of mirth. "I wish I had been present." He laid his handkerchief on the arm of his chair with sudden concern. "You can't be tied to the incident, can you?"

"It was dark, but it doesn't matter. His lordship's clothing and boots were wrapped in his tailor's boxes and delivered to his townhouse the next morning. He can hardly claim to have been robbed when the items taken were returned."

The old earl smiled. "And given his self-importance, I doubt he'll be sharing the experience with his cronies. No matter how he tries to tell the tale, he'll come out looking like a coward." He leaned back in his chair and steepled his fingers. "I only hope it will help

Kate."

"I left him with a warning to provide for his wife." Will paused. "He will receive another, more painful lesson if it becomes necessary."

"Are you ready for your debut at the Riverton Ball?" Hargrove asked, changing the subject almost as though he didn't want to acknowledge just what Will was capable of.

"There may be a problem."

The older man sat forward in his chair. "But you said you couldn't be tied to the Glenville incident."

"No, I said it wouldn't matter if I were. He suffered no harm, and nothing was stolen. There are no charges to be held against me." Will rubbed his jaw. "The problem is a woman."

Hargrove grinned. "Aren't they all?"

Will didn't smile back. The situation was too serious, too important. "She is asking questions. Questions about Lazarus."

"Perhaps she is a young woman in need of his help," the earl offered.

"No. It was just the opposite I'm afraid. I'd been injured—"

"Injured?"

"Shot."

"Shot! Good lord, my boy. When? How?"

"Nearly a week ago. How doesn't matter. What does matter is Olivia St. Germaine is now asking questions. Questions that could cause a great deal of trouble."

"St. Germaine? Sir Philip's sister?"

"Yes."

"Does she know about her brother? What we

suspect him of?"

Will shook his head. "No. Fingers and I made a few comments to gauge her reaction. She defended him. One would think the man was the closest thing to God walking among us the way she carried on about him and his fervent dedication to those wounded in battle."

"It will be a shame when she learns the truth."

"I'm not interested in whether she learns the truth."

Hargrove stood and paced in front of the fireplace. "What can we do?" He stopped in mid-step. "I forbid you to harm her. She's innocent in all of this."

"You forbid?" Will said in a quiet voice as he leaned forward in the chair. Those who knew him, knew when he became quiet was when he was most dangerous.

The earl took a step back. "Perhaps 'forbid' was the wrong choice of word."

Acknowledging the unspoken apology with a nod, Will leaned against the smooth leather seatback. "She'll come to no harm from me." A smile quirked at the corner of his mouth. "She doesn't heed threats very well."

"You threatened her?" Hargrove's voice shook with outrage.

"I would never hurt a woman. You, of all people, should know that."

"Yes, of course. But what of your...friends?"

"Neither she nor any other woman will ever come to harm by my men or by my command."

"Perhaps I should speak to her."

"Not necessary." He rose and crossed to the door. "Contact me in the usual manner once arrangements are made for the Riverton Ball."

"I've already accepted the invitation and let it be known I will be bringing a guest. The only arrangement that needs to be made is where to have my coach pick you up." The earl moved to the center of the room. "Why isn't it necessary?"

"I'm rather certain I succeeded in frightening her off." Will opened the door and walked into the vast marble hall.

"How?" Hargrove rushed after him.

Will took his coat from the waiting footman and shrugged into it. "She now knows how dangerous it is to attract my attention."

"How?" Hargrove repeated. The word was little more than a squeak.

Will smiled. His friend seemed as nearly outraged as Miss St. Germaine had been, though she had had the more wicked tongue of the two. He still bled at her parting remarks. Though she didn't know it, he had had Harry follow her home from the warehouse to ensure she arrived safely. His smile faded. She had found the one weakness in him. His regret for what he could not change.

He signaled to the footman to open the front door and turned to go.

"William?"

"Do not worry so, my lord," he said in a mocking tone. "It was what proper women fear most."

"And that is?"

"A kiss from someone like me."

He left the townhouse without a second glance and disappeared into the darkness, regret weighing a little more heavily than usual.

Chapter Five

Olivia nodded and smiled at Lord and Lady Bromley as they passed, then slipped out the French doors onto the terrace. She moved into the shadows near the balustrade, took a deep breath, and released it slowly. Already, she could feel the tension draining away. She said a silent prayer of thanks that the weather had turned warmer in the past week.

A close intimate gathering of three or four people was much more to her liking, yet here she was at another of Amanda's famous balls. It hadn't been all bad. She'd been successful in her escape from the teeming mass of people who were too busy trying to impress each other to notice her absence. *Thank heavens.*

Setting the glass of champagne she'd carried all night on the flagstones near her feet, she leaned against the stone barrier. She closed her eyes and let the cool air wash over her and tease the loose tendrils of her hair. She smiled, remembering how Amanda had declared her soiree would be an utter failure without Olivia's presence. It was a shame her friend was such a miserable liar.

Voices and the sound of the door opening behind her pushed her down the stairs into the garden. She wasn't ready to give up her solitude so soon. Wending her way around a box hedge, she sat near a small fountain. If she wasn't already viewed as something of an oddity, she supposed sitting here alone as though waiting for a lover would set gossiping tongues to wagging.

But she didn't care. Here was where she wanted to be. The nearly full moon shone almost as brightly as the sun. Crickets chirped, and occasionally the slight breeze ruffled the leaves. The silence was punctuated by the sound of laughter or conversation as people strolled past the hedge, but for the most part, it was quiet and peaceful.

And that was what she needed. She longed for peace, an escape from of the horrible memories of war. It was rare that she found it for more than a few minutes at a time. She'd learned to treasure the silence, to steal away from the prying questions, the pitying looks of the matrons who considered any woman unmarried as a creature to be ashamed of.

She sighed and stood. As much as she loathed the idea, she should return to the house. Amanda would send Lord Riverton after her if she disappeared for too long. And somehow, no matter how large the crush, her friend always knew when she left the ballroom in search of her ever-elusive peace.

Moving around the end of the hedge, Olivia dug through her reticule for her timepiece. Perhaps it was late enough for her to make her excuses and take her leave. Curling up with the latest Minerva Press novel seemed a much more preferable way to spend the remainder of the night.

Her fingers closed around the timepiece, and she tilted it toward the moon, using the light to read the watch face. Focusing on the hands, she stumbled to one side as someone bumped into her. A hand clasped her elbow, steadying her.

"Thank you," she said as she watched the drunken gentleman who'd bumped into her continue down the path without so much as an apology.

She turned to her rescuer to express her thanks properly and froze. The one person who haunted her thoughts as easily as her battlefield memories stood before her.

"You!" She pulled her arm from Lazarus' light grasp, determined not to notice how his hair shone blue-black in the moonlight, how different he looked in proper evening dress.

With a small smile playing about his lips, he bowed. "At your service, my lady." His eyes sparkled, reminding her of the black Jet necklace the Duchess of Cornwall wore that very evening.

"I'm not a 'Lady,'" she retorted. She couldn't believe he had followed her here. Here to Amanda's first ball of the Season.

Lazarus' eyebrows rose. "You're not?"

Then she realized what she had said and how he had deliberately mistaken her meaning. "I don't hold the title of 'Lady' as you very well know." She glanced up and down the path. "What are you doing here?" she asked in a low undertone.

"I am an invited guest."

"Invited?" Olivia's voice rose, and she quickly lowered it. "Invited by whom? Amanda, Lady Riverton, knows nothing about you."

"Why do you assume I am dishonourable and would come where I am not invited?"

"Did you not leave me to find my own way home

when I came to your warehouse to check on your wound? Surely, you of all people, know the dangers to a woman unaccompanied at night especially in that area of London. I don't think there is much honour in that."

Lazarus stiffened at the insult, but Olivia was past caring. He had risked her life that night, and she had barely managed to reach her home before suffering an attack of panic and fear that had felt suffocating in its intensity. Even now she felt her breath starting to come too quickly, her nerves sending signals to flee. No, she wouldn't let him know how he affected her. He would only find a way to use it to his advantage. She drew in a deep breath and held it, before releasing it slowly. She had to remain calm.

"Prescott. There you are." Lord Hargrove approached, a handkerchief dangling from his fingers. "It is hotter than Hades in that ballroom." Realizing the other man wasn't alone, he smiled. "I see you've made an acquaintance." He came to an abrupt stop and looked between the two.

Lazarus stepped smoothly into the sudden silence. "Yes. We were introduced by—"

"A mutual friend," Olivia finished. She curtseyed to Hargrove. "It is good to see you in company again, my lord."

"Ah, yes. It is good to see you as well." The earl lifted her hand to his lips with a distracted air. He turned to Lazarus. "I came to tell you I was taking my leave." He looked at Olivia, then at Lazarus. "But perhaps I should stay a bit longer."

"No need, my lord. No need at all."

Hargrove opened his mouth then paused. "Very well," he said after a long moment.

Though she didn't see anything overt, Olivia was certain some sort of silent communication had occurred between the two men.

The earl turned toward her. "I shall bid you good night then and wish you a pleasant remainder of your evening."

She curtseyed again. "Thank you, my lord."

Hargrove nodded to his friend, then turned on his heel and headed back toward the terrace.

"What are you doing out here alone?" Lazarus asked as soon as the other man was out of earshot.

"What are you doing here at all? How are you and Lord Hargrove acquainted?" Olivia countered. "I told you to stay away from me."

"Should I have allowed you to fall when you were knocked aside by one of your Society 'gentlemen'?" he asked in a mocking tone.

"No. Thank you again." She hated the thought of thanking him when he had her knocked unconscious and then played a part in her humiliation only a few days ago.

He smiled and rubbed the side of his finger against the edge of his lower lip, drawing her attention to the deep dimples in his cheeks. "I get the impression you don't quite mean that."

"Olivia!"

Turning at the sound of her name, Olivia tried to suppress a grimace. Amanda was headed straight toward them, determination in every stride.

"Someone you wish to avoid?" he asked.

"No. She is a friend." *Very nearly my only friend.* "But your presence will be hard to explain."

Lady Riverton drew to a halt at the edge of the

path. "Olivia?" There was a wealth of question in the single word.

Realizing she still stood in the grass with Lazarus, Olivia stepped onto the path. "Amanda, your ball is a smashing success. I'm certain it will be the talk of all Society. Those who didn't attend shall be green with envy."

Lady Riverton ignored her and looked at Lazarus. "I don't believe we've met."

Olivia jumped into the breach. "Lady Riverton, may I present—"

"Mr. William Prescott, at your service," Lazarus said as he raised her hand to his lips though his gaze never left Olivia's.

"I'm certain your name wasn't on the guest list."

"Amanda," Olivia gasped. She'd never known her friend to be rude.

"Forgive me, Lady Riverton." Lazarus gave a slight bow. "I'm afraid I pressed Lord Hargrove into allowing me to accompany him this evening. He hasn't been well since the death of his daughter."

"You are acquainted with Lord Hargrove?" Amanda asked, her surprise registering in her voice.

"A friend of the family."

"I hope you enjoy the rest of the ball." She linked her arm through Olivia's. "Come, there is something you must see."

Rather than draw attention, Olivia allowed herself to be led away. "What is wrong?"

"You were standing in the shadows talking with a strange man, and you ask what is wrong?"

"We were properly introduced by Lord Hargrove." She looked back over her shoulder. Lazarus, or should she think of him as Mr. Prescott now, followed at a discreet distance.

"There is hardly anything proper about Hargrove. He flaunts his mistresses all about Town," Amanda snapped.

"That is just gossip. Do you honestly believe the way the man has been grieving for his daughter that he is keeping a mistress?"

"It doesn't matter if it is or isn't true, you should know that. Look at all the things that are said about you that aren't true. If you keep associating with the wrong type of people, your reputation will suffer even more."

Olivia came to an abrupt halt. "The wrong type of people?" She tried to keep control of her temper. "Who exactly are the wrong type of people? Are they those people who must earn their living through trade, those people who exist on the fringes of Polite Society like Lord Hargrove or Mr. Prescott? Or people like me whom all you great members of the *Ton* look at with pity and treat as one of your own but then gossip about as soon as we are out of sight?"

"Don't be ridiculous. That is not at all what I meant." Lady Riverton stepped closer and asked in a concerned voice, "Are you suffering nightmares again? Is that what this is all about?"

Olivia bit back the urge to scream in frustration. Amanda was a dear friend, but at times she was woefully self-absorbed. Hearing movement behind her, she spun around. "Do you always skulk about eavesdropping?"

"May I help you with something?" Amanda smiled, ever the hostess.

Lazarus gazed at Olivia for a long moment, then

glanced at Lady Riverton. "I believe you already have." He gave a slight nod of his head and climbed the stairs leading to the terrace.

Olivia watched him until he was swallowed up by the teeming mass of people populating the ballroom. She didn't understand what he meant by his strange remark. How had Amanda helped him?

"Come inside. I believe you need a glass of sherry." Her friend smiled and added in a laughing whisper, "I tell Riverton I use it for medicinal purposes only."

She sighed and followed the younger woman inside. She hadn't the heart to fight or to inform her that she had never used sherry for medicinal purposes. Whiskey, yes. Even brandy once, but sherry, never.

She'd no more than stepped through the French doors when the babble of numerous conversations rose and swelled. Telling herself she did not care if she was the subject of those conversations, she inhaled deeply. The smell of too many overheated and perfumed bodies assailed her senses, and she forced back a gag. Allowing Amanda to shepherd her through the crowd, she looked back over her shoulder and longed for the peace of the garden.

Lazarus stood near the doors. He raised his glass of champagne in a silent salute. She quickly looked forward again.

****

Will watched Olivia walk away. He'd ceased thinking of her as "Miss St. Germaine" since the night she'd come to his warehouse on the docks. The rather modest deep blue gown emphasized her figure. He forced his gaze upward away from her shapely hips.

Her dark brown curls gleamed in the hundreds of candles in the chandeliers overhead. His fingers had itched to caress her hair much like the wind had done earlier when she first appeared on the terrace.

Realizing he was staring, he turned and scanned the crowd. It wouldn't do to become distracted. There was no sign of His Grace, the Duke of Sandhurst. Will pushed down the familiar wave of anger that always threatened to erupt at the mere mention of the man's name.

Perhaps an innocent question or two would lead to the duke's whereabouts. It was a known fact that Sandhurst never declined an invitation from Lady Riverton. Her gatherings were full of the important people he would want to impress. It also allowed him to keep abreast of the latest gossip and scandal. And more importantly, made him privy to information to be used against his peers in due time.

Will wandered around the perimeter of the room, searching for the man he suspected in his sister's disappearance. He stopped by the table of refreshments and exchanged his empty champagne flute for a glass of punch. Under the guise of taking a sip of the liquid, he gazed out over the crush of guests. He grimaced at the awful taste and set the glass back on the table, wishing he'd brought along his flask of brandy.

Out of the corner of his eye, he thought he caught the familiar figure of the duke. He turned quickly and plunged into the crowd, murmuring excuses as he passed. As he closed the distance between himself and his quarry, he slowed his pace. He had no wish to approach the man. Yet.

He halted a few feet away, willing the man to face

him. The man turned. It wasn't Sandhurst after all. Frustration ate at him, but he didn't allow it to push him into making foolish mistakes. He would bide his time. He needed to keep his wits about him if he hoped to find Mary; he could wait a little longer.

He stood there long after the person he'd mistaken as Sandhurst walked away. The mass of people ebbed and flowed around him. Will moved in a slow circle, looking about him.

Olivia stood near Lord and Lady Riverton as they conversed with an elderly couple. His gaze nearly completed its circuit of the room when he froze. There near the entrance of the ballroom. Lord Sandhurst. There was no mistaking him this time, puffed up with self-importance, he smiled at a young girl who looked to be no more than sixteen and her very happy mother.

Will headed toward his nemesis. A sense of calm settled over him. He'd waited far too long for this moment. He would finally meet the Duke of Sandhurst as an equal. Not in social standing, but in something much more important—power. And then one day, one day soon, he would kill him.

He stopped directly behind the blushing young girl, certain Sandhurst could not help but notice his presence.

His Grace looked up, and their gazes met. The duke stumbled over his words.

A slow smile curving his lips, Will nodded in acknowledgement and walked away. Sandhurst knew he had gained entrance to his world. And for tonight, that was enough.

Drifting from one group of people to another, he listened to the conversations, hoping to learn something useful about his enemy. Even with Hargrove's introduction, he was treated with distant politeness. He knew he only had to let it be known that he possessed a modest fortune, and he would be as fawned over as the Prince Regent himself.

Unfortunately, he didn't want that information bandied about. Especially now that he was trying to leave his criminal past behind. Having to explain how he had amassed those first few hundred pounds would ruin his reputation as a legitimate businessman.

"Excuse me, sir." A hand tapped him on the shoulder.

Will turned.

"Mr. Prescott?" the footman asked.

"Yes."

"I have a message for you." The footman held out a folded sheet of parchment.

Will glanced at the servant's outstretched hand. "Do you know who it is from?"

"His Grace, the Duke of Sandhurst."

"This should be enlightening," he murmured, taking the note.

The footman bowed and walked away. Will moved to the edge of the ballroom. He flipped the folded sheet of vellum over. There was nothing written on the outside. For a long moment, he stared at the wax seal depicting the duke's crest.

The lion standing on its hind legs, a bird crushed under one paw reminded him of a time he'd rather forget. He rubbed at the sudden burning sensation at the back of his neck and closed his eyes for a brief moment. He hated the insignia almost as much as the man it stood for.

Feeling curious and a small sense of dread he refused to acknowledge, he snapped the wax seal in half and unfolded the message.

"Laz—"

Will looked up at the sound of Olivia's voice. "Mr. Prescott," he corrected quietly.

"Mr. Prescott." She glanced toward the doors leading to the terrace. "I wonder if I may beg a favor of you," she finished in a rush.

Fear lurked in her eyes, her face pale. Her agitation was palpable.

"What has happened?" he asked.

She looked to the French doors again.

He reached out to touch her arm, remembered at the last moment that the familiarity of the gesture wasn't proper, and dropped his hand.

"Would you be so kind as to allow me the use of your carriage?" She twisted her fan in her hands. Will heard the delicate ivory ribs snap and doubted she was even aware of it.

"You don't have a carriage of your own?"

"Lady Riverton sent her coach to pick me up. I was to spend the night." She stared into the night before meeting his gaze, her blue eyes imploring. "Please. I need to leave."

He shoved the missive from Sandhurst into his frock coat pocket and maneuvered her through the crush of guests and out of the ballroom. "Did someone make improper advances?" he asked in a low voice.

She shook her head.

Taking her pelisse from the waiting footman, he helped her into it. He shrugged into his own coat and ushered her out to his carriage.

The wind whistled through the newly blossoming trees. Thunder crashed overhead. Olivia jumped back with a whimper, nearly colliding with him as he followed behind. He put his arm around her waist and hurried her to the coach, propriety be damned.

"Take us to the St. Germaine residence," he said to the driver, closing the door behind him.

As the carriage moved forward, he lit one of the interior lamps. Olivia sat huddled in the far corner, her eyes squeezed closed, her lips moving soundlessly.

"Miss St. Germaine. Miss St. Germaine." He raised her chin with gentle fingers. "Olivia, tell me what happened."

She opened her eyes and stared at him. Only she wasn't looking at him, she was looking through him. It was as though he wasn't there. A crack of thunder filled the silence, followed by a flash of lightning. She clutched at his hand, her lips moving faster.

It dawned on him then. She was afraid of the storm, of the thunder in particular. He ducked his head to hide a smile of relief and moved onto the bench beside her.

The thunder rolled overhead while rain battered against the roof of the carriage. Olivia covered her ears with her hands and rocked back and forth. Putting his arm around her, he pulled her close, trying to offer the comfort of his presence. As a child, he had always been less afraid when he wasn't alone.

Realizing she was still whispering to herself, he leaned closer.

"It's only thunder. It's only thunder. It's not cannon fire. It's not cannon fire. It's not cannon fire," she repeated over and over.

Chapter Six

Cannon fire? Will didn't know what she meant by
that. He watched over her, not sure how else to offer
comfort from the storm.

The carriage pulled to a stop, and he sent up a
small prayer of thanks that the St. Germaine townhouse
was not a great distance from the Riverton home. Once
he saw her safely inside with a cup of tea, Olivia should
be fine. He looked down at her white face as the
footman opened the door, an umbrella in hand to shield
them from the elements. Tea be damned, she needed a
bracing glass of brandy.

Will stepped down from the coach and helped her
out. Making certain the footman was keeping her
sheltered from the rain, he pulled up the collar of his
coat and followed them. They entered the townhouse
just as a loud crack of thunder bellowed overhead,
shaking the timbers of the building.

Olivia whipped off her pelisse and strode down the
hall. "Ellie, where are you?" she called. "We must
hurry. They will be arriving soon."

"I'm here, Mum. I've already started with the
bandages." The young maid who'd helped out the night
he'd arrived injured handed a stack of white linen
folded into small squares to Olivia.

Bandages? Will shrugged out of his great coat,
handed it to the footman, and walked down the hall.

"Good. I know I can count on you to keep a level head." Olivia opened the door off to the left. "We'll have them put the wounded in here. Remember, I need to see the most serious injuries first."

Ellie bobbed her head. "Yes, Mum."

Wounded? Will glanced at Olivia and then the maid. What was going on?

"I'll need my instruments," Olivia called over her shoulder as she climbed the stairs.

"I puts them on a table next to the cots." Ellie gave Will a wary glance, then dashed up the stairs after her mistress.

Cots? Instruments? Who was she expecting that would be wounded? Was she like her brother after all? Taking advantage of those who could ill afford proper medical care? Will took the stairs two at a time. He reached the top just in time to see the two women disappear into a room near the end of the hall. He quickened his stride.

Stopping in the doorway of the room, which from the décor could only be the library, he took in the scene before him. Elaborate cabinets with glass doors guarded rows upon rows of books. A plush blue carpet lay underfoot while matching drapery hung at the two windows on the far side of the room. A fire burned low in the hearth.

Olivia stood near a credenza, sorting the folded linen into small piles while Ellie hovered in the background. Will spied a sideboard with various decanters. Olivia may not need a brandy any longer, but he did.

"Stop!"

Will froze. He'd taken no more than a few steps

71

into the room when she shouted the command. He watched her weave her way across the room as though she was walking around objects in her path.

She stopped in front of him, her gaze roaming over him. "Are you injured?"

He looked at her. His bullet wound was healing, but she knew that. "I do not believe so," he answered carefully.

She let out a sigh of relief. "Oh. Then you must be here to help."

"I..." Will didn't know what to say. She acted as though she had no idea who he was or why he was there.

She pulled him along behind her as she threaded her way back to the waiting piles of linen. Placing a handful of the folded squares in his hand, she glanced around. "Here, this man needs pressure applied to his wound." Olivia walked away.

Will stared after her. What man? The room was empty save for the two of them and the maid.

Olivia stopped and looked back at him. "Hurry." She turned away only to look at him once more. "You don't suffer from the vapors at the sight of blood, do you?"

Not certain what was happening, he shook his head. She moved back to where he stood and grasped his wrist, leading him to a spot a few feet away. Taking a few of the linen squares from him, she pressed them down against nothing but thin air.

"This will help stop the bleeding. Do not worry about hurting him. You must keep pressure on the wound." She placed his hand over hers, then slid hers out from underneath.

Will grabbed at the cloth, not wanting it to fall to the floor. He worried how she would react if that happened. He looked over at her. She smiled and nodded and moved off to help another man who didn't exist. He wasn't certain how long he stared at her as she moved around the room, applying bandages and sewing wounds that only she could see.

A tap on his arm drew his attention. The maid stood near him, a wad of linen in her hand.

"Ellie—"

"Bridget. Me name is Bridget."

"What's wrong with Miss St. Germaine?"

"I don't know. She acts like this sometimes when it be stormy."

"Ellie."

Bridget jumped and turned away. "Yes, Mum?" she asked, hurrying to her mistress's side, though mindful enough to move around the imaginary cots of wounded men.

"I..." Olivia blinked, gave a slight shake of her head, then looked down at her hands.

The faint sound of thunder in the distance drew her gaze to the window. She bit her lip. "It happened again, didn't it?" she whispered.

"Yes, ma'am," Bridget said in a somber voice.

Olivia glanced around the room, her gaze settling on Will. He returned her gaze. He heard tales of men returning from war who relived the experiences they suffered there. Could that be what happened here? Her cheekbones flushed with color, and she turned away.

"Will you help me to my bedchamber?" she asked.

Bridget put her arm around Olivia and led her from the room. She looked back over her shoulder, her gaze

73

pleading.

Will nodded. He would keep her secret.

"Should I be asking Mr. Jennings to bring ye a wee bit of brandy to help ye sleep?" Bridget guided Olivia out of the room.

"That might be best." Olivia sighed and allowed the servant to usher her down the hall.

Will stared at the empty doorway. He turned away, determined not to let the appearance of her fragile mental state deter him from implementing the plan that had grown like a seed in his mind. A seed planted by Lady Amanda Riverton this very evening.

He had planned on striking a bargain with Miss Olivia St. Germaine. One she wouldn't be able to refuse if she valued her reputation. She would help him gather information from her acquaintances in the *Ton* about Sandhurst, and he wouldn't expose the fact that she had spent time with him and Fingers without a proper chaperone, though he was injured at the time.

The idea had blossomed as he listened to Lady Riverton's tirade regarding her friend's association with the wrong sort of people. Olivia may not be aware of it, but he knew Lady Riverton wouldn't hesitate to treat her like a social pariah should any more scandal attach itself to the St. Germaine name.

Given Lady Riverton's status, he had no doubt the other members of Society would follow her lead. He guessed Olivia was only accepted now due to her ladyship's good grace. And it wouldn't take more than the veriest whiff of the wrong sort of gossip to change that.

One last faint rumble of thunder drew his gaze to the entryway. The hall stood dark and silent. Olivia had sounded so...lost.

He turned away, running a hand through his hair. He couldn't let himself be deterred from blackmailing her into helping him. He had already waited too long to get close to the duke to let such an opportunity simply slip away.

Remembering the note he'd received from Sandhurst just before leaving the Riverton ball, Will pulled the crumpled sheet of parchment from his pocket. He smoothed the folds and held the sheet under the wall sconce. The note was brief, to the point.

Do not do something Mary would hate you for and you would regret.

Sandhurst

The words mocked him. The bastard had all but admitted he knew where Mary was. The missive only hardened his resolve to find his sister and make the duke pay. Pay with his very life.

****

Olivia dropped her quill onto the desktop and stood. From the sound of the commotion coming from the entrance hall, the man known as both Lazarus and Mr. Prescott was not going to be put off any longer. Smoothing her hands over her skirts, she rounded the desk and headed out of the room. She came to a stop at the top of the stairs.

"Miss St. Germaine is not receiving callers today, I tell you."

"And I am telling you, I will not leave without seeing her."

"I would prefer not to have you put out, but if you insist on this course, I'll have no alternative." Jennings signaled to the footman to come forward.

"It's all right, Jennings," she called. "I will see him." She turned on her heel and strode back to the study. She needed a few minutes to compose herself before facing the man.

Touching a hand to her forehead, she paced behind the desk. What could she say to explain her actions of the night before? Footsteps in the hall sounded his arrival, and she quickly sat. He may have insisted on seeing her, but she would do her best to control the meeting.

"Please come in." She gestured to the hard-backed chair in front of the desk.

He glanced from the chair to her. "Do you always torture your guests by making them sit on such uncomfortable pieces of furniture?

"You are hardly a guest. I allowed Jennings to permit you entrance because I didn't want to give my neighbors the satisfaction of having something to gossip about when Jennings and Daniel removed you from the premises."

Lazarus sat on the corner of the desk and leaned toward her. His finger tapped her chin. "Do you honestly believe they would have been able to do so?"

She moved back, away from his touch. She didn't bother to respond to his question. They both already knew the answer. "Why are you here?"

"I see your manners need as much polish as mine." He slid from the desk, walked across the room, and closed the door.

"I would prefer the door open." Olivia stood.

"I would prefer our conversation is not overheard."

"I have nothing to hide from my staff. They are already in possession of my worst secret."

He looked at her for a long moment as though he was trying to decide how much to say. "I'm searching for someone, and I believe the Duke of Sandhurst has the information that will help me locate her."

"Why are you here and not at the duke's residence then?"

"I've already approached him without success. You may be able to help me get the information."

She stared at him in disbelief. "I'm afraid you are mistaken if you think the duke will give me more than a passing glance. I may attend some of the same entertainments, but I am hardly among his acquaintances."

"But surely your friends, such as the Rivertons, count him among their number."

"Perhaps."

"I thought we could strike a bargain of sorts. You have a secret you need to keep from Polite Society, and I need a way to gather information."

Olivia stared at him, outrage and a strange sense of disappointment stealing over her. "Ah. I understand now. I give you entrée into Society, and you will not tell anyone how I am losing my mind."

Lazarus moved to stand in front of the desk. "How are you feeling today?"

How dare he show concern when he just proposed to blackmail her. She stalked toward the window and stared out at the street below. "You needn't concern yourself, sir. I suffer from nightmares and the occasional slip back into the past, but I rarely howl at the moon like a mad dog any longer."

He clasped her upper arm and turned her to face him. "I do not ask to insult you—"

"No, you ask only to remind me that you will tell the *Ton* if I do not bow to your blackmail." She pulled her arm free.

"You paid me a kindness by attending to my bullet wound and then sought me out to ensure I was healing properly. Why do you not think I might want to repay that by being concerned for your health?"

"Because I am nothing but a pawn in this strange game you are playing with the Duke of Sandhurst. You, sir, are not a friend of mine, so don't pretend to be. People do not blackmail their friends." She crossed to the door and held it open. Lazarus had more than overstayed his welcome.

He moved with a powerful grace she tried hard not to notice. Wresting the door from her grasp, he closed it with a quiet click.

She glared at him, grabbed the handle, and opened the door mere inches before he slammed it closed with the flat of his hand against the wooden panel. Leaning his weight on it, he smiled at her. "Do not tempt me into a tussle with you over the door." His smile grew wider. "Though on second thought, I may enjoy it."

Looking away from his coal dark eyes, Olivia tried to fight the burning sensation spreading across her cheeks. She moved away, eager to put space between them. "I do not understand how you can blackmail me and then in a matter of seconds play the flirt."

His smile disappeared. "Must you harp on about blackmail? Can you not see it as an agreement to help one another?"

"Help one another? How are you helping me? By not having me ostracized by a society that barely accepts me as it is?"

"Perhaps I can help you in another way." He moved toward her, his gaze predatory.

Olivia backed up until she hit the edge of the desk. Afraid to take her gaze from him, she reached for some type of weapon. From what the Bow Street Runner had told her, Lazarus could be dangerous. She just never expected him to hurt her.

Her fingers closed over a paperweight shaped like an apple. It was small, but heavy, being fashioned from sterling silver. Could she use it to cosh him over the head if necessary?

As though he had read her thoughts, he grabbed her hand and forced the trinket from her grasp with ease. He turned it over in his hand, tossed it up in the air, and caught it. "You weren't thinking to hit me in the brain box with this, were you, Olivia?"

"Don't be ridiculous." She hoped the tremor in her voice didn't give away her fear. Leaning back to put as much space between them as possible, she cleared her throat, gathered her courage, and continued on as any good soldier would. "I do believe I haven't given you leave to use my Christian name."

"Surely after seeing me without a shirt, not to mention having your hands all over my body, we are beyond formality at this point." He tossed the paperweight onto the desk, his eyes alight with laughter.

"My hands..." she sputtered. He made it sound as though they had been intimate when nothing could be further from the truth. She'd cared for his injury, nothing more. "You are no gentleman to say such things."

His smile disappeared, and his gaze turned serious.

"I've never claimed to be one. It is best you remember that." He took a step back.

Olivia took advantage of the movement and slid three steps to the left.

He watched her, his gaze hooded. "I noticed you seem to be enamored of Lord Michael Huntley."

"Lord Michael?" She automatically used the name she'd called him since childhood instead of his proper address. How could he have learned of her *tendre* for Huntley? She always made certain to treat him no differently than anyone else. "We have known each other since we were children. I do not know what you mean."

"I'm certain you were being discreet, but when you thought no one was paying attention, your gaze rarely left him at the Riverton Ball. A woman doesn't watch a man like that unless she has feelings for him." He paused. "More than likely, feelings that aren't returned."

She lifted one shoulder in a careless shrug and turned away. "So now you know another of my secrets. It must please you to have even more ammunition to hold over my head."

"That's not why I mention it."

She turned back. "Then why do you?" she snapped. "To torture me, punish me perhaps for asking questions about you, seeking you out to make certain your wound was healing properly?"

"You will be doing me a favor by ensuring I get invitations to the same events Sandhurst does."

"I would hardly call it a favor, as my only other option is having my private life given to the gossips to salivate over."

Lazarus scowled. "Must you natter on about my supposed blackmail of you?"

"Supposed?"

He ran a hand through his hair. Olivia watched the black strands run across his fingers and found herself wishing she could do the same. Would it feel as soft and silky as it looked? She shook her head as she realized what she was thinking. Good lord, perhaps she should be in Bedlam. How could she be attracted to a man who could crush her with just a word in the wrong ear?

"I'm trying to make amends for forcing you into helping me. I thought I would help you make Huntley jealous."

Olivia burst out laughing. Putting a hand over her mouth, she bit her lip in an effort to gain control. "Please do not take this as an insult. But Lord Michael is hardly going to be jealous if he sees us together."

"Why not? You are a beautiful woman."

She clenched her jaw and felt her lips tighten into a thin line. "Flattery is not necessary. Lord Michael sees me as nothing more than a childhood friend, an honorary sister, if you like. It would be a waste of time and an embarrassment to me to try to make him jealous."

Lazarus opened his mouth, and she rushed into speech, cutting him off. "I'll help you gather the information you seek, not because you plan on filling my head with lies of my great beauty, but because I have no other choice." She held up a finger. "But I do have one condition you must agree to."

"I don't think you are much of a position to put on conditions on what you will do."

She nodded her head in acknowledgement. "What you say is true. And although you claim you are not a gentleman, you do say you are a man of honour."

He glared at her. "What is your blasted condition?"

"You will help me locate my brother."

He rubbed a finger back and forth just below his lower lip, his expression thoughtful. "Help you?"

Olivia conceded she needed him to do more than help her. "Being the person you are, I'd like you to find Phillip. I fear he has somehow gotten himself involved in something he may not know how to get out of."

"The person I am?" Lazarus' voice was quiet with just a hint of impatience.

"I didn't mean that as an insult, but you must admit you would hear things among your…friends and…acquaintances that I would never know of."

"True." He lifted her hand and held it between them. "What benefit do I receive if I agree to your condition?"

"I will secure as many invitations as I can as you requested."

"And?"

"And what?"

"Helping me gain entrance to various social events was already part of the bargain before you insisted on your condition."

"What else do you want?"

He lifted her hand to his lips and gazed at her. "Honourability makes for a lonely bedfellow."

She snatched her hand back. "I will not become your mistress. Not even to find my brother."

He gave a careless shrug. "Pity."

She crossed the room, needed to put space between

them before her temper took control and she told him to go to the devil. As much as she loathed to admit it, she needed his help to find out what Phillip had gotten himself involved in.

"Do not fret. I will do what I can to learn your brother's whereabouts."

She stalked back to him. "I am not fretting. I'm trying to decide how much I would care if you spilled my secrets. I have but one true friend associated with the *Ton,* so my life would not change so much if I am no longer welcome among them. I'm not certain I want to help you secure invitations to events given by the *Beau Monde.*" She crossed her arms over her chest, daring him to do his worst.

Lazarus smiled, and Olivia felt the first frisson of unease. He walked past her, stopping just behind her. She started to turn, but he held her in place. "You will help me or I will do more than tell your secrets," he said in her ear.

"I no longer care if you do."

"Are you certain?" he asked in a silky voice. "Perhaps I will locate your brother and ensure he meets a less than pleasant end."

She whirled around then. "You wouldn't."

"You've been asking questions about me, surely you've learned just what I'm capable of. My reputation was not acquired by issuing empty threats. I have earned it by word and by deed, and I am quite pleased with the results it brings me."

The Bow Street Runner's words came back to her. Durant had said it was rumoured Lazarus had blinded a man and worse. How could she have thought to try to bargain with the man? Now, she may have put her brother's life in danger. "If I secure you invitations, you won't harm Phillip?"

"You have my word."

Olivia took a deep breath. "Then I shall do my best to ensure you are invited to the same entertainments as the Duke of Sandhurst."

"I knew you would agree to my proposal if given the proper incentive."

Chapter Seven

Olivia paced in front of the rows of books that took up the entire east wall of the library. She seemed to be doing a great deal of pacing lately. Coming to a halt, she closed her eyes and took a deep breath, letting it out slowly. Calm. She must stay calm.

She had done as Lazarus insisted—secured an invitation for herself and a guest to an upcoming ball. Now she felt as nervous as a green recruit before his first battle.

It had been nearly a week since he proposed his so-called bargain. She'd received no response to her note, sent two days earlier, informing him of the engagement. Should she seek him out? Would he tell her how he planned to proceed once they arrived at Lady Bingham's townhouse?

She rubbed the area above her left eye. The tension of her current situation and lack of proper sleep had combined to give her a headache. The nightmares had returned with a vengeance these last two nights. She placed the blame at Lazarus' feet for their sudden reoccurrence.

She sighed and glanced around the room. The fire flickered in the grate, sending glimmers of light into the late afternoon gloominess of the room. The club chairs and small writing desk were shrouded in shadows. Perhaps she should light a candle. Outside, the rain pattered against the windows, but thankfully, there was no thunder.

Curling up on the settee, she closed her eyes and tried not to contemplate how she managed to get into such a predicament. A knock on the door pushed her into a sitting position. "Come in," she called.

"A man come to the servants' entrance," Bridget said. "He is wantin' to talk to you. Says it's important."

Lazarus. Olivia jumped to her feet. "Where is he?"

"I left him waitin' in the kitchen."

She hurried down the hall. Pushing through the kitchen door, she came to a stop. It wasn't Lazarus waiting to see her, but Patrick. "Yes?" she asked. His earlier threat to hurt her if she didn't stop asking questions made her wary.

"Lazarus be needin' ye."

Olivia shook her head and backed up a step. She wouldn't be going anywhere with him. She didn't trust him.

"He's waitin' for ye. We 'ave to hurry." He crossed the room and grabbed her by the arm, pulling her toward the outside door.

"Daniel," Olivia yelled.

Bridget grabbed a heavy skillet off the table and hefted it over her head just as the door to the kitchen burst open. The footman stood there, his chest heaving, fists clenched. Jennings followed close behind.

Patrick glanced from the two men, to the pan, and then to Bridget. He freed Olivia instantly and moved away, his hands held outward. "You don't understand. Lazarus needs yer help. The hackney is outside." He pointed to the two men. "Ye can bring them if ye must."

Olivia stared at the younger man. His expression was full of worry. Surely, he didn't mean to hurt her if he was willing to allow Daniel and Jennings to accompany them.

"You'll be needing yer doctoring things."

Had Lazarus been shot again? She turned to the footman. "Bring my cloak and a coat for yourself. I will get my medical case." She looked at Patrick. "We'll be ready to leave in a moment." As she left the room, she swore she saw a flicker of relief cross his face.

Her case in hand, she hurried back to meet the others. Worry pulled at her. Lazarus had had barely enough time to recover from his last bullet wound. She took her cloak from the footman, swung it over her shoulders, and headed for the servants' entrance. Daniel and Patrick jostled against one another as they followed. Ignoring the sounds of pushing and shoving, she opened the door and froze.

Lazarus stood in the opening, his hair and clothes wet from the rain.

"I need your help."

He stepped into the room, his coat wrapped around the large bundle he carried. He shifted the weight, and the side of his coat fell back, revealing the battered face of a young girl.

Patrick rushed forward. "I tried to get her to come."

Lazarus glanced at Olivia, then back at the youth. "Fingers will need you."

The young man nodded and disappeared into the rain without another word.

Olivia took one look at the girl and spun on her heel. "Follow me." She left the room, then called over her shoulder, "Daniel, bring a towel for our guest."

Entering the infirmary, she set about lighting the lamps on the sideboard and credenza. Lazarus stood in the doorway, his arms cradled around the girl.

"Put her down here." She patted the cot, set her medical case down on the nearby table, and opened it.

He lay his burden down on the cot and with gentle fingers, peeled back his coat. The girl whimpered, her hand clutching at his shirt.

"Shh. You're safe here." He uncurled her fingers from his shirtfront and dropped a kiss on her forehead.

He met Olivia's gaze. "Her name is Rachel."

Olivia nodded, trying to control her temper at the sight before her. The girl's nose and mouth were bloody, her right eye dark purple and swollen. Another bruise darkened her left cheekbone. Her wrist lay at an odd angle across her chest. She couldn't have been more than twelve years of age. "Who did this to her?"

Lazarus shook his head. "It doesn't matter."

Olivia looked up from dabbing the blood from the girl's nose. "It *does* matter."

"It doesn't concern you."

Straightening, she glared at him. "You bring a young girl who has obviously been beaten to me for help, and you say it is no concern of mine? By bringing her here, you make it my concern."

Ignoring her, he took the towel the footman held out. He wiped his face and ran the towel over his hair. Droplets of rain hid in the dark strands, reminding her of shining diamonds in the lamplight. Realizing she was staring, she swallowed and quickly set to work washing away the last of the blood from Rachel's mouth and nose.

"Please send for Mr. Durant," Olivia said as the

footman moved to the door.

"Wait," Lazarus commanded. "Durant, the Bow Street Runner?"

"Yes."

"He's not needed."

"What? Of course a member of the law is needed. The person who did this needs to be punished."

He looked at Rachel for a long time. When he raised his head, his eyes were black chips of ice. "He will be."

Olivia quelled the urge to step back. His anger pulsed through the room like a living thing. Now was not the time to press him to do the proper thing. With one last glance at his stony expression, she set about splinting the young girl's wrist. It was obviously broken and would take a great deal of time and care to heal properly.

Setting aside the extra cloth she'd used to wrap the splint, she watched him from under her lashes. She wasn't sure how he would react to her next request. Clearing her throat, she met his gaze. "I'd like you to step out into the hall for a few moments."

He shook his head. "I'm not leaving her. I promised I would stay with her, and I will."

"I understand that...but I need to check to see if she was..." She trailed off, not sure how to put her fear that Rachel had been raped into words.

He stiffened. It was as though he understood her worry without her having to voice it. "That didn't happen."

"Are you certain?" she asked, hating to press the subject.

"Yes," he rasped. "Patrick stopped the bastard in

time."

Feeling an enormous sense of relief, Olivia brushed a few strands of hair from the girl's cheek. "Would you be willing to turn your back? I'd like to remove her dress and check for other injuries."

A muscle jumped in his cheek telling her he was only just managing to keep his anger in check. He nodded and turned away.

Wasting no time, she removed the ragged gown and ran her hands over Rachel's chest and limbs, trying to ascertain if she had suffered other injuries. A deep blue contusion ran from just under her ribs nearly to her waist. Olivia applied a gentle pressure along the length. Rachel moaned in response.

Lazarus started to turn, then stopped, his back stiffening at the sound of the young girl's pain. "You're hurting her."

"Not intentionally, I assure you. I'm trying to ascertain if she suffered breaks in her ribs." Olivia draped a sheet over her. "You may turn around now."

He looked at her over his shoulder, then turned to face the cot. Curling his hand around Rachel's limp fingers, he gave it a gentle squeeze.

Touched by his kindness to the girl, Olivia moved away to give them a measure of privacy. Under the pretense of having something to do, she lifted a nearby ewer of water, poured it into the basin, and washed her hands. "She will be fine in a few weeks' time," she said in a reassuring tone. "She has some terrible bruising, but I do not believe any ribs are broken."

When he didn't respond, she looked up from drying her hands. He stood by the bed, staring down at the injured girl.

"Is she the person you are looking for?"

"No." He brushed back the hair from Rachel's forehead. "Though she is very much like her." He raised his head and met Olivia's gaze, his expression unreadable. "Is she able to travel?"

Taking note of his closed expression, she swallowed the questions his response set clamouring to life. "If she will not be traveling far and if she has a safe place to stay and recover."

"She does."

"She should stay abed for at least a week."

"Would you be willing to see her again to ensure she is healing properly?"

"Of course." Olivia couldn't keep a smile from her lips. "You know how I insist on checking up on my patients."

He dipped his head in acknowledgement, a small smile touching his mouth in return.

Chapter Eight

"If I had known *he* was to be your guest, I wouldn't have helped you get an invitation."

The words were spoken low enough, but Olivia was certain Lazarus had heard them, though he gave no sign of it. Perhaps because he was too busy scanning the overcrowded ballroom for the Duke of Sandhurst.

"I had to practically get on my knees and beg Lady Bingham for that invitation," Amanda hissed from the side of her fan.

"And I appreciate it, as I've already told you numerous times." Olivia forced her lips into a smile and hoped she at least appeared to be having a pleasant conversation.

"May I get you ladies some refreshment?"

She met Lazarus' gaze and knew he was trying to find a polite way to give them some time alone. She smiled for real this time. "That would be lovely, thank you."

"Not for me. If I need a glass of that insipid punch Lady Bingham always serves, my husband, *Lord* Riverton, will get it for me."

Lazarus inclined his head. "As you wish." With a quick bow, he turned away.

Olivia watched him disappear into the crush knowing he would take the time away to do a more thorough search for the duke.

"I can't believe you asked him to be your escort."

"Would you accompany me to the retiring room?" she asked, barely holding onto her patience.

"Whatever for?" Amanda moved closer. "Are you feeling ill? Though if I had to be polite to that man for one second longer, I would be the one worrying about casting up my accounts."

"You haven't said a polite word to or about Mr. Prescott all evening."

"It hardly matters. The man is completely uncouth." With a languid hand, Lady Riverton waved her fan back and forth.

Olivia's grip tightened on her own fan until she felt certain the delicate ribs would snap and yet another one of the useless accessories fashion demanded she waste funds on would be ruined. "I am not engaging in a public row with you. Either you come with me and discuss this privately, or refrain from making such snide remarks."

"Oh, very well, I'll accompany you," Amanda said in a put-upon tone. She turned toward the far end of the room as the musicians began to play. "I hope we don't miss the first waltz. You know how I love to dance the first waltz."

Olivia took a deep breath and practiced her breathing exercises. She found it helped her control her temper as well. "After you," she said, gesturing for her friend to lead the way.

Ten minutes later, she closed the door to the suite of rooms being used by the ladies in attendance for the evening. She made a quick circuit of the area, taking in the lush carpet and jewel-toned velvet drapes. Matching chairs and settees were clustered together in the rooms encouraging one to sit and partake of the latest bit of scandalous gossip.

Ensuring they were alone, she made her way back to the door and leaned against it. If someone tried to enter, she would have enough warning to change the topic of conversation.

"Well?" Amanda tapped her foot impatiently.

"What is wrong with you this evening?" Olivia countered. "Why are you acting this way?"

"I'm concerned for you. Your association with Mr. Prescott will do your reputation no good."

"And why is that?" She felt the need to pace, to work off her anger, but she stayed put. "Is it because he is a mere mister? Do not forget I am but one step removed from being a commoner."

"Your brother holds a title that makes you gentry at the very least."

"And it is only through his knighthood that I am accepted by the *Ton* at all."

"Don't belittle yourself." Amanda huffed. "That's your biggest fault. You continually place yourself among the lower classes. And I mean that in the most literal sense."

Olivia folded her arms over her chest. "If you harbor some grand illusion of orchestrating a marriage between myself and one of Riverton's titled friends, drop the idea right now. It won't happen."

Amanda crossed to the cheval mirror that sat in one corner. She gave a small moue of disgust and fluffed out the skirts of her butter yellow gown. "It could happen if you weren't so stubborn. You are a well-bred young woman." Turning one way and then another, she gazed at her reflection. "If you were to emphasize those attributes, instead of playing the wallflower, you would have any number of suitors."

"Really?" Olivia raised her eyebrows in disbelief. "And which gentleman is willing to overlook the fact that I engaged in the manly behavior of doctoring others instead of making my debut like a proper young miss, not to mention my penchant for speaking my mind?"

"Just the other evening Viscount Ruskin mentioned how lovely you looked at the last ball I gave." Amanda smiled in triumph.

"Viscount Ruskin isn't interested in me. He's looking for anyone who is willing to act as a stepmother to the five hellions he calls his sons."

"That is true." Lady Riverton tapped her chin with her fan as she leaned her hip against the end of a settee. "But I am certain there are others who would clamour for your attention if you didn't act so...so..."

"Strange?" Olivia supplied.

"That wasn't the word I was searching for. But you do have to admit, you act like a high-strung horse at the merest hint of a thunderstorm."

Olivia lifted a shoulder in what she hoped was a nonchalant shrug. "Everyone has something they fear. Thunderstorms are mine."

She stumbled forward as someone pushed against the door. Turning quickly, she grabbed the handle and pulled it open. Dismay filled her at the sight of a frowning Lady Jersey standing before her. Forcing a smile to her lips, Olivia gave a quick bow. "Forgive me, my lady.

Without giving the formidable woman a chance to respond, she ducked around her and headed back to the ballroom.

"Olivia, wait." Amanda hurried down the hall after her.

"Are we not finished discussing my unsuitable escort and my off-putting manner?"

Amanda bit her lip as though it had just occurred to her how harsh her words had sounded. She laid her gloved fingers on Olivia's arm. "You know I only mention these things because I want the best for you."

"Yes, I know." Hoping to distract her friend before she began to sulk, she linked her arm through the other woman's. "Shall we return to the ball? You don't want to miss the waltz."

Amanda brightened. "Oh, the waltz. I nearly forgot. And I still have to find Riverton. He is most likely in the card room." A small giggle escaped her, and she strode away with a waggle of her fingers.

Olivia watched her walk away. She never realized how much her friend manipulated the people around her. Until now. Now, that she had started doing things Amanda didn't approve of. Things that could ruin her reputation and taint the Riverton name by association.

"How do you plan to make Huntley jealous if you're hiding about in the hallway?"

Olivia turned toward the voice. Lazarus leaned against the wall, his arms crossed over his chest.

"That is your plan, not mine. I don't waste time on futile endeavors. At least not anymore," she added softly.

He moved closer. "What 'futile endeavors' did you waste time on before?"

She gave a slight shake of her head. She didn't want to remember. She only wanted to forget.

He lifted her chin with gentle fingers. "You can trust me," he said, his voice barely above a whisper.

She felt herself falling under the spell of his dark eyes. When his gaze fell to her mouth, as though drawn there beyond his control, everything around her ceased to exist. He dipped his head, bringing his mouth within a hair's breadth of her own. Heat pooled low in her stomach.

"Olivia!"

She jumped back with a guilty start.

Lord Michael Huntley stood a few feet away, a scowl marring his handsome features. Her face burned with mortification.

"Michael," she said, in a voice little more than a high-pitched squeak.

He strode forward and took her by the hand. "Have you taken leave of your senses?" He led her a few steps away when he came to a sudden halt. He looked down at his arm where Lazarus grabbed it, then raised his gaze.

"The lady was with me."

He shook off Lazarus' hold. His expression that of a person who had smelled a foul odor. "I don't believe we've met," Huntley said, with a curl of his lip.

Olivia jumped into the breach. "May I present Lord Michael Blakely, Marquess of Huntley. Michael, Mr. William Prescott."

Neither man greeted the other. Instead, Huntley turned toward her. "What are you doing?" he demanded. "Your reputation can ill afford another scandal."

"I...We were looking for you."

"Really. It looked as though you were about to be

ruined."

She gasped. A sharp pain pierced her heart. Did Michael, her Lord Michael, think so little of her?

Lazarus grabbed Huntley by the neck and slammed him into the nearby wall. "Apologize to her."

"Go to hell."

"Apologize." He tightened his grip, his fingers digging into the other man's neck.

Gasping for breath, Huntley pushed at Lazarus' hand without success. He cut his gaze to Olivia. "S...sorry."

Lazarus released him, and he stumbled back, his hand clutching his throat as he took great gulping breaths.

She touched him on the shoulder. "Michael, are you all right?"

He nodded and cleared his throat. "I'm sorry if I offended you, but you must admit if I hadn't come along, you'd have done something regrettable."

"You may be right." She glanced at Lazarus. He stood watching her with an unreadable expression. The Runner's words came back to haunt her. Mr. Durant said he was quick to violence. She didn't know why Lazarus had rushed to defend her when he himself was only using her to gain information. He hadn't a care for her reputation.

He moved to her side. "Shall we return to the ballroom? I'm sure Lady Riverton is missing you."

"I'm certain you are right," she agreed, suddenly eager to be lost in the overcrowded room. She sent a hesitant smile in Michael's direction and turned away.

The sound of flesh meeting flesh followed by a groan sent her spinning around. Michael sprawled in a half sitting position on the marble floor holding his jaw.

Lazarus flexed his hand and moved to her side. "Shall we?" he asked as if nothing had occurred.

"You hit him!"

"You accepted his apology. I didn't."

Huntley climbed to his feet and made a show of adjusting his clothing. He sent a malevolent glare in Lazarus' direction before pushing past them. He turned back. "I sincerely hope you don't do something you have cause to regret, Olivia. For if you do, I'll not lend my good name to help you. Not when you refuse to listen to my advice."

Taken aback, Olivia could only stare at the man she'd once dreamed of spending her life with.

He gave her a mocking bow and walked away.

"Don't let him upset you," Lazarus said. "He's a jackass, and no advice from him would be worth taking."

"He's a marquess. He could have you sent to gaol before the night is over."

Will smiled and tucked her hand in the crook of his arm. "Would you worry over me?"

"I would have to come to see you, and I'd rather not. I'm told Newgate is a horrible place."

Looking down at her, he sobered. "That it is," he murmured. He didn't want her anywhere near Newgate. She'd already seen more than a lady should, thanks to her brother. He stopped in mid-stride, bringing her to a halt. "If I am ever in Newgate, promise you won't come."

"Have you done something that would warrant your being sent there?"

He knew she was asking about more than his

confrontation with Huntley. How could he tell her he'd done more than assault a lord? Much more and worse. Unable to stop himself, he reached out and tucked a stray curl behind her ear. It felt as silky as it looked.

"Promise me you won't come," he repeated, tracing the rim of her ear and down the side of her neck. Damn she smelled good. He leaned closer, inhaling the scent of lavender and something else he couldn't quite identify.

Olivia's eyes drifted closed, and she tilted her head, allowing him better access. "I can't," she said, her voice a low whisper.

His fingers followed the line of her collarbone. The modest neckline of her pale green gown taunted him. "Why?" He allowed his hand to glide over the exposed slopes of her breasts. He shouldn't be touching her like this. She was too high in the instep for the likes of him. But he couldn't stop.

She opened her eyes, stared at him for a long moment, then took a step back out of his reach. He saw the desire in her eyes and wanted nothing more than to make Huntley's remark a reality. The image of her lying on the crisp linen sheets of his bed, her hair unbound tempted him. He turned away, angry with himself. She was a means to an end, nothing more.

He stiffened at the touch of her hand on his arm. "Do you still want to know why I would have to come and see you?" she asked, her voice husky with the remnants of desire.

"Why?"

"To get Rachel's direction." She looked up at him from under her lashes, a smile playing about her lips. "After all, you know the lengths I will go to check up on my patients."

Will laughed. The sound echoed off the walls, and he found the tension that had tied him in knots fading away.

A few minutes later, they walked through the entrance to the ballroom. A quick scan of the room gave no sign of Sandhurst. Had his information been false? He'd been told Sandhurst never missed an event given by any of the premier hostesses of the *Ton*. And even he knew Lady Bingham fell into that category.

Will looked at Olivia. The chandeliers overhead caught the highlights in her hair and set them aglow. She stood quietly by his side, her hand still resting on his arm. She was like no other woman he'd ever met. It felt good just to stand beside her. She glanced up at him and smiled, before turning at the sound of her name.

"Have you heard?" Lady Riverton rushed to Olivia's side, her cheeks flushed with excitement over the latest bit of gossip.

"What should I have heard?" Olivia asked, amusement in her voice.

"Lord Willoughby was found beaten behind his home." Lady Riverton lowered her voice. "They say his face is nearly unrecognizable."

At the mention of Willoughby, Will edged closer.

"Amanda, are you certain?" Olivia asked. "You know how gossip tends to rely a great deal on embellishment."

"It's true. Riverton has seen him. He says the viscount is disfigured."

"Has a physician been called to attend him?"

Will held his breath as he waited for the answer.

"Yes," Lady Riverton replied as she watched Lady

Jersey pass by. "I must go." She rushed off, eager to spread the latest scandal.

"Why would anyone do such a thing?" Olivia asked as she watched her friend cross the room.

Will turned her to face him. He gazed into the blue depths of her eyes and willed her to understand. And said the one word that would condemn him. "Justice."

Her eyes widened as realization dawned. "Rachel."

He nodded, waiting for her to turn away in disgust.

"I cannot agree that what happened to Lord Willoughby was right, but I do understand the reason behind it."

Will hadn't realized he held his breath until her words released it from him. She didn't see him as some sort of monster. She understood. He smiled, feeling suddenly light hearted. It was a feeling he was unaccustomed to.

He glanced over her head. Huntley stood near the refreshment table nursing a glass of the god-awful punch being served, his gaze boring into Olivia's back. Could Huntley's earlier behavior have stemmed from jealousy? Perhaps trying to make Huntley jealous on Olivia's behalf wouldn't be so difficult after all. It was the least he could do to repay her for her kindness to Rachel as he had no intention of telling her where her brother was once he was located. His first loyalty was to Finch, the man Phillip St. Germaine had stolen a large sum of money from. If St. Germaine survived that encounter, then he would consider letting Olivia know he'd been found.

Will leaned forward until his mouth was a hair's breath away from Olivia's ear. "Your Lord Michael is staring at you as though you are the last bottle of brandy, and he is dying of thirst."

She glared at him. "It is not very gentlemanly to jest about such things."

"And I keep telling you, I'm no gentleman." Barely resisting the urge to touch his tongue to her earlobe, he took her hand in his. "Shall we dance? It will give you a chance to observe Huntley and see for yourself that I'm not making sport of you." He didn't give her time to respond, gently pulling her toward the area where dancers were already moving in time to the music.

She put her hand over his. "I don't know how to dance."

"Neither do I, but I think we can manage a passable enough waltz to drive Huntley mad."

"But the orchestra is playing the wrong type of music for a waltz."

"That I can take care of." He winked, leaving her staring at him open-mouthed in surprise as he backed away.

He turned and headed for the group of musicians. A few words and a gold sovereign later, he hurried back to Olivia's side. He reached her just as the music he requested began to play.

Taking her hand, he lifted it to his lips. "Shall we?"

At her hesitant nod, he led her out onto the dance floor. A few careful steps later, she was still as stiff as the corset she wore. "Would you at least look like you are enjoying my company?"

She looked down at their feet. "I'm afraid I'll step on your toes, or make you trip, or worse, cause us both to fall."

"I don't care if you step on my toes." He moved his hand from her waist and lifted her chin to meet his gaze. "I won't trip and..." He lowered his voice. "I won't ever let you fall."

He felt her tremble, the heat of her body so close to his, the weight of her stare, and wished they were anywhere but here amid too many prying eyes and waging tongues. He wanted to pull the pins from her hair, see it fall over his hands, feel the silkiness of it between his fingers.

Resisting the urge, he tightened his grip on her waist, bringing her body closer to his. The movement, unplanned as it was, only served to torment him more. Olivia's eyes widened at the closer contact. She took the opportunity to put space between them as they moved into a less than graceful turn and bit her lip, looking anywhere but at him.

Certain she had read his desire for her in his eyes, he tried to put her at ease. "There you see; you haven't trod on my toes once."

"Why are you being so nice to me?" she asked his left shoulder, still unwilling to meet his gaze.

"Why would I not?"

"Because you don't have to be." She looked at him directly then. "I have no choice but to help you gain entrance to Society, or you'll spill my secret. One word dropped into the right ear is all you'll need to do to ruin me. Being pleasant to me doesn't change the fact that we are here together due only to your blackmail tactics."

Will frowned and came to a halt as the music ended. "Can you not forget about our agreement for just a moment?"

"It is hardly an agreement since I was left with no choice but to bend to your wishes."

Clasping her elbow, he led her to an empty area at the side of the room near a large grouping of leafy potted plants. "Keep your voice down. Do you want to be overheard? You won't have to worry about me giving the gossips your secret to slaver over; you'll do it yourself in your efforts to castigate me."

"Me? Castigate you? The great Lazarus that everyone fears?"

A frisson of unease slithered up Will's spine and around his throat. The blasted cravat he wore suddenly felt much too tight. "What do you know of my doings as Lazarus?"

Had the questions she'd been asking about him revealed what he'd done, what he was still willing to do if necessary? No, she couldn't know or she wouldn't have come near him much less let him escort her tonight, blackmail threats or not. Feeling calmer, he bared his teeth in a parody of a smile. "Not enough apparently, since you do not fear me. As you should."

Lord Huntley appeared at the side of the first potted palm. "Olivia, may I speak with you?"

"I think you've said enough to Miss St. Germaine this evening." Will cut off whatever she might have said.

"I would like to speak with you, too." Olivia shot him a cutting look before moving away, her hand clasped around Huntley's arm. "Shall we move out to the terrace? I find I'm in need of some air."

Will watched them weave their way through the crowd, feeling Olivia's anger like a cudgel to the back of the head. He smiled. He couldn't wait to match words with her again. Something about her made him feel more alive than he had in a very long time.

He glanced at the wall to his right and stilled at the sight of his reflection in an ornate, gold framed mirror. He was grinning like an idiot. Like a lovesick fool. Scowling, he turned away and went in search of something stronger to drink than insipid punch or watered down champagne.

He needed to spend less time trying to make Huntley jealous and concentrate on why he was really in attendance. Olivia had gained him entrance to one of the major events of the season, and he needed to take advantage of the opportunity.

Making his way to the card room, he hoped to find a few pigeons to fleece along with a glass of good brandy. But given the other refreshments being offered, there wasn't much chance of finding the latter.

Will glanced from the cards he held, to the face of the heavily scrolled pocket watch he'd won in the last hand, to the doorway of the card room. It'd been nearly three hours, and there had been no sign of Olivia. While he hadn't lost much money, he hadn't played his best either and blamed her for his distraction. He found himself constantly checking to see if she hovered near the door looking for him.

Perhaps his plan to make his lordship jealous had worked too well. A sudden image of Olivia in Huntley's arms burned through his mind and knotted his stomach. At that thought, he placed his cards on the table, bid the men around him good night, and headed back to the ballroom.

He passed a closed door from which a man's voice drifted followed by feminine laughter. Will stopped. Olivia and Huntley? He grasped the doorknob just as Fingers appeared at his side.

"We need ta talk."

"Meet me in the garden." Will raised an eyebrow at Fingers's appearance, dressed in servants' livery as he was.

A couple entered the hallway, drawing Fingers's attention. "She's nae in there," he said in a low voice as he passed by and continued down the hall.

Will stared after him. How did Fingers know what he was thinking? He supposed it was one of the reasons they worked well together. He nodded at the couple as they walked past, intent on finding a secluded place for a tryst no doubt. It never ceased to surprise him that though the members of the *Ton* thought themselves well above the rest of society, they indulged a good number of lower class vices.

He entered the ballroom, skirted around the clusters of people, and headed for the terrace. He spotted Olivia at the edge of one such group where Lady Riverton held court. She looked tired. He would meet with Fingers then return to take her home.

Slipping through the French doors, he strode down the marble steps leading into the garden. Not wanting to draw undue attention, he walked at a sedate pace along the flagstone path. As he rounded a bend, Fingers stepped out of the shadows, dressed in his usual clothing.

Will scanned the area, while his partner did the same.

"Sandhurst is makin' plans to move against ye."

After his brief encounter with the duke earlier in the evening, Will wasn't surprised by the news. "What did you find out?"

"I saw him with one of Hammond's men. They

looked like they was hagglin' over somethin', deal of some sort."

"Hammond's men?" Will felt whatever hope he'd harboured in making peace with his former adversary slip away. He would have no choice but to retaliate if the other man moved against him. It seemed a meeting was necessary and quickly. "Go to the Silver Slipper; tell Hammond I want to see him tonight."

"Ye think he'll be there?"

"He'll be there. He visits Belle."

"I hadna heard Belle was back ta seeing visitors."

"I have to admit I was surprised, especially her taking up with the likes of Hammond."

Fingers grinned. "A wee bit of jealousy are ya feeling?"

Will grinned back. "No more than you."

"Aye," Fingers agreed. "Belle is a fine woman."

"For one who runs a whorehouse."

"Don'na be casting stones, Lazarus. Yer glass house will tumble down around ya."

Given the changes he'd made lately, he was all too aware of the precarious position between his life of a few months ago and his life now. "Tell Hammond I'll be there in two hours."

"And if he willna wait?"

"He will. I have something he wants."

Chapter Nine

"Be angry with me, but don't sulk. I realize you would have preferred to have Huntley escort you home."

Olivia turned away from the window and glared at him. Fire snapped in her blue eyes. The effect was ruined, however, as she grabbed for the hand strap to keep from sliding across the bench seat when the coach careened around a corner.

"Where did you hire your driver?" she asked as she resettled her skirts.

He smothered a grin. "Patrick handles the reins well."

"For a man bent on killing his passengers," she muttered.

Though he heard her, he couldn't resist teasing her. "What did you say?"

"Patrick? Did you say your driver's name is Patrick?"

"I don't think that is quite what you said before."

Olivia stared at him for a moment. "The same boy you ordered to see me home after I came to your place of business?" She sat forward, her arms crossed over her middle. "The same one who you sent to threaten me when I was asking questions about you?"

"I didn't send him to threaten you. He did that on his own."

"Why?"

Will shrugged. There was no way he could explain the fierce loyalty he engendered among his men without revealing his past.

"Does he often act without your knowledge?"

Wary now, he sat up from his lounging position across from her. "What are you insinuating?"

"Perhaps Patrick is still acting without your knowledge because he thinks he needs to protect you."

"What makes you say so?" Had she overheard something she shouldn't have?

She gave him a pointed look. "His actions."

He frowned in confusion. Had the boy threatened her again? He'd spoken to the young man, ordered him to watch over her, to keep her from learning too much, but he'd been quite clear that she was no threat to him or any of the others. "What has he done?"

She turned back to the window and gazed out. "He frightens me," she said in a low voice as though it cost her a great deal to admit such a thing aloud.

"Why?"

It was Olivia's turn to shrug. "The way he watches me...sometimes...I think he could quite easily kill me and go on about his day without giving me another thought."

"What?" Will roared as the carriage came to a shuddering stop.

She jumped. "Perhaps it is just my overactive imagination." She gave him a wan smile. "As evidenced by my actions during the last thunderstorm, we both know I have one."

The coach door opened, and Patrick stood in the doorway, lowering the steps.

At the sight of him, she shrank back into the corner. Will doubted she was even aware of her actions. She truly was afraid of the tall young man.

"Thank you, Patrick." He glanced at Olivia as she hunted through her reticule in an obvious attempt to stay in the carriage. "Check on the horses."

The youth gave him a strange look, then left to do as he was told.

As soon as he was out of sight, Olivia catapulted from her seat and out the door as though her skirts were on fire. By the time Will stepped down from the carriage, she was already moving into the house. She stopped on the threshold and gave him a quick wave before closing the door. Clearly, he wasn't going to be invited inside. It was just as well. Hammond would wait for only so long.

He returned to his seat in the carriage. "To the Silver Slipper," he ordered with a quick rap on the ceiling.

"Aye," Patrick called back and set the horses into motion.

Will tried to focus on the coming meeting with Hammond, but his thoughts kept drifting to Olivia and her fear of Patrick. She wasn't the sort of woman who was false in her emotions. She was truly afraid of the youth. It seemed a conversation with his young driver was in order.

Twenty minutes later, he stood outside Belle's establishment. It may have been one of the best whorehouses in London, but one couldn't tell by looking at it. It looked like any other townhouse one would find on the outskirts of the fashionable area of town. Needing his wits about him for the upcoming meeting, he pushed all thoughts of Olivia from his mind and lifted the brass knocker.

The door opened, and the butler stood there. "The ladies aren't receiving visitors this evening."

"Hello, Weatherly. Belle should be expecting me."

"Ah yes, of course, Lazarus." The butler stumbled back in his haste to open the door wider. "Come in. Her ladyship and Mr. Hammond are waiting for you in the rose parlour."

Will removed his coat and hid his grin at the title Weatherly insisted on using when referring to Belle. While she was definitely a woman, she was no lady. No lady did the things she did in bed and enjoyed them with such gusto.

The servant took his coat and handed it off to a footman. "If you will follow me…"

Will walked behind the butler as he led the way to the parlour. Tapping his pocket to ensure the pistol he'd put there earlier was tucked out of sight, he hoped he wouldn't need it. The last time he and Hammond had met, two men had died, and he had suffered a bullet wound. Though it had brought Olivia into his life, he didn't want this meeting to have the same outcome.

Weatherly gave a quick rap on the door before opening it. "Lazarus has arrived." He stepped aside for Will to enter.

Belle rose from a pale pink divan. She stood there for a moment ensuring he saw she had nothing on beneath the filmy black gown she wore, then crossed the room to meet him. "Lazarus. It's been far too long." She wrapped an arm around his waist and kissed him. A hungry kiss that promised much more if he wanted it.

Will tore his mouth from hers. "While I appreciate

the offer—" He looked at the man lounging in a leather chair in front of the fire. "—I don't share."

Belle gave a throaty laugh. "You don't know what you're missing." She slid a hand down the front of his trousers and cupped him. "Perhaps I can persuade you."

Will removed her hand. "Perhaps not." Was this part of some plan devised by Hammond? To have Belle distract him? To what end?

"You always were a bit of a prude in the bedchamber, weren't you?" Belle floated back to the divan.

Hammond rose. Dressed in the height of fashion, he could have easily passed for a member of the *Ton* if one viewed him from the left side. If one viewed him from the right, however, they would see him for the brutal man he was. A scar ran from his eyebrow, across his eye, to end at his lip. "Fingers said ye be wantin' to do business." He gave a pointed look at Will's side. "A bullet puts a bloke in the right frame o' mind, I always be sayin'."

"The outcome of our last meeting has nothing to do with this." Will moved to stand in front of his adversary. "I've come with an offer because it is to my benefit, not yours."

"So ye be sayin'. Don't mean I be believin' ya."

"I find talk of offers and deals to be tediously boring." Belle moved to the door. "Finish your business quickly, Hammond, or I shall have to find something...or someone...to relieve my boredom." She dropped the gown from her shoulders, stood there in the nude for a moment, then with a wink over her shoulder, she was gone.

"Say yer piece. I got things to be doin' and ain't no

one who does it better than Belle."

Eager to get this over with himself, Will sat in the chair opposite from the one Hammond had vacated. "I understand the Duke of Sandhurst has contracted with you to...shall we say remove me as a source of irritation to him." He looked at Hammond for some sort of confirmation but received none.

The other man walked to the sideboard and poured a glass of scotch and downed in it one swallow. "And if that be true?"

"I've come to persuade you it's in your best interests to renege on the bargain."

"Me best interests? I'd be sayin' it's in yer best interests." Hammond refilled the glass. "And I never go back on me word." He brought the scotch with him as he sprawled in his chair. "Mebbe I be wantin' to have you 'removed' as much as the ole duke."

"I will relinquish my hold on the east end of the docks, leaving it for you and your men to use as you please." Will pretended a nonchalance he didn't feel. He needed to be able to concentrate on Sandhurst without having to worry when Hammond or one of his men would strike and where.

Hammond sat up at the words. "Ye'd give up all claim to it?"

"I would if you agree to break your contract with the duke, which would mean you couldn't have one of your men carry it out in your place."

"I'd be havin' control of it, with no meddlin' from you?"

"Yes, with one minor condition."

"O' course. And what be that?" Hammond asked with a sour twist of his lips.

"My men and I will leave you to run the east end of the docks as you choose, but if you or yours attack me or mine or if you start running whores there, I will take control back in *any* manner required."

"I'll be thinkin' on it. The duke offered a lot o' blunt to be rid o' you." He tossed back the scotch as though it were nothing more than water.

Wanting the matter settled, Will pushed his advantage. He knew how much the other man wanted control of at least part of the waterfront. "You'll make the decision now, or there will be none to make."

Hammond watched him, his gaze impenetrable, while he ran a finger up and down his scar. "Wot's keepin' me from killin' ye right now and takin' over the docks."

"The same thing that's keeping me from killing you." At the inquiring look from the other man, Will continued. "Neither of us wishes to end up swinging from the end of a rope for murder."

Hammond grinned. "Aye, ye be right about that."

"Since we both know how trustworthy you are. If you decide to go back on your word to me and I am found dead, my men will ensure you hang for it whether it be at the order of the magistrate or by their hands."

The grin disappearing from his face, Hammond sat forward. "Ye shouldn't be threatenin' a man ye wants to do yer biddin'."

Will leaned forward as well. "That is no threat," he said in a low, measured tone.

Hammond resumed his earlier lounging position. "I'll be havin' me men on the docks tomorrow."

"We have an agreement then?" Will pressed for the

other man to say the words, knowing he wouldn't risk his own life to go back on them.

"Aye. We have an agreement." Hammond stood and crossed to the door. "Ye can find yer own way out." He picked up the gown Belle left behind. "I gots a woman or two to tup." He walked into the hall.

Just as eager to leave as his adversary was to get into Belle's bed, Will stood. He'd taken only a few steps when the other man appeared in the doorway.

"Oh, and Lazarus, I ain't seen or talked to no dukes or their men in me life. I guess ye gave me the docks fer nuthin'." He left the room, roaring with laughter.

Will let him go. Giving up control of part of the docks was a small price to pay for peace of mind. Knowing how much Hammond had coveted them for years, he was certain the other man would keep his word and not make a move against him or his men.

Now it was time to teach the duke a very painful lesson.

Chapter Ten

"It's true. Sandhurst has left London."

Will breathed in through his nose in an effort to quell his rising temper. "You're certain?"

"Aye." Fingers stood just inside the door.

Will stood, anger pushing him into movement. He paced between his desk and the fireplace. "He will pay for what he's done to Mary. If it takes my very last breath, he will pay."

"He canna run forever," Fingers said in a quiet voice.

"Find him before the coward decides to leave the country. Bribe, threaten, do what you have to, but find that bastard and bring him to me."

Fingers nodded and moved to leave the room.

"Find Patrick and tell him to be here in the morning." Will took another deep breath and resumed his seat behind the desk.

"I was gonna have him help find the duke. He's verra good at that sort o' thing."

"So he is." Will picked up the ruby-encrusted dagger he always kept on his desk and tapped it against his hand. "He and I will have a discussion first." It was time to make certain the lad knew what the consequences were if Olivia continued to feel threatened.

"He's still young, still learnin', ya ken?"

"I do understand, but he needs to learn there are boundaries and consequences if he crosses them."

"But—"

Will held up his hand. "I'm going to talk to him, nothing more...this time."

Fingers opened his mouth. Will cut him off. "Give Patrick my message and find Sandhurst. You, of all people, know how important this is to me."

"Aye. I do. But you mustna lose your humanity in your quest for revenge."

"I believe that was lost long ago." Will touched the back of his neck, realized what he was doing, and clenched his hand into a fist.

"If yer not careful, ye will become just like him," Fingers said in a low voice.

"Him?" Will questioned, though he knew exactly who Fingers was referring to.

"The man who raised you."

"He did *not* raise me." Will's voice rose with each word. "He beat me, starved me, tortured me, but he did not raise me." He stood and slammed both hands on the desk, his chest heaving with anger. "Now get the hell out and find Sandhurst."

Fingers stood there a moment longer before leaving and closing the door behind him with a quiet click.

Will closed his eyes and forced himself to swallow the anger, the humiliation he felt at what he'd suffered as a youth. He learned long ago control was the answer to everything. Control over himself, his emotions, over his men and his empire. And he'd worked at developing the iron will that allowed him to live without losing that control and allowed him to do what he had to.

He slumped into his chair, rested his elbows on the

desk, his forehead in his hands. If he could just find Mary, get her out of whatever asylum Sandhurst had her committed to. He wanted so badly to find her, to make it up to her for whatever atrocities she'd suffered, to take care of her for the remainder of her life. Perhaps then he could begin a new life for himself. But he couldn't move on, couldn't let go of the past until he knew she was safe, until she was with him again.

He wished...no, he didn't wish. He'd learned a long time ago wishes were for children and fools. Distracted from his thoughts by a sound, he lifted his head, listening. A storm was coming. He sat for a moment as the import of that ominous rumble became clear. Jumping up from the chair, he snatched his coat from where it hung on a hook near the door and left the room.

****

Will eased the door open, slipped inside, and closed it behind him. He leaned against the polished oak door for a moment. A fire burned in the grate, sending shadows dancing against the walls. He took a step forward, the bed beckoning to him like a lover.

What was he doing here? She was no doubt sound asleep. Drawn to the bed, he would just look at her to ensure she was fine and then take his leave. As he moved closer, he realized what he thought was a body was actually a mound of pillows and bedclothes. He whipped back the sheets. Empty. Where was she? Was she in her lover's bed while he risked the wrath of the storm to come here? To be certain the thunder hadn't sent her back to her memories of the past.

Anger flared to life at the thought of her lying with another man. He tamped it down. He had no right to feel anything for her. She was too high in the instep to even consider him a friend much less anything more. The only reason she didn't give him the cut direct was because of their bargain. He turned to go when he heard it—a whimper like that of a child. Tilting his head, he concentrated on the silence. Had he imagined the sound? Thunder crashed overhead, and rain began to beat against the windows. There it was, the same sound, only louder now.

He crossed the room and stopped in front of the only other door in the room. He set his ear against the wooden panel and listened. The strangled sob that came from within had him turning the knob and stepping inside.

Tens of candles stood in a circle on the floor in the middle of the small room, filling it with enough light that it could have passed for mid-afternoon. Pale yellow drapery hung at the windows and was repeated in the carpet. In the far corner with her legs hugged to her chest, sat Olivia, her face pressed to her knees. Another whimper escaped her as thunder rumbled and lightning flashed through the room.

A strange sense of what he could only describe as relief filled him as he slowly made his way to her. She was here, not with a lover. Here, safe with him.

He eased up beside her before crouching down. "Olivia," he said in a gentle voice.

She jumped at the sound of his voice. "W-what are you doing here?" Her eyes were huge, her face pale.

"I wanted to ensure you were all right." At her strange look, he gestured to the window. "The storm."

"You shouldn't be here."

"You shouldn't be alone." He sat on the floor next

to her.

A crack of thunder reverberated through the room, and she squeezed her legs harder, rocking back and forth. "Please let it end soon. It's not cannon fire. I'm home, I'm safe," she whispered the last words over and over.

Her misery tore at his heart. Wanting to offer what comfort he could, Will shifted closer and wrapped an arm around her back. She stiffened and moved away. Stung by her actions, he tried not to let it show. All that mattered right now was that he help her through the storm. Not sure how to offer comfort without touching her, he sat beside her, hoping his presence would be enough.

Lightning flashed, and she clutched at his hand. Hers felt small and helpless. He folded his fingers around it. It was as cold as ice. He needed to get her warm. He gave her hand a squeeze, released her, pushed to his feet, and lifted her into his arms. When she leaned her head against his shoulder, he knew her fear had won the battle. He skirted the candles and carried her to the bed in the adjacent room.

He laid her down, and she rolled on her side, continuing to whisper to herself about the storm. Will pulled the coverlet over her. "I will return in a moment." He reached out to touch her but touched the edge of the bed instead before turning away.

Once back in the smaller room, he extinguished the candles save for one. As he stood, he realized it was her dressing room. An enormous chest of drawers stood on the opposite wall, shoes from dancing slippers, to walking shoes, to half boots stood in a neat row like soldiers waiting for inspection. A tub for bathing was in the near corner. He quickly turned away, but an image of her surrounded by steaming water as it lapped against the tops of her breasts floated into his mind.

He gave his head a shake to dispel the image and blew out a breath. Thoughts like that shouldn't include the likes of her. Taking the candle with him, he left the room and closed the door. He set the beeswax taper into a holder on a small table.

Olivia's shaky exhalation drew his attention. He removed his coat, sat on a dainty chair he wasn't sure would hold his weight, and removed his boots, never once letting his gaze leave her. Her eyes were squeezed shut, the fingers of her fist pressed against her mouth.

The mattress listed as he climbed onto the bed behind her. He settled her back against his chest, the blankets an effective barrier between them. He wrapped his arm over her and cupped her hand in his, rubbing his thumb against the soft skin of her palm. He knew she was lost to the storm when she let him comfort her without complaint.

A loud crack of thunder sounded overhead seeming to make the house shudder. Olivia shrank back against him as though seeking his warmth. Will pulled her closer, his breath stirring the tendrils of hair at her temple. As the storm eased, Olivia drifted off to sleep.

Loathe to leave her, he lay beside her for a long time after the thunder faded away. It seemed as if his heart beat in rhythm with her breathing. He closed his eyes and reveled in the feeling. He couldn't remember if he'd ever felt this way before. He wished he could stay until the morning but knew it would do irreparable damage to her reputation to be found in bed with a man. And to be forced to wed the likes of him, she'd become a social pariah in an instant.

He pressed a gentle kiss to her hair and rose from the bed with care so as to not disturb even the mattress. He pulled on his boots, slung his coat over his arm when her voice froze him in place.

"Thank you for taking care of me, Lazarus." Her eyes were already closing as she drifted back into a peaceful slumber.

"Will," he corrected though he doubted she heard him. With one last look at the sleeping beauty he was leaving behind, he slipped from the room and into the night.

Fingers stood waiting for him where he'd left his horse in the neighboring stable. He nodded to the young lad who was doing his best to keep Fingers away from Titan. Will flipped a shilling to the boy for watching over the horse for him. The youth caught the coin in mid-air and disappeared into the depths of the stable.

"I've readied the list for ye," Fingers said. "Patrick is waitin' around the corner with the coach."

"You expect me to leave tonight?" Will brushed a hand down Titan's nose.

"'Tis for the best, is it not?" Fingers asked, sending a pointed look in the direction of Olivia's home. "You shouldna be dallying with the likes o' her. That kind of woman expects marriage to be part of the deal."

"I wasn't dallying with her. I was…" Will trailed off, not wanting to divulge Olivia's secret, her fear of thunder and the horrors the sound of it forced her to relive.

"As ye say." Fingers didn't bother to hide his disbelief.

Will tossed Titan's reins to his friend. "I trust you

will take care of things while I'm gone?"

"Of course."

"Keep Harry on Olivia. Tell him to follow her, see she comes to no harm. Let it be known she is under my protection."

Fingers opened his mouth, closed it, then gave a nod of acquiescence. "Verra well."

"I'll send word if I find Mary."

"Mayhap ye should be checking the convents and nunneries, too. We canna be leaving her in a place like that either."

"It would be a damn sight better than an asylum," Will said, though he agreed a convent was no place for Mary. "I'll see you in a few days." He turned and left the stable.

"Don'na be losing ye temper. Ye tend ta do things ya shouldna when that happens," Fingers called after him.

Will ignored the warning. He'd do whatever he had to, to gain entrance to the asylums on the list. They were his best hope of finding his sister, certain as he was that Sandhurst had hidden her away in one of them. Though it wouldn't hurt to investigate any convents and such in the areas near the asylums.

He took one last look at the window he knew to be Olivia's bedchamber. He hoped there would be no storms while he was gone. The thought of her having to go through them alone tore at him for a reason he couldn't quite explain, not even to himself.

Chapter Eleven

"What are you doing here?" Olivia jolted into an upright position, the blanket held nearly to her chin, at the sight of Lazarus entering her room.

Without a word he moved to the bed, climbed on it, and pulled her to him, her back to his front.

She broke free and nearly fell off the bed in her haste to get away from him. "What are you doing?" she asked, her voice shrill.

Will slowly sat up. "It's been a difficult day. I wanted to see you."

"You're in my bed. I'm...I'm not dressed." Her hand clutched the neckline of her night rail closer."

"I'm not *in* your bed. I'm on your bed, on top of the bedclothes. You are *in* your bed, under a sheet and blanket." He looked her up and down, taking in what little he could see of her plain cotton nightgown. "And you are dressed. Even your hair is still properly contained." He gestured to the braid resting on her breast.

"I'm not. I'm in my...my..."

"You're not nude, are you?"

"Of course not." Her cheeks turned red, and she looked away.

"Then you're dressed."

"It's not proper for you to be here, at this time of night." She picked at the lace edge of the pillow, not meeting his eyes.

"Have I ever claimed to be the proper sort?"

"No." She met his gaze. "But despite my past, I am."

"I want to hold you, nothing more. You're safe with me. You have my word."

"Your word as a gentleman?"

Will ran a hand through his hair and sighed. "You know I am no gentleman."

He didn't know why he came to her tonight. Yes, he did. He hadn't found a single trace of Mary at any of the places Fingers had put on that damn list. The thought of her still out there alone, going through who knew what kinds of hell had driven him to seek out the one good thing in his life right now—Olivia St. Germaine. He needed to feel her softness against him, needed her to make his sense of failure easier to bear.

She watched him, her blue eyes filled with indecision.

"Trust me."

Olivia looked at him. He sensed her indecision and laid his hand, palm up, on the bed.

"What I know about you is rumour and hearsay. How can I trust you?" she whispered. "How can I trust that you aren't using this situation to your advantage? That I won't regret trusting you in the days to come?"

"I would not do anything to ever cause you regret."

She stared at him for a long moment, and for the first time, he couldn't tell what she was thinking by the expression on her face. Finally, she placed her hand in his, giving him her answer without words. He waited until she lay down and then settled them both on their sides. Olivia lay in front of him as stiff-necked and unyielding as a clergyman.

"Why are you here?" she asked. "I've not heard a word from you in four days."

"You know I'm searching for someone."

"Yes, a girl."

"I wasn't in town these last days. I had information I'd hoped would help me find her, but it proved inaccurate."

"Do you still believe the Duke of Sandhurst is involved in your friend's disappearance?"

"My sister."

"What?" Olivia twisted around to look at him over her shoulder.

"The young woman I'm looking for, she is my sister, Mary. And yes, I believe Sandhurst had everything to do with her disappearance."

"Why?"

"It doesn't matter."

Olivia sat up, the coverlet pressed to her breasts. "Yes, it does. You're blackmailing me into helping you gain entry into various social events. I deserve to know why you believe Sandhurst is involved."

Will sat up as well. "I'm not blackmailing you." God, he was growing to hate that word. "We've struck a bargain to help each other, you and I."

"Some bargain. I had no choice but to accept if I didn't want my secrets revealed and if I wanted your help to find out why Phillip has suddenly left London with no word to me about his return or where he is."

"And I had no choice but to come to you for help."

"That cannot be true. I'm certain there are any number of members of the *Ton* that would help you."

"Only those whose vowels I hold, and those men

are so desperate to maintain their lifestyles or the appearance of them they'd tell me anything I wanted to hear as long as I promise not to call in their markers. I haven't the time to spend chasing false rumours and lies. Mary has been missing since Christmas. I need to find her as soon as possible."

"You haven't heard from her since then?" Olivia settled back onto her side. "It's been nearly five months."

"Yes, it has, and I grow more worried with every day that passes."

"I'll send a note to Amanda in the morning to see if she knows of any entertainments the duke may be attending. Perhaps I can wrangle an invitation or two."

"Thank you." Will lay down and pulled her close.

She stiffened. "I think it's best if you leave."

He rubbed a hand up and down her arm. "Let me stay for a while longer. It's late…I don't want to be alone right now." The last slipped out before he could control his tongue.

He hated how vulnerable he sounded. He hadn't asked anyone for anything since he was a lad who was too stupid to know better. People didn't help one another out of kindness but out of greed and what it could gain them. And yet, here he was begging for her company. When he had comforted her during the thunderstorm, held her in his arms as he lay beside her, it had felt as though she belonged there, that she was the other half of himself he hadn't known was missing until that moment. He needed her now as she had needed him then. Just being here beside her gave him solace, helped alleviate the choking sense of failure. He had had such hopes of finding Mary this time.

Olivia closed her eyes and took a leap of faith. "You may stay for now."

His arm came around her waist, his warmth seeping through the bedclothes. She relaxed against him, hoping he could feel the strength she was trying to give to him. Though she swore she felt his lips against her hair, he didn't move his hand once in an attempt to caress her. Olivia found herself hoping he would and feeling strangely disappointed that he hadn't. Instead his palm rested gently against her arm near her elbow. She knew the instant sleep claimed him, his breathing settling into a deeper rhythm.

She would wake him soon. He needed the rest. She doubted he'd slept more than a few hours during his search for his sister. His clothing was wrinkled and travel worn. At least two days' growth of whiskers stubbled his cheeks, and his eyes had deep shadows of exhaustion under them. There had been a wealth of sadness in his gaze. She knew how it felt to be helpless in a situation beyond one's control. It wouldn't hurt to allow him a few minutes to sleep. She found herself leaning back against his warmth, her eyes drifting closed.

****

Olivia followed the little man who'd introduced himself as Harry down the hall. Being in the same hall in the same warehouse Fingers had taken her to the night she had demanded to see Lazarus made her feel a little less hesitant than when Harry had appeared at the servants' entrance stating he'd been instructed to take her to Rachel to check on the girl's progress.

Why hadn't Lazarus mentioned he wanted her to see Rachel last night when he'd suddenly appeared in her bedchamber? Her cheeks warmed as she remembered falling asleep in his arms. She had no idea when he left. She'd woken this morning alone with no sign of having a midnight visitor the night before.

Harry glanced back at her. She couldn't help noticing he kept casting looks at her like she'd suddenly sprouted two heads. She touched the chignon at the back of her neck, making sure the pins still held it in place, then touched the front of her gown, ensuring she was presentable. The way he kept looking at her made her feel as though she was walking about in her unmentionables.

He stopped in front of a door, knocked once, then opened it. He moved back, allowing her room to enter.

"Ain't never heard of no woman doctoring," he muttered as she passed him.

Olivia smiled at the comment she was sure he hadn't meant her to hear. It explained his strange behavior and why he kept staring at her. Knowing it was that and nothing more, she felt at ease, her nervousness draining away. The one thing she was confident in was her ability to provide proper care for Rachel. After the injuries she'd treated on the battlefield, a broken wrist and a few bruises, terrible though they were, were easily seen to.

She moved into the room and set her case on a table just inside the door. Though small, every effort had been made to turn the area into one of comfort. Two chairs were pushed in against the table. A bed took up the far wall, while a leather chair sat near a chocolate colored divan. There, Rachel sat in rapt attention.

A male voice filled the room, reading from one of

the latest novels of the day. Olivia moved closer not wanting to interrupt, but something must have given her away.

The person stopped reading and looked around the side of the chair. "Miss St. Germaine," he said, standing.

"Good afternoon, Fingers."

"I was just keepin' the wee one company 'til you arrived." He turned back to the young girl. "I'll be back soon, Rabbit." He handed her the book and crossed to where Olivia stood. "Lazarus be wantin' to see ye when you're finished," he said, then left the room.

"How are you feeling, Rachel?" Olivia moved to the divan, carrying one of the chairs from the table with her.

"Me arm is still painin' me."

"May I look at it as well as your other injuries?"

Rachel held out her arm. Olivia sat in the chair. "How are you liking the story?" she asked in an effort to take the girl's mind off the examination.

"Oh, Fingers, he's a right good reader. He makes them words come alive in me head."

"Does he read to you often?" Olivia moved on from Rachel's wrist to the bruise on her cheek, checking that her eyes were clear.

"Aye, when he's not workin' for Lazarus. He keeps me company. I get jumpy when I be here alone. That's why he calls me 'Rabbit.'"

Olivia could imagine how much the young girl kept both men hopping. "May I check your ribs?"

Rachel nodded. "I have to be warnin' ye. They be a frightful sight." She pulled a sheet that had been kicked to the bottom of the divan up to her waist then lifted her loose gown to expose her ribs.

Her entire left side was mottled with bruises ranging in color from bluish-purple to yellows and greens. Olivia gave her a small smile of encouragement. "Do they cause you any pain?" she asked, gently probing the area.

Rachel inhaled sharply. "Just when you be pressin' on 'em, Mum."

"I'm sorry. I didn't mean to hurt you." Olivia pulled the gown down to meet the edge of the sheet. "You seem to be healing well."

"So I don't have to be stayin' abed anymore? I needs to get back to work."

"I don't think you're quite ready to start working yet."

"But I be needin' to. Please, Mum."

"What type of work do you do?"

"I was a maid at…" Rachel touched the bruise on her cheek. "I don't know. Mebbe I can sell oranges."

"How old are you?"

"I turns fourteen this summer." Rachel's voice sounded proud.

Olivia couldn't believe Lord Willoughby had beaten a thirteen-year-old girl. Though she didn't know the man well, she would have never guessed he was capable of such a thing. While she abhorred violence of any kind, she couldn't help feeling grateful Lazarus had handled the manner in the way he had. Perhaps the next time his lordship raised a hand to someone, he would remember his own beating at the hands of another.

Due to servants' talk, Olivia doubted Rachel would find another position in service, but she didn't want her reduced to selling oranges either. "I will talk to Lazarus about finding a new post for you."

"Oh, will you? He won't even allow me out of this here room."

"I can't guarantee he'll listen to me, but I will speak to him about it." Olivia stood. "I shall take my leave so you can get back to your book." She carried the chair back to the table and picked up her case.

"If you need me, tell Fingers, and he'll bring me here, all right."

"Yes. Thank you."

Opening the door, Olivia wasn't at all surprised to see Fingers waiting for her. She lifted a hand in farewell to Rachel and stepped into the hall.

"She is well?" he asked.

"Yes, she's doing very well, considering her injuries and how she acquired them."

He scowled at that. "Lazarus is waitin'."

"Heavens, we can't have that, can we?" Olivia couldn't keep the remark to herself. It was amazing how the man had people jumping to his every whim. She wished she knew how he engendered such loyalty among the people who worked for him.

Ignoring her sarcasm, Fingers led the way down the hall and around a corner before stopping in front of yet another door. He gave the same series of knocks as a few weeks ago and opened the door, without waiting for a response.

"Miss St. Germaine," he said, giving her a slight push inside.

Olivia stumbled forward then turned just in time to see the door shut.

"You must forgive him. He sometimes forgets his manners."

She raised her brows at the comment and faced the room. Lazarus stood near an enormous oak desk, the fingers of one hand tracing an odd pattern on the edge of the desk. He wore black as usual, the sleeves of his shirt folded up to reveal the corded muscles of his forearms. The collar was undone, and there wasn't any sign of a cravat in sight. The drapery at a large window on the right side of the desk had been opened, bathing him in sunlight as it spilled into the room. She never believed herself capable of flights of fanciful imagination, but at that moment, he struck her as a fallen angel, dressed in darkness but seeking heaven's light.

"Rachel is recovering well and eager to work," she said, looking away from him. She felt unaccountably nervous in his presence. "I doubt she'll be able to secure a post in any of the households of Mayfair. I have a friend in Bath that owns a small bakery. I can send her a letter asking if she'd be willing to hire Rachel on."

"Thank you for the offer, but she'll not be leaving London and all she knows because she was beaten."

"I'm not implying that at all." Olivia was aghast that he felt she was trying to hide the young girl away in shame. "I was just trying to help."

"She's not your responsibility. You needn't worry about trying to help."

"She became my responsibility when you brought her to me for care," Olivia snapped, his high-handedness setting off her temper.

"You stated she is all but recovered, so any responsibility on your part has ended. I will see that she is taken care of in the future." He moved to lean against the desk, his arms folded across his chest. "There will be no more discussion on the subject."

"Fine." Olivia stalked to the door. "I will contact you once I receive a response from Lady Riverton regarding any upcoming entertainments." She yanked the door open.

"Are you not going to check my wound?"

His words halted her progress as nothing else would. She turned back. "It's been nearly a fortnight. It should have started healing well before now. It isn't still bleeding, is it?"

"No, it hasn't bled since the night Fingers brought you here." He crossed the room, unfastening his shirt.

"What are you doing?" Her voice came out higher than normal. She felt the sudden urge to flee from the room.

"You asked that I take my shirt off the last time you examined the wound. I assumed you would want me to do the same today."

"Yes, yes. Of course." Flustered, she forced her gaze away from the sculpted planes of his chest only to have it land on his flat stomach and the muscles there. She jerked her gaze to the window, feeling the need to fan herself. Her cheeks heated as he came closer.

"I believe you actually have to look at the wound in order to see how well it is healing," he said in a dry voice.

"I was waiting for you to remove your shirt."

His lips twitched, but he didn't remark on her obvious lie. She didn't understand why she was affected so by his nearness, by seeing him in a state of undress when she had never been affected by any of the men she cared for on the battlefield, and she'd seen a good number of them without any clothing at all.

Clearing her throat, she did her best to assume a professional attitude. He was her patient, nothing more. "Turn a bit to your left," she instructed as she looked at his side.

She touched the wound with gentle fingers and felt him shudder. "Sorry, my hands are cold."

"I know of a way to warm them." He took her hand in his, but before he could do anything more, she pulled free.

"So do I," she said and rubbed her hands together in a brisk manner for a few minutes. "They should be warmer now." She probed the edges of the newly healed scar. "Does it still cause you pain?"

He laid his hand over hers, flattening it against his skin. "It's feeling better now."

She slid her hand from beneath his, ignoring the wild fluttering of her heart. "Who removed the stitches?" she asked, determined to keep the encounter impersonal.

"I did two days ago."

She nodded and walked around him to examine the exit wound on his back where the lead ball had passed through his body. "They should have stayed in until at least today, but I see no signs that you aren't healing well." She didn't know which she felt more relieved about—that he would be completely recovered soon or that she could leave and not have to be in such close proximity to him when he was without a shirt.

He turned and moved closer. Olivia backed up a step. He kept coming, crowding her until she backed into the nearby wall.

"What are you doing?"

"You ask me that question quite often, do you know that?" He plucked a pin from her hair and dropped it onto the carpet.

"Stop that." She touched her chignon. It seemed to still be in place.

He grinned and removed another pin.

She made a grab for it, but he dropped it to the floor.

"Do you realize I've never seen you with your hair free?" He pulled another pin free.

Olivia felt her hair start to uncoil and slip free from the remaining pins. "Because it isn't proper."

"When has anything I've done with you been proper?" he whispered.

She trembled as his lips brushed her ear. "You and I have done nothing."

He leaned forward until their lips were all but touching. "Haven't we? I distinctly remember us sharing a bed, not once but twice."

She wanted to close the distance between them, wanted to feel his mouth on hers, wanted to know at long last what it would feel like to be kissed by him. Instead, she turned her head away, praying he would move back and at the same time hoping he wouldn't.

"We didn't truly share a bed. You were always above the counterpane," she said in a voice that shook a little despite her attempt to keep it even.

"But I wanted to be under it." He traced small circles on her breast, coming closer and closer to her nipple causing it to contract into a tight bud. "I wanted to be under you."

Her eyes drifted closed with each completed circle, his touch sending heat curling low in her stomach. She knew she should stop him, remove his hand, do anything to stop the madness of the sensations spiraling within her.

"Olivia." He touched the very center of her nipple.

Even through the fabric of her gown, she felt a jolt of sensation. "I love how you say my name."

His hand stopped moving.

She opened her eyes to find him staring at her, his gaze dark and unreadable. Had she spoken aloud? She hadn't meant to. "I...um...everyone pronounces my name 'Ahlivia,' but you say 'Ohlivia.'"

He ran the barely there touch of his thumb across her lips. "Olivia," he whispered. His fingers skimmed down her arm leaving gooseflesh in their wake until he clasped her hand in his. "Olivia."

"Yes?" The word was no more than a breath of air.

He placed her hand on his chest, holding it there when she tried to pull free. "Touch me."

"I...I...it's not proper."

He closed his eyes just as she swore she saw desire flare within them. "Please."

She lifted her other hand, let it hover over his skin. Oh how she wanted to touch him, to feel the muscled hardness of his body. Even now where he held her hand against him, she felt as though he branded her with the blazing heat from that single point of contact.

He released a deep sigh, her hand rising and falling with the motion, and opened his eyes. With a derisive smile, he released her. "I apologize. I've forgotten my place." He gave a small bow and turned away.

She felt bereft at the loss of his touch. Without thinking, she laid her hand on his back. He stiffened but didn't move away.

"Where is your place?" she whispered, not knowing if she asked him or herself. She'd always felt as though she didn't fit in with the members of society, and she didn't fit in with the servant class either. She was stuck somewhere in between, often feeling barely tolerated by the *Ton* and put on a pedestal she didn't deserve by her few servants for what she'd experienced in war.

She ran her fingers down the length of a scar running from the top of his shoulder to just below it. Of their own volition, her fingers moved to touch each nick and mark on his back, ending at the most recent one she'd cared for herself. He stood still, his only movement the flexing of muscles as she traced his scars. His head hung forward. She found herself leaning closer and closer until her cheek rested against his back.

He shuddered and reached back for her hands, folding her arms around him as he pressed her hands one over the other to his stomach. The muscles there jumped at the contact. He held her without uttering a word.

Olivia felt strangely at peace. She couldn't explain it, but holding him this way while he held only her hands, she felt…protected and protective.

Slipping one hand free, she slid it up his chest to his throat. His pulse thrummed against her fingertips, and his breathing grew ragged, but still he didn't move. She touched his jaw, the faint stubble of his whiskers pricking her fingers.

"Lazarus," she whispered his name, not knowing why, but needing to.

He lifted his head and turned in her arms, hunger etched across his features. "Will. My name is Will," he said in a hoarse voice.

"Will," she repeated, wanting something she didn't know how to voice.

He knew he shouldn't, but he couldn't hold back any longer. He pressed a kiss to her lips. A gentle touch, then again, and again, each kiss making his hunger grow until he wanted to devour her, to lose himself in her as he had no other.

His hands slid into the silky mass of her hair. He'd wanted to touch her like this for far too long. Angling his head, he deepened the kiss, his tongue slipping into her mouth. She gave a low moan and pressed closer. Her hands slipped from his shoulders to twine around his neck. Her fingers grazed his nape, sending a shower of ice through his veins.

Pulling her hands away from the back of his neck, he broke the kiss, resting his forehead against hers while he fought to control his breathing. "I burn for you." The words escaped him unheeded.

"And I melt for you," she whispered in return. "I've never responded to a man's nearness the way I do you. I cannot explain it." She looked down. "How did you get so many scars?" she asked, tracing a finger across an old knife wound that sliced across his pectoral muscle to the edge of his nipple.

"They are a matter of course in my business." He watched her touch him and felt himself harden even more than before.

"And the scar on the back of your neck?"

Will froze. He had been certain he'd removed her arms from around his neck before she realized what her fingers had touched. Of all the scars he carried, he hated that one the most. "I fear you are mistaken. I have no scar there."

"You do. I felt the ridges of it for just a brief moment, but it is there. You didn't mind me touching the others, why do you lie about this one?"

He pushed out of her embrace and stalked toward the window, raking a hand through his hair. How could he tell her what was done to him? It would show what a true coward he was. She would never look at him the same way again.

He felt her come stand beside him and suddenly the words, words he'd never spoken before, came tumbling out of him. "My father died in a horse-riding accident when I was but five years of age. My mother, my sister, and I went to live with her brother and his family. He was a vicar and had limited funds to support us all so when a baronet showed an interest in her, her brother was quick to marry her off."

He gazed out the window, not seeing what was really there, but instead the past playing like a farce across the stage of his mind. "The baronet was an abusive bastard who started beating my mother within days of the marriage."

"I'm sorry." Olivia slipped her hand into his.

"I was seven years old the first time I took Mary and tried to run away. He had his coachman find us and bring us back to him. I was given nothing to eat for four days and had to watch Mary eat every meal I was denied."

"Oh." The sound of distress escaped Olivia without her notice.

"I didn't mind. I was glad Mary wasn't punished. She was three years younger than I and didn't understand what was happening. When he lost his temper, he no longer just beat my mother; he would take his rage out on me, too. For every blow he landed, I made plans. Plans to get Mary and me away from him for good."

"Why did your mother not try to protect you?"

"She had become a shell of her former self, jumping at shadows, barely speaking, afraid of what would cause the baronet to strike out at her. One day she just disappeared as though she ceased to exist. I never knew if she left Mary and me or if the baronet succeeded in finally killing her."

Olivia squeezed his hand.

"I was ten when I took Mary and ran away again. We got farther than before, but that bastard found us. He told me I belonged to him, and I always would belong to him. But he didn't punish either of us. Instead he seemed almost sorry for what he'd done to my mother and me in the past. He took me to Tattersall's and bought me a pony."

"Perhaps he was trying to make amends," Olivia murmured.

"You couldn't be more mistaken." Will moved away, keeping his back to her. He didn't want to see her face when he told her the worst of it. He clasped his hands behind his neck, his fingers touching the scar that made him the man he was. "You see, he used that pony to torture me. He starved it from the very first. Whenever I tried to help it by feeding it, even weeds from the nearby fields, he whipped the animal until its hide was nothing but bloody flesh. He made me watch," Will whispered the last, still hearing the high-pitched screams of the horse as it felt the lash. "I could stand it no longer, so one day I took his hunting rifle and shot

Star in the head. I figured a quick death was so much better than the prolonged death he was suffering."

"Star was your pony," Olivia said, her voice thick with tears.

Will nodded. "The baronet became enraged when he saw what I'd done. He said I robbed him of one of his possessions so I would have to take its place. He had me dragged to the blacksmith. He branded me, and I lived in the barn like an animal." Will turned to face Olivia then, ignoring the tears streaming down her face. "I carry his mark on the back of my neck. And every day he reminded me of that fact by flashing the signet ring he used as the brand in front of me."

"Oh, my God. How did you get away from him?"

"I planned, and when the time was right I spirited Mary away. I waited until he went to London on business, to ensure we would not be caught. Once I had Mary safely hidden, I went back and waited for him to come to the barn. I had a knife, and I was ready. I stabbed him over and over and over again. I was twelve years old. Do you see what kind of man I am?"

Olivia moved to stand in front of him. "You had no choice. He would have killed you eventually."

"Do not make excuses for me. Since then I've done a lot of things that, if I were not blackmailing you, would send you running from me in fear. I'm not a good man."

She sniffed and wiped away the last of her tears. "I think you have so much good inside of you. I don't think you even know how much."

"Do not make me into someone you wish I was instead of who I am," he said, angry that she didn't see him for the brutal man he was despite what he'd just told her.

"Will." She touched his jaw, making him meet her gaze, her eyes a darker blue than he'd ever seen them. She moved closer until there was no space between them. He felt every inch of her along his body. "I know you are a good man. I know it here." She touched her heart. "Prove it to me. Kiss me again."

Never one to turn down a lady, he took her mouth with his. Lost in the haze of desire, it took him a moment to realize someone pounded on the door while calling his name. He broke off the kiss. "What is it?" he demanded.

"Hammond's men have taken Harry. Fingers has gone to try and get him back."

"Son of a bitch," Will muttered and set Olivia away from him. He strode across the room and opened the door just enough to speak to Patrick without letting the young man see into the room. "Tell Muldoon and Banner to meet me on the dock."

He closed the door and scooped his shirt from the floor where he'd dropped it earlier. "I have to go."

"I know." Olivia twisted her hair into a knot at the back of her head and began gathering her pins, putting them in her hair as she found them. "Shall I stay in case Harry needs medical attention?"

"I think it would be best if you leave." Will shoved his arms into his shirt. "I don't know what Hammond is up to, and I don't want you caught up in it. I know you fear Patrick, but I have no one else to see you home."

"Do not worry about me. Go. I know you need to."

Will nodded and headed for the door, fastening his shirt as he went.

"Please send for me if you need me...to care for

anyone."

At her words, Will moved back to where she stood. "Thank you." He gave her a hard kiss on the mouth and left the room.

Chapter Twelve

Olivia picked up her medical case from the chair by the door and looked around the room. Though Will wished her to go home, she found herself wanting to stay, to wait until he returned and know that he was all right. She sighed and tucked her hair behind her ear. Without all of her hairpins, the tight coil she'd pulled her hair into was already coming loose.

Unwilling to have Patrick escort her home, she decided to leave before he arrived. She opened the heavy oak door and froze. He stood on the other side, a scowl twisting his lips at the sight of her.

"Lazarus said to take ya home."

Determined not to let him see how much he frightened her, Olivia straightened her spine and gave him a direct look. "If you will see me to the nearest hackney, there's no need to trouble yourself further. I'll pay you for your escort to it."

"I don't wan' your blunt." He grabbed her arm and yanked her into the hall.

She tried to pull free, but he only tightened his hold. She winced as his fingers dug into the tender flesh of her inner arm. Without a doubt, she'd bear bruises on the morrow.

"I'll not be putting you in a hackney. Lazarus said to take ya home, and I mean to." He frogmarched her down the hall and out the door before she had a chance to respond. Once outside he manhandled her into a battered carriage and took the seat opposite. He rapped on the roof, and the coach moved forward.

Her nerves jumping, Olivia tried to regulate her breathing. Losing control of that was the first sign of a pending panic attack. She couldn't let him see any sign of weakness, knowing he would pounce on it like any other predator hunting its prey. Deciding to play the meek female as he expected her to be, she stayed quiet.

He too said nothing. For long moments, he watched her, his gaze causing her skin to crawl with gooseflesh. She glanced out the window, wishing the horses would go faster. She wanted nothing more than to be away from the young man who stared at her with such hatred.

"I know what you do when you're alone with him."

"No, I don't think you do." She kept a tight rein on the fear growing within her.

"Every woman who wants a bloke's attention knows she can get it by lifting her skirts." He raked his gaze over her starting at her feet, lingering at her breasts, before meeting her eyes once more. "I'm thinkin' you're no different."

Resisting the urge to cross her arms over her chest to hide herself from his view, she rubbed her hands together instead, wishing she'd thought to wear the kid leather gloves Amanda had given her as part of "a lady's proper wardrobe." As a barrier they would be flimsy at best, but they would have been better than what she had now—nothing.

She cleared her throat and hoped she wasn't about to engage in bear-baiting. "I fear you are mistaken. I am treating his bullet wound, nothing more."

He gave her a skeptical look. "An armful like you? Always sniffing around, asking questions, trying ta learn more about him. I'm thinkin' you're interested in a lot more than the hole in his side." He stuck his boot under the hem of her gown. "I'm also thinkin' I might want to be seeing what's under your skirts that's leading Lazarus away from what's important." He lifted his foot, causing her gown to rise along with his boot, giving him a clear view of her stocking covered legs.

She slapped her skirts down and slid down the bench away from him. "Do not touch me."

"I wasn't touching ye." He left his seat opposite and was beside her in a flash. "Yet."

Olivia held out one hand to stave him off and balled her other hand into a fist. One thing Phillip had insisted on when he'd taken her to war was that she learn to fend off a man's advances. And unfortunately, she'd had plenty of opportunities to put his lessons to use.

Patrick grabbed her outstretched arm and twisted it behind her in an instant. "Ye'll listen to what I have to say and do what I tell ya. Ya hear?"

Her breath hitched in her throat as he yanked her hand upward. Pain shot down her arm to her hand, but she refused to make a sound. Blinking back tears, she forced herself to focus.

The hackney came to a sudden stop throwing them both off balance. Olivia jumped up and pushed out of the coach, not caring where they were. Almost boneless with relief, she realized they were in the private lane behind her home used to reach their small stable. She hurried forward, the servants' entrance in sight, eager to put as much distance between herself and Patrick as she could, as fast as she could.

She'd taken only a few steps when she was yanked backward by her hair. Olivia cried out. A hand closed around her neck, and Patrick pulled her tight against him. Clawing at his hold with one hand, she jammed her elbow back into his ribs, brought her hand down to slam into his nether region. Anticipating the movement, he shifted at the last moment, and her fist bounced harmlessly off his thigh.

She froze as she felt the point of a knife against her neck. His hand shifted and clutched her jaw under her chin. "You'll listen to what I has to say."

Olivia inhaled at the sharp sting of the blade puncturing her skin.

"Are ye listening?"

"Yes." The word came out a whisper.

"You will stay away from Lazarus. Stop asking questions ye shouldn't be asking about him." He dragged the knife downward, slicing the tender flesh. "Do ya understand what will happen if ye don't do as I says?"

Feeling blood run down her neck, Olivia knew she had lost any chance to fight back. "Yes."

In all that she had endured on the battlefield, she never expected that she would die at her brother's home by the hand of a common thief.

"Remember it." He released her jaw and shoved her forward.

Olivia fell to her hands and knees. She scrambled to her feet and ran toward the servants' entrance. Looking over her shoulder, she fumbled for the handle. He was gone, the coach nowhere to be seen. She pressed a hand to her neck, applying pressure to the wound, and glanced around. She was completely alone.

She took a steadying breath and went inside. "Bridget," she called as she closed and locked the door.

The young maid came into the room from the butler's pantry, a soft cloth used to polish the silver in her hand. "Oh, my." She dropped the cloth and hurried forward. "What happened? Are ye all right? Who done this to you?"

Knowing she must look a sight bleeding as she was and her hair in disarray, Olivia gave the servant a wan smile and tried to hide the fear still coursing through her. "I'm fine. It was…an accident, nothing more." She glanced away as the lie fell from her lips. "I'm sure it looks worse than it is. Will you help me clean up?"

"Yes, of course. Do ye want to go to your room or Sir Phillip's patient room?"

"His examining room would be best. The supplies we'll need are there." She pushed away from the door and headed toward the small room at the front of the house.

Not hearing any movement behind her, she looked back. Bridget stood just inside the kitchen, leaving her barely visible from where Olivia stood. "Are you coming?"

"Yes, Mum." The maid lingered a moment longer.

Olivia swore she heard whispered voices, but the young woman hurried down the hall without a backward glance making her doubt she'd heard anything at all. She moved into Phillip's examining room and picked up the ivory handled mirror her brother would use to check his appearance before seeing a patient. She couldn't remember how many times she had teased him about worrying over his appearance like some dandy. He would always respond with a smile and tuck the mirror into a nearby drawer.

She held the mirror so she could see her neck. While the hand she'd kept pressed to the wound was smeared with blood, the cut didn't look deep, and the bleeding had nearly stopped. She'd been lucky. If Patrick had started cutting under her jaw instead of behind and below her ear, he would have sliced through the main vein in her neck, and she would have died of blood loss in a matter of minutes.

Bridget took the mirror from her without a word and handed her a warm, wet cloth in its place. She held the mirror up so Olivia could see the wound and gently wash away the blood.

"I don't believe it needs stitching." She set the cloth aside.

"I'm happy yer not hurt bad. Ye gave me a fright when I seen you all bloody like ye were." Bridget bustled around the room gathering the necessary supplies for a bandage. She laid them on the cot used for examinations. "Ye sure yer all right? There's a lot of blood on your dress."

"I'm fine. A little flustered, a little embarrassed, and a little sore, but for the most part, I'm fine." Olivia picked up the mirror the maid had set aside. Instead of focusing on the wound on her neck, she looked at her gown. The neckline on the right side was stained a rusty brown where the blood had soaked into the material. There were also traces of blood on her collarbone that she hadn't quite washed away.

She picked up the small piece of cotton and held it out. "I'm afraid you'll have to apply the bandage. I'm not sure I'll be able to do it while looking in a mirror."

Bridget took the square of cotton and pressed it with gentle fingers to the cut.

The door burst open with such force, it slammed against the wall. Bridget let out a loud squeak, and Olivia jumped and grabbed the scissors from the cot. She shoved the young maid behind her before she realized it was Will who stood in the doorway.

His anger hummed through the room like the buzz of bees trapped in a jar. "Leave us."

The young servant took to her heels without a word. She flattened herself against the door frame as she passed him, careful to keep a wide berth between them, then took off down the hall.

Will crossed the room, took the scissors from Olivia's shaking fingers, set them down, and tilted her head back to better see her neck. Bruises that could only come from a man's hand lined one side of her jaw. He touched the tender skin with a gentle finger. "Who did this to you?" he growled.

"I need to get Bridget. I need her help to apply a bandage."

"I will help you." He crossed to the table. Picked up the pitcher of water and poured it into the basin. "Tell me what to do," he said, washing his hands. He needed to do something to keep his anger in check. He could feel his temper rising out of control every time he looked at her bloodstained gown.

She picked up the cotton pad the maid had dropped in her haste to leave the room and put it the wastebasket. With quick economical movements, she retrieved a clean pad and set it on the cot along with a length of gauze. She pressed the cotton square to her neck. "I'll just need you to hold this in place and then help me tie off the gauze."

It took considerable effort, but he managed to keep his emotions under control as he moved to her side and held the cotton square against her skin while she applied the gauze. A few short minutes later, she stepped back from him. "I should only have to wear it for the remainder of the day." Then as though to reassure him, she added, "It is little more than a scratch."

But it had the opposite effect. "A scratch!" The words exploded from him. The hold on his temper slipped away. "You very nearly had your throat cut, and you say it's nothing more than a scratch? Have you even seen yourself?" He towed her from the room, across the hall, and into the small parlour she used to receive the occasional guest. He stopped before the large looking glass over the mantel, positioning her in front of it.

She gave herself a cursory glance then turned away. "I realize I look a sight, but truly the wound is very superficial. How is Harry?"

"I don't give a damn about Harry right at this moment." He grabbed her arm. "You will tell me who did this to you, and you will tell me now."

"Will, you're hurting me."

He released her in an instant and backed away. The last thing he ever wanted to do was hurt her in any form or manner. Furious with himself for losing control, he stormed to the side table and poured a glass of scotch. He tossed the drink back in one swallow, drew a breath between his teeth as the alcohol burned like a flame down to his stomach, feeding his anger. "Why won't you tell me what happened?" He slammed the glass onto the table, and she jumped. "Was it one of the members of the *Ton?* Those bastards always think they can take what they want," he muttered the last more to himself than to her.

Olivia shook her head and stared at him, her teeth worrying her bottom lip.

A terrible thought occurred to him. Had the taking of Harry been nothing more than a ploy to get to Olivia? Hammond had to have known he would go after Harry. But could his nemesis have known she would be at the warehouse at that particular point in time?

"Was it Hammond? One of his men? Was it someone you knew?" With each question, his voice became louder. He lost the last vestiges of control when she looked at him with fear in her eyes, like he'd been the one to slice open her neck with a blade. "'Ow ken ye be protecting 'im?" He closed the space between them, his fingers wrapping around her arms. "I 'ave ta know. I'll be murdering the bastard."

Olivia raised her hands to either side of his face and kissed him. A kiss that caught him completely off guard. A kiss that drained the anger right out of him. A kiss that set off the strange yearning he felt whenever he was around her.

She lifted her mouth from his all too soon but stayed close, their lips a hair's breadth apart. "Feel better?" she asked.

He gazed into her beautiful eyes at an utter loss as how to respond. He pulled her closer, wanting nothing more than to hold her in his arms and keep her safe. She slid her hands down to his chest, laid her head against him, and sighed. He rubbed his chin against the silky softness of her hair and felt his anger and fear drain away.

"You lost your H's," she murmured.

He froze. She was right. So consumed with fear of what could have happened to her, he'd reverted back to the way he'd spoken before he realized that his manner of talk proclaimed him as one of the lower classes. He'd taught himself the proper way to speak. Determined to erase any sign of his poor upbringing, he spent hours mimicking the lords and ladies whose pockets he'd picked, particularly the way they spoke. Not once in thirteen years had he ever used less than proper speech. Until now.

She must have felt him stiffen because she raised her head and looked at him. "I meant no insult. It was just an observation, nothing more."

He stepped away from her, feeling the heat of embarrassment crawl up his neck. "My apologies for my loss of control."

"Will." She tried to close the distance between them, but he moved further away with every step she took. As though sensing his discomfort, she took a seat on the settee. "You never did say if Harry is all right."

"He's fine. I don't care about Harry right at this moment. Why won't you tell me who attacked you?"

"It doesn't matter." She stood. "I'm glad Harry wasn't hurt." She paused as a sudden thought occurred to her. "How did you know I was hurt?"

"Your footman sent a message."

"Daniel? Why would he do that?"

"That night I saw you home from the Riverton's ball, the night you…" he faltered, not certain how to go on.

"The night of the storm when I had one of my episodes, when I thought there were wounded soldiers to be cared for." Olivia hugged her arms to herself.

"Yes, then. I told Daniel how to get word to me if you ever needed help. And because he knows I'm trying my best to keep my life from touching yours. By the looks of that..." He pointed to the bandage. "I am failing miserably. But that will change once you tell me who hurt you. Whoever did this to you will become an example to others who think that attacking you is the best way to get to me."

"I've heard rumours about your brand of justice, and I know what you had done to Willoughby. I want no part of it. I want no one hurt or worse, killed because of me."

"Your wishes have no bearing in this."

"Then you and I have nothing left to discuss. Jennings will show you out."

Will stalked across the room to stand in front of her. "Why are you in a great hurry to be rid of me? Are you expecting someone?"

"I'm not expecting anyone. It's well past calling hours. I think it's best if you go and that we refrain from contacting each other."

"Refrain from contacting each other?" he echoed her words, disbelief and an unnamed emotion flowing over him. He couldn't imagine not seeing her on a daily basis. He would not let her leave him. And he'd hold her to him by any means necessary. "Do you forget we have a bargain?"

"No, I haven't forgotten. But neither one of us seems to be much help to the other in our search for our loved ones." She sank down onto the plush divan cushion and pushed her hair off her face.

"You've been a great deal of help to me. You gave me entrée to the Riverton's ball, which in turn allowed me to make contact with Sandhurst. The fact that he has fled London only proves he had something to do with Mary's disappearance." Will sat beside her. "Although it may not seem like it, I am trying to find your brother. I have men searching for him and have a…an acquaintance who is also looking for him. It can be difficult to find a person who doesn't want to be found."

"But why would Phillip be hiding? What could he possibly have gotten involved with that would cause him to leave without a word?"

Unable to tell her the truth about her brother, Will took her hand. "Sometimes a man can get into a situation that he doesn't know how to get out of. Sometimes we think it's best to leave and take our trouble with us in an attempt to protect those we're leaving behind." As the words left his lips, he couldn't help wondering if he were also talking about himself. He left Mary to work as a governess rather than keep her with him as he tried to make a better life for them both.

"Phillip is a doctor. What trouble could he possibly have gotten into that he feels it's best to leave me here alone?"

"I don't know," Will lied. He couldn't tell her, her brother was addicted to the laudanum he prescribed to patients, making him a man desperate enough to do anything to get it. "But whatever it is, perhaps he thought this is the only way to protect you."

Olivia jumped to her feet. "I don't need

protecting." She paced in front of the fireplace. "I just need to know where he is and that he is all right." She glanced in the mirror and scowled at her reflection. "It's ridiculous for him to think I am unable to help him after all that I faced alongside him on one battlefield or another."

Will stood. "It is no more ridiculous than you refusing to tell me who attacked you." He moved to stand beside her. "Who are *you* trying to protect?"

She closed her eyes for a moment. When she opened them, they were a dark blue and filled with utter sadness. She reached out to touch him, closed her fingers into her palm, and dropped her hand to her side. "You," she whispered.

"Me?" he said, taken aback. He was the last person he expected her to name. "Was it Hammond then who hurt you? You have no need to protect me from the likes of him. I've been tangling with him for years. One could say we understand each other."

"I don't believe I've ever met him."

"He has an unusual scar on his face. Did the man who accosted you have a scar?"

Olivia shook her head and looked into the mirror. Will couldn't help feeling she was purposefully avoiding his gaze. He watched while she tried to set her hair to rights but after a few futile attempts, gave up.

"I shall have to buy new hair pins. I doubt I have but three left," she muttered under her breath.

He grasped her shoulders and gently turned her to face him. "Olivia, I'm not a patient man at the best of times and seeing you injured makes me even less so. Tell me who did this to you and why you feel you need to protect me from him."

She took a deep breath. "It was...Patrick. It was Patrick. I'm sorry. I'm so sorry."

"Patrick!" Shock sent him stumbling back a step.

"I'm sorry. I didn't want to tell you. I know how much he means to you."

"But why?" He raked a hand through his hair. He had taken the youth under his wing, tried to teach him there was a better life to be had than one as a thief. Had come to feel like an older brother to the boy.

"He warned me to stay away from you, to stop asking questions about you, which I haven't done since I was trying to find you that first night."

"And if you don't stay away from me?" Will asked, anger burning away his initial shock.

She swallowed and touched her bandage.

"He threatened to kill you if he saw you with me again." It was a statement, not a question.

Olivia nodded, her expression solemn.

"I couldn't understand why you were so afraid of him." Will spoke the words aloud though he was in truth talking to himself. He turned away, raking a hand through his hair once more. He knew what he had to do. "You will have nothing to fear from Patrick in the future. I guarantee it." He strode toward the door.

Olivia ran across the room and grabbed his arm. "Wait. You cannot blame him for what he did. He was only trying to protect you. He sees me as a threat to you."

He shook her off. "Then he should have come to me and told me of his concerns."

"Perhaps he was trying to show his loyalty to you by taking care of the matter himself."

"After what he did to you, why are you defending

159

him?" His voice was calm, quiet even. But he was furious. He was beyond even that, but this time he was in control. And he would remain so.

"I don't want you to hurt him because of what he did."

"He'll be lucky if I don't kill him. If you would like him to apologize, I will make certain he does." He pulled her into an embrace. "I'll make this right," he said against her hair. "You will never have to fear him or any of my men again."

Olivia pushed out of his arms. "You said you wouldn't hurt him."

"No, I said I wouldn't kill him."

"Will."

"As long as he keeps his distance from you and causes you no more harm, I'll not hurt him. But if he doesn't…"

The implied threat lingered in the air.

Chapter Thirteen

Olivia stared out the window at the colorful blossoms filling the garden without seeing them. Had she made a mistake in sending a missive to Will telling him she'd arranged for them to attend the Smithfield musicale? She hadn't seen him since he left in search of Patrick four days earlier.

She still wasn't certain how she felt about telling him it was Patrick who had attacked her. She tried hard not to think of it, but it preyed on her mind a great deal. She sighed and pushed her worry over Will's response and what it might have driven him to do out of her mind. She needed to concentrate on his lack of response to her note instead. Perhaps she'd given him too little notice to agree to attend this evening's entertainment, but she'd barely managed to secure the invitations at all.

The sound of Jennings clearing his throat drew her attention. "This arrived for you." He held out a silver salver with a folded piece of parchment on it.

She took the note and broke the plain black seal. It was from Will declining to attend. A strange pang of disappointment thrummed through her chest as she read it. As Sandhurst was no longer in London, he no longer saw the need to suffer the company of the *Ton*.

Had Sandhurst truly left London, or was Will telling her a falsehood so he didn't have to spend time with her? Deciding to test her suspicions, she crossed to the small desk in the corner of the parlour where she often wrote correspondence. "Is the messenger waiting for a response?"

"If you mean the grubby lad who brought the note, then yes." Jennings didn't bother to hide his distaste.

"Good." Dipping a quill into the inkwell, she penned her response, sanded it, and sealed it with a drop of wax. She opened the desk drawer and withdrew a coin. "Give this to the boy along with the coin. Be sure to tell him it's of utmost importance."

Jennings took the letter and coin and left the room. Olivia didn't expect Will to respond to her note, but at least she had in her own way let him know she didn't quite believe him. She had always known in her heart if he had to make a choice between one of his men and herself, she wouldn't be the person he'd pick. Patrick, with his actions against her, had forced Will to decide who was more important to him. His men were willing to lay down their lives for him and she...she was just a means to an end, a way to secure invitations to various social events as a way to reach Sandhurst, nothing more.

She sighed. For the first time in her life, she felt lonely. Wished for someone she could confide in without having to temper her words or tell half-truths to for fear of being ostracized by society or looked on as someone who was on the verge of losing her mind. "Oh, Phillip, why are you never there when I need you the most?"

Certain Will had no interest in keeping their bargain, she headed back to the desk and pulled a fresh sheet of vellum toward her, dipped her quill in the ink, then hesitated. Would Mr. Durant be able to help her find her brother? Would he be willing to take on a case where there was no sign of a crime having been committed? Did Bow Street Runners even take on cases looking for people who hadn't been in contact with their families for weeks? Phillip was a grown man after all and free to come and go as he pleased.

She set the quill aside and rubbed her forehead. Perhaps it was best to wait a few more days before contacting the Runner.

****

"Miss, miss."

Olivia rolled over. She blinked to bring Bridget into focus.

"He's here. Lazarus, he be waitin' for ye."

"What?" She sat up.

"He be dressed mighty fine, too, if ye don't mind me sayin'."

"What time is it?" She looked around, realizing the room was rather dim. How long had she slept? She'd only meant to lie down long enough to ward off the headache she felt hovering all afternoon.

"'Tis eight-thirty."

"He must be here to attend the musicale." Olivia pushed off the bed. "Hurry, help me change my dress. I'll need to do something with my hair." She rushed to the wardrobe and sorted through the gowns hanging there, discarding one after another. "Heavens. Why didn't he send a note saying he'd changed his mind?"

She chose a blue gown and laid it on the bed. "Tell him I shall be ready forthwith." She glanced at the maid standing by the bed. "Go."

"But I thought ye wanted me to help ya dress."

"I do. Just go tell him then come back."

Bridget turned to leave.

"Wait," Olivia called. "Undo my dress first. I'll take this one off while you're gone." She turned around, her back to the young maid.

Bridget quickly unfastened the gown and hurried from the room.

Olivia removed the dress and stepped out of it, leaving it in a puddle on the floor. Normally, she took great care of her clothing, but there was no time. She slipped the more formal gown on and holding the bodice against herself, went in search of the matching kid slippers. Dropping them by the bed, she poured water into a small basin and washed her face and hands. Drying them, she sat at the small table that held her lotions and perfume and quickly pulled a brush through her hair. *What was taking Bridget so long?*

A knock at the door sent her whirling around in her chair. The door opened, and Bridget slipped inside. "Thank goodness, what took you so long?"

"I hurried as fast as I could, miss."

"I know you did. I'm sorry." Olivia turned back toward the mirror. "Can you help me with my hair? I don't know what happened to my hairpins. I seem to have lost most of them."

She looked down at the table, not wanting Bridget to see her cheeks color at the lie. She knew exactly what happened to them. Most of them were somewhere on the carpet in Will's office and the others...well, she didn't want to think how she'd lost the others. A shiver traced itself up her spine as she remembered Patrick grabbing her by her hair.

"Himself asked me to give ye this." Bridget held

out a small box wrapped in plain brown paper.

"Himself?" Olivia took the box and set it on the table in front of her.

"Lazarus." The maid moved behind her. "If'n you'll stand up, I kin fasten yer dress."

Olivia stood. She pulled the string tied around the package and removed the wrapping. When Bridget finished, she retook her seat on the small stool and lifted the lid of the box. A card with the bold strokes of Will's handwriting lay on top. "*To replace the ones I took.*"

Olivia quickly set the card face down on the table. The last thing she needed was to have to explain what the card meant. "Oh." Nestled in a bed of pink satin were the most beautiful hairpins Olivia had ever seen. An intricately carved enamel rose decorated each pin. They ranged in color from the palest white to a deep ruby red.

Bridget plucked one from the satin nest and began to thread it through Olivia's hair.

"Wait. I can't keep these. They are far too dear."

"Don't be daft. They's a right nice gift, and the darker ones will set off yer hair real pretty like." The maid took another pin from the box.

"It wouldn't be seemly to accept such a gift from a man who isn't my relative."

"Do ye want ta keep 'em?"

"Yes, of course. They're beautiful."

"Then keep 'em." Bridget picked up another pin and another, setting them in place. "Who would know where ye got 'em? I ain't got no one to tell."

"It would be rude to give them back after he went to all the trouble of purchasing them, wouldn't it?"

Olivia asked, more to convince herself than anything else.

"Aye, it would." Bridget stepped back to admire her handiwork. "There ya be."

Olivia looked in the mirror for the first time since opening Will's gift. Her hair was gathered at the back of her head and fell in a waterfall of curls to her shoulders. "Bridget, I don't know how you managed to make me look so beautiful in such a short amount of time, but thank you."

"'Twas easy when ye have beauty to start with." The young maid tilted her head. "But I think ye be needing one more thing," she said and left the room.

"I have just the thing," Olivia said to the empty room before realizing she was alone. Shrugging, she slipped on a pair of small pearl earbobs. She moved from the stool to step into the slippers she'd left by the bed, then crossed to the clothespress and withdrew a pair of elbow length matching gloves. She slipped them on and turned to find Bridget setting her pelisse on the bed.

"Hurry now. Let me be putting this on ye, and ye'll be ready ta go." The maid held up a length of royal blue ribbon.

"What is that for?"

"You'll see." She wrapped the ribbon around Olivia's neck and secured it in the back. "Yer hair'll cover the tiny knot holding it in place."

"I don't think I should wear a ribbon around my neck. It's not appropriate."

"Look in the mirror, then decide." Bridget gave her a gentle push toward the dressing table.

Olivia stared at her reflection. She almost didn't

recognize the woman looking back at her. The ribbon set off the deep blue of her gown and hid most of the knife wound though it looked much better than it had four days ago. "I'll wear it," she said, making the decision in an instant.

She turned away from the mirror, scooped up the pelisse from the bed, and gave Bridget a quick hug. "Thank you for helping me."

She left the room, leaving the young maid blushing and speechless. Olivia hurried down the stairs to where Will waited in the parlour set aside for unexpected callers. Just outside the door, she took a deep breath in an effort to calm her nerves and entered the room. "I'm sorry I kept you waiting. I had decided not to attend after you declined my offer of the invitation."

Will turned away from the window. Their eyes met. His gaze traveled over her like a caress making her feel as though he had reached out and touched her. She moved, closing the distance between them. He touched the ribbon at her neck and his expression closed, becoming shuttered like always, leaving her to wonder if she had imagined the desire she saw in his eyes or if she wished something more there.

"You made a very good point in your response to my note. Tonight's event will provide me with a chance to try and learn Sandhurst's whereabouts." He took the cream colored pelisse from her and helped her into it. "You're wearing the hairpins."

"Some of them." Olivia touched her hair. "They are quite lovely, thank you."

"As are you." She was so beautiful. He wanted to hold her, to take her in his arms, to touch her, but he couldn't do any of those things. He knew he shouldn't, but he desperately wanted to.

She made him wish he didn't have a criminal past, made him want to be a better man. To be a better man because of her, just for her. He gave a slight shake of his head. Though he was trying to become a legitimate businessman, he knew he could never escape his past completely. It was foolish to think otherwise. And even more foolhardy to expect Olivia to accept it without a qualm. "Shall we go?"

She glanced at the clock sitting on the mantel. "Yes. I'm afraid we'll be a few minutes late."

"I thought it was fashionable among the *Ton* to be late."

"Some believe it best to be late so they can be certain all the other guests will see them arrive. I prefer not to be the center of all that attention."

"My apologies for making us late then." With a hand on the small of her back, he guided her down the hall and out of the house to the waiting carriage.

"It is my fault. I wasn't dressed…" Her voice trailed off as she looked up at the driver.

"Fingers will be handling the reins tonight."

The man sitting in the driver's box inclined his head in acknowledgement. Will allowed Olivia a moment to see that he spoke the truth, then ushered her into the coach. He watched as she took a seat and adjusted her skirts. Sure she was settled, he rapped on the ceiling, and the carriage began to move. "You mentioned you were undressed," he prompted.

"What? I said no such thing. I said I wasn't dressed—"

"Which is exactly the same thing as being undressed," Will interrupted. He enjoyed teasing her.

Her cheeks bloomed a lovely pink color, and she became flustered in her embarrassment. It was nice that despite all she'd been exposed to during her time at war that she still blushed at the things she didn't consider proper to discuss.

"How is Harry?" she asked in an obvious attempt to distract him.

"Do not trouble yourself over him. He made the mistake of gambling with some of Hammond's men and then refusing to pay his losses. I paid his markers so now he will owe me."

"I'm glad he wasn't hurt."

"Fingers believes I should have let Hammond's men teach Harry what happens to men who try to cross them, but I think he learned the lesson well enough without having to suffer a beating or worse."

"You care for him. You want everyone to think you are cold and unfeeling, but in truth you are devoted to those you consider your family." Olivia said the words as a statement, not as a question as though she believed he was capable of caring for another.

Her belief in him, that he wasn't a cold-hearted bastard out to take advantage of the misfortune of others, sent a pang through his heart. He rubbed the spot in the center of his chest, trying to ease the strange feeling.

"You women always want to see the best in a man. I paid Harry's debt to keep Hammond pacified, nothing more." Will spoke the lie as though it were the truth. "I haven't the time to deal with the likes of him right now. Finding Mary is much more important."

"I see." It was clear she didn't believe him. "Thank you for having Fingers drive your carriage this evening rather than...your regular coachman." Olivia looked away from him, her fingers touching her neck in an unconscious gesture.

Will reached out and turned her chin to face him. "I promised you that you would be safe. Removing Patrick from his normal duties is part of that." He hesitated a moment before continuing, "I'm sorry I didn't take your fear of him seriously, that it took you being attacked by him for me to see it. I asked you once before to trust me. Now, I'm telling you, you can trust me."

"I do trust you. I must."

"Why *must* you?"

"Because I've never allowed anyone the liberties you've taken," she whispered.

"Did you allow them if I took them?"

She nodded. "I allowed them because I wanted you—"

The carriage door swung open. "Yer Highness," Fingers said to Olivia, before sweeping into a low bow.

Will started. He hadn't even realized they'd come to a stop. He glared at his factotum and exited the carriage. He turned and helped her from the coach.

"None of your men like me a great deal, do they?"

"I cannot explain Patrick's dislike of you as I do not understand it myself. Fingers, however, feels I am doing you a disservice by spending time with you. Calling you 'your highness' is his way of reminding me of that." Will settled her hand in the crook of his arm and joined the other couples heading toward the door of the Smithfield townhouse.

"How can that be? We are helping each other learn the whereabouts of our siblings."

"As true as that may be. He feels I risk your reputation by forcing you to procure invitations and the like so I may hunt Sandhurst among his own kind."

"And what do you think?"

"I think he may be right, but I will not forfeit the opportunities your friendship with Lady Riverton gives me."

And I will not give up spending time with you regardless of what anyone thinks is best for you.

Chapter Fourteen

For the first time since Phillip left London without a word, Olivia felt the keen sense of loss of his companionship. She had always felt they were closer than most siblings, given what they'd faced on the battlefield together. But it had been nearly three months since his disappearance, and she hadn't received a single note from him.

She hoped Will was having better luck at finding his sister though if his demeanor at the Smithfield musicale was anything to judge his success by, he was no better off than she was herself. Things had gone from uncomfortable to untenable by the end of the evening. From the moment they arrived, they had been the object of scrutiny with the other guests paying little attention to the Smithfield sisters' attempts at singing, reciting poetry, and playing the pianoforte. While the other women present had been polite, they spent most of their time whispering about her in tones just loud enough to be heard. With each comment, Will had become quieter and quieter, his expression carved in stone by the end of the recital.

Perhaps he had been correct in first refusing her invitation. He certainly learned nothing about Sandhurst, and she had gained nothing but a headache by the time he brought her home with barely a word spoken between them.

For the past seven days, she had wandered from one room to another, unable to settle at anything. She'd even consented to an outing to Hyde Park with Amanda and Lord Riverton two days ago in a desperate attempt to keep from thinking about Will and what he might be doing. Perhaps he had decided she was of no use to him after all. Perhaps she hadn't heard from him because he was out of town once again searching for Mary.

Olivia sighed and pushed open the door to Linton's Book Shop. Hopefully with something new to read, she'd stop staring out the windows worrying over things she had no control over. She didn't know when she became a woman who fretted over things, but she decided she didn't like it.

Bridget made a pointing motion with her hand and headed to the other side of the shop. Olivia browsed among the shelves nearest the door, finding a few books that piqued her interest when a prickling sensation ran down the back of her neck.

Feeling as though she was being watched, she glanced around the book lender's shop. Overstuffed bookshelves lined the walls while chairs were arranged in comfortable groupings inviting one to sit and read or share their love for a particular volume of work. The overflow of novels that didn't fit on the shelves were stacked in haphazard fashion on various tables throughout the establishment.

Other than the proprietor who sat behind a heavy oak desk in a far corner, his head buried in the book he held between two gnarled hands, there didn't seem to be anyone else present. Olivia took a deep breath, breathing in the scents of leather, paper, and ink. She dispelled the uncomfortable feeling of being the object of scrutiny with a small shake of her head.

Her dealings with Will and the feelings of dislike by his men were making her unaccountably jumpy.

Deciding to take both books she held, she went in search of Bridget. Olivia headed toward one of the side rooms where ladies' maids were known to congregate while their mistresses browsed the shelves and exchanged gossip. She took a quick look inside the room. No sign of Bridget. *Where could she be?*

Olivia moved to the back of the room and the free standing shelves that created a mazelike warren of corridors. "Bridget," she called in a whisper, not wanting to disturb anyone reading among the stacks of books.

Hurrying past one row, she rounded the corner and called again. She moved from row to row looking for the young maid with no success. Perhaps Bridget was in the section of children's books. Yes, that must be it. While her reading skills had improved, she still struggled a great deal, and children's books would be easier for her to read. Olivia moved to the end of the nearest shelf and froze.

A man stood just a few feet from her. He stared at her over the open book in his hands. The feeling of being watched hadn't been a product of her overactive imagination. She spun around and rushed back the way she'd come. She picked up her skirts and ran up one corridor and down another, praying she was headed back to the main area of the shop.

Rounding the end of the towering bookshelf, she looked over her shoulder to see if anyone followed her. The space behind her was empty. Breathing a sigh of relief, she took one last glance back and ran into the solid form of a man.

His hands came up to grasp her arms. Olivia wasn't sure if he held her to keep her from falling or to keep her from escaping. She gave his chest a hard shove and pulled free. "What do you want?"

"What makes you think I want something from you?" he asked.

"You were watching me back there."

"Was I now?" A grin played at the corners of his mouth.

"Yes, you were and now you are in front of me, keeping me from passing." Olivia took stock of his appearance. If she needed to describe him later to a Bow Street Runner perhaps, she wanted to be able to give as many details as possible. He was tall, but not overly so. While dressed in the latest fashion, the colors he wore were not. The dark gray could have meant he was still in mourning, but somehow she doubted it.

"Mayhap you are keeping me from passing. It is possible I just happened to look at you back there for no particular reason at all." He crossed his arms over his chest.

"You were holding your book upside down which means you weren't even attempting to read it."

The man dipped his head in acknowledgement. "Lazarus said you were intelligent."

"W-w-who?" Olivia stood on her toes in an attempt to look over his shoulder, hoping to see someone, anyone, she could call to for help if necessary.

"Come now, there's no need to pretend. I know you and he are friends." He took a step forward.

Olivia stumbled back, eager to keep some modicum of space between them. "He and I aren't friends. We are no more than acquaintances, and I am hesitant to claim even that."

"Are you hesitant because you're afraid of having your name bandied about with his? That claiming a friendship would somehow sully your reputation?" Anger flared in his eyes.

A harsh bark of laughter escaped her before she could stop it. "Apparently Lazarus hasn't told you everything about me. My reputation is already plagued by scandal, and I am barely tolerated by the members of society and then only because they have little choice in the matter if they don't wish to be ostracized themselves. A friendship with Lazarus could hardly do more damage."

The man raised an eyebrow. "You might be surprised," he murmured.

"Now that you've satisfied your curiosity about me, may I pass?"

"Actually, I came in search of you to ask a favor."

"Let me guess. Lazarus has gotten himself shot again and needs medical attention." Olivia sighed. "I need to find my maid, and then we can go to him."

"Lazarus is well. At least he was when I last saw him two days ago. The favor I ask for is for myself."

"But I don't even know you." Olivia hated the plaintive sound in her voice. How did tending to a man's bullet wound lead her to this?

The man gave a formal bow. "Finch at your service."

Olivia inclined her head in acknowledgement of his manners. "What can I do for you, Mr. Finch?" She hoped it wasn't a question she would regret later.

"No mister. Just Finch." He looked around as

though he wanted to make sure no one was in hearing distance, then gave a negative shake of his head. "Would you join me for dinner?"

"Dinner? That's the favor you want?"

He smiled, laughter lighting his blue eyes. "No, I'd like to make my request over dinner. I'm hoping a good meal will induce you to agree to help me."

"I'm sorry. I don't accept invitations from complete strangers. I'm more than happy to hear you out, but…" She let her voice trail away.

Reaching out, he took her hand in his, the warmth of his gloved hand permeating hers. "What can I do to convince you to share a meal with me?"

She gently extricated her hand. "If Lazarus will agree to join us, I will have dinner with you."

All expression slipped from Mr. Finch's face. "I'd prefer if he didn't join us."

Olivia took a step back. It was as she suspected. The man before her was no friend of Lazarus, an enemy more likely, and one hoping to use her against him.

As though he read her thoughts, he closed the distance between them. "I mean neither you nor Lazarus harm. I am his friend. In fact, we are also in business together. The Two Deuces, perhaps you've heard of it?"

"The gaming hell?" She eyed the bookshelf to her right. Were there any books heavy enough to knock him unconscious?

He grimaced at her words. "It's much more than a gaming hell."

She slid an oversized volume on the Roman Empire from the stack. "If you are truly friends with Lazarus, why do you not want him to join us?"

As though knowing her intention, Mr. Finch took the book from her and set it back on the shelf. "Every man has secrets he wishes to keep that way."

"Even from his business partner?"

"Since it has little or nothing to do with the business, yes."

If there was any one thing Olivia was grateful she learned during her years on the battlefield, it was how to tell those people who were genuine from those who were trying to manipulate you to serve their own purpose. Sensing he was telling the truth, she hoped she wasn't about to make one of the biggest mistakes of her life. "If I agree to have dinner with you, would you allow me to bring someone else?"

"It would depend on who that person would be?"

"My biggest footman along with a loaded pistol, should there be need of it," Olivia said, completely serious.

Mr. Finch laughed. "You may bring your footman and his pistol." He wiped his eye. "Now I see why Lazarus speaks so highly of you. A practical woman is hard to find."

"He thinks no more of me than any other woman of his acquaintance. We are helping each other look into familial matters, nothing more."

"Hmm."

The fact that Mr. Finch couldn't have been more obvious in his disbelief rankled. Olivia started to say more but changed her mind. Her protests would only serve to make him believe her even less than he did now.

"Shall I call for you this evening then?"

"Where will we be dining?" She had no intention

of getting into a carriage with a stranger, friend of Lazarus or not. If a busy street hadn't deterred Patrick from threatening her that first time, who knew what could happen in a closed carriage.

"As I can hardly take you to a gentleman's club, I thought we'd dine at The Brass Key."

"Very well. I shall meet you there at seven this evening. Is that acceptable?" Olivia raised an eyebrow in question. If she was going to have dinner with the man, it would be on her terms.

"You're not concerned about being seen in public with me?" Mr. Finch asked.

"Should I be?"

He raised a shoulder in a half-hearted shrug just as Bridget came rushing around the opposite corner.

She skidded to a stop inches before crashing into Mr. Finch. He held out a hand to steady her, but she took a quick step back. "There you is, Miss. I was thinkin' ye'd gone and left me." She reached past Mr. Finch and grabbed Olivia by the arm, pulling her forward with surprising strength. "We gots ta go. You's gonna be late meeting Lady Margaret."

At a complete loss as to why Bridget was acting the way she was, Olivia allowed the young maid to all but push her around the corner and up the next corridor.

"Seven this evening, Miss St. Germaine. I'll be waiting," Mr. Finch called after her.

She managed a quick look back and a nod of acknowledgement before Bridget rushed her out of the aisle and into the next one. Within minutes they stood outside in front of the carriage, barely taking the time to purchase the two books Olivia forgot she even had and one for Bridget.

The footman quickly opened the door and lowered the step. "Thank you, Daniel."

She took a seat and adjusted her skirts while she waited for Bridget to settle herself as well. The young woman kept looking out the window as though watching for someone. Had she been accosted in the shop while Olivia had been speaking with Mr. Finch?

As the carriage began to move, the maid released a huge sigh and slumped back against the plush cushions.

"What happened? Why are you so overset?"

"What happened?" the maid squeaked. "Do ye know who ya was talkin' to?"

"Mr. Finch. He said he was a businessman and friends with Lazarus. He needs to ask a favor of me."

"Any favors that man wants, ye don't need to be knowing about, much less doin'." Bridget sat forward. "Him being friends with Lazarus should tell you he ain't someone ye should be knowing."

Olivia tried to hold her temper. While she was grateful for the maid's concern, she did not like being taken to task by her. "Nonetheless, I agreed to meet him this evening and hear him out."

"Oh, me lord." Bridget made the sign of the cross in front of herself. "Trouble loves ye the way me brother loves eatin' jam tarts."

It was all Olivia could do not to roll her eyes at her companion's theatrics. "I'll be fine. Daniel will accompany me."

"I'm guessing there ain't no way I can change your mind."

Olivia shook her head. "I agreed to meet him, and I will. I didn't, however, agree to help him with whatever he's going to ask of me."

"I'm sorry for saying so, miss." Bridget looked down at her hands. "But you keep helping men ye don't know, ye may find yourself in the briars with no way out."

Olivia couldn't argue with the logic of that. She still carried a slight mark on her neck to prove it. She was already having second thoughts about agreeing to have dinner with a man she didn't know, hadn't even been properly introduced to. How trustworthy was a man who stalked a woman in a bookstore in an effort to get her alone, even if it was just to talk? "What do you know of Mr. Finch?"

"He says he's a friend of Lazarus. That's reason enough to stay clear of him."

"But you asked Daniel to send for Lazarus the night I was accosted."

"Aye, I did. I hoped if he knewed ye was hurt, he'd put it about ye was under his protection. I didn't want ye getting hurt again."

"Well, your thinking must have been right because the man who attacked me hasn't come near me again." Knowing servants were well versed in the gossip about London, Olivia asked the one question she wasn't sure she wanted to hear the answer to. "What do you know of Lazarus?"

"No more'n you. He come to the house in the middle of the night, gut shot, looking for Sir Phillip. His man held a pistol on you. They knocked you in the head. Ain't that enough to know he ain't a good man?"

"I don't know. Sometimes good men get into situations beyond their control. War is a lot like that. As a soldier, a man has no choice but to follow orders even if he doesn't want to, else he's branded a traitor, a coward, or worse, a deserter if he walks away from a battle." Olivia rubbed her temple. She felt a headache forming over her left eye.

"He ain't no soldier, and there ain't no war here in London. I don't think he follows orders, I think he gives them."

"Be that as it may, he's agreed to help me find Sir Phillip in return for me helping him gain entrance to certain society gatherings. I can hardly go back on my word."

Bridget slumped back against the seat. "I guess not, but it don't mean I won't keep worryin'."

"Thank you. I appreciate your concern." Olivia closed her eyes, willing the headache to subside before it took hold. A sudden thought struck her, and she opened her eyes. "Who is Lady Margaret? I'm sure I had no plans to meet anyone today."

"Oh." The maid looked around the coach, not meeting her gaze. "She be me cat."

****

Olivia stood outside The Brass Key, feeling much like she had when she attended to her first patient on her own. She pressed a hand to her stomach in an attempt to settle the nerves tumbling about there. She touched a hand to her hair, then to the modest neckline of her light blue gown. What was she doing here, about to partake of a meal with a complete stranger? Why hadn't she sent a note to Will, asking him if he did indeed know Mr. Finch as the other man claimed? What if this was all some sort of plot to force Will to do something he didn't want to do, or couldn't do?

"Miss Olivia? Are you all right? I can take you home."

Olivia gave Daniel a reassuring smile, her gaze taking in his great height, broad shoulders, and big hands. If she needed protection, he was more than able to provide it. "No, I'm fine. You do have the pistol I gave you?"

"Yes..." He hesitated. "I'm just not sure why you gave it to me. Are you expectin' trouble like the night I was visitin' my sister?" He referred to the night Will had first appeared in Olivia's life.

"I'm not certain. I hope not. I just want you to be prepared to use the pistol if you need to, not just to protect me, but yourself as well."

"I'm ready." He patted his side where the gun sat under his livery jacket.

"Let's go in then, shall we?" She took a deep breath and opened the door.

Aromas of freshly baked bread, well cooked meat, and vegetables filled the air. She sniffed again. One thing she wouldn't regret about this evening would be the meal. Anything that smelled this wonderful had to taste just as good.

A balding man hurried forward, his clothing neat but showing wear at the cuffs. "May I help you, my lady?"

"Yes, I…um…" Olivia stumbled over her words, not sure if she should correct the man in his form of address.

"She will be dining with me this evening."

Olivia turned to find Mr. Finch standing behind her. Had he only just arrived, or had he seen her attack of nerves outside? His expression gave nothing away.

"Very well. I have a private dining room ready if you'll follow me." The proprietor turned and led the way through the crowded common room to a door off to the side.

Mr. Finch gestured for her to follow the man while he would follow her with Daniel bringing up the rear. Her heart beating madly, she swallowed and walked after the balding man.

He opened the door and led them inside. The room was painted a pale yellow with light green accents. The table linens were in the same color scheme, and in the center of the table beside a small candelabra stood a vase of daffodils. A fire burned in the grate, making the room warm, but not uncomfortably so. He moved to the table and pulled out a chair for Olivia.

"Thank you," she said as she sat.

Mr. Finch took a seat opposite her while the footman stood against the wall near the door.

"We are offering beef stew with bread this evening, but if you'd like something else, I'm sure my wife wouldn't mind," the balding man said.

"The stew and bread would be lovely, thank you." Olivia raised a brow at Mr. Finch waiting for him to order something different. He seemed to have more refined tastes than simple peasant food.

"I will have the same. I'd like a bottle of your best wine and bring a bowl of stew for him." Mr. Finch gestured toward Daniel.

"Do you have a small table you could bring in?" Olivia asked.

"Is this one not to your liking, my lady?" the proprietor asked, his brow creased with worry.

"Oh, no. The table is beautiful. It's for my footman. No one should have to stand while having a meal."

"Of course, my lady. I'll have one brought in right away." The man bowed and scurried from the room.

"My lady?" Mr. Finch mocked.

Olivia scowled. "I could hardly correct him. He seemed nervous enough in your presence."

A knock sounded at the door before it opened. The balding man entered, carrying a bottle of wine. Two young men followed, struggling to carry the extra table into the room. They set it across the room and hurried out. A girl no more than ten years of age quickly set the table with plain white table linens. She shot a glance at the owner, who Olivia assumed was her father, before setting a tiny vase of blue wildflowers on the table and leaving the room.

She returned seconds later carrying a tray laden with food. With a minimum of movement, she deftly placed steaming bowls of stew in front of Olivia and Mr. Finch while her father poured the wine he'd opened. She set a basket of bread on the table and backed away with a curtsey. She stopped at the other table and placed the remaining bowl of stew and bread basket on the table and sent a smile in Daniel's direction before disappearing from the room.

Olivia hid a grin behind her hand. She imagined the young girl would be quite the headache to her father when she grew older and young men started to notice her.

"Send your man out if you need anything else," the owner said as he set the wine bottle on the table. With a final bow he left the room, closing the door behind him.

"Sit," Mr. Finch ordered, pointing Daniel toward the other table.

The footman leaned against the wall and examined

the nails on one hand.

"Please do sit down and enjoy your meal," Olivia said, doing her best not to laugh at Daniel's overt insolence toward Mr. Finch.

He crossed the room, moved the chair around the table so he sat facing them. He took a bite of bread, his gaze never leaving Mr. Finch.

The other man stared back, anger tightening his features. The two men were evenly matched in height and build, and while she had brought her footman as a form of protection, she didn't want them to come to blows. She wanted the evening to pass uneventfully, with nothing coming of it but a pleasant meal and conversation. She touched Mr. Finch on the arm. "Perhaps you can tell me your favor now?" She hoped the question distracted him enough to cool his temper.

"I'll not discuss it with him in hearing distance." Mr. Finch lifted his glass and drank half the contents before slamming it on the table.

"Then I shall take my leave since that was the only reason I agreed to come this evening." Olivia set her serviette on the table.

He put his hand over hers causing her to halt in mid-movement. "I don't trust him."

"I do, and if you want my help, you'll have to do the same." She pulled her hand from under his and rose to her feet. She made a staying motion to Daniel who now stood, his chair toppled to the floor behind him.

"I'll not have my personal business bandied about by servants."

"Daniel knows all of my secrets and has never spoken of them outside my home."

Mr. Finch gave her skeptical look. "You are

incredibly gullible for someone of your age. Servants love to gossip as much as the people they work for and especially *about* the people they work for."

"Perhaps they do, but my servants do not. That I do know, despite my *advanced* age," Olivia replied, stung by his comment.

"I meant no insult. Sit down and enjoy your meal."

"One thing you should know about me, Mr. Finch, is that while I spent time on the battlefield, I was never a soldier. I do *not* take orders from anyone. I believe you and I will be more comfortable as strangers who share a mutual acquaintance. Good night." She crossed the room, the footman at her side.

"Wait," Mr. Finch called as her hand closed around the door handle.

She stopped but didn't turn around. She heard his chair scrape against the floor as he stood.

"I apologize if I offended you."

She faced him. "*If* you offended me? *If?*"

"Obviously I have." He gave a small bow. "I apologize for my choice of words. Will you please come, sit down?"

Crossing to the table, she held on to her temper with both hands. "You regret your choice of words but not saying them?"

He scrubbed a hand down his face. "You need to learn to accept an apology." He held up a hand when she opened her mouth to speak. "Out of fear of saying anything else to offend you, can't you accept the fact that I'm trying to say I'm sorry."

"You need to learn a better way to do it." Olivia resumed her seat, her vanity still smarting. She turned and nodded to Daniel who moved back to his table and righted the overturned chair.

Mr. Finch sat with ill grace. "I'm not accustomed to bowing and scraping to anyone, much less a woman."

"I'm not asking you to. An apology should be sincere, else it's not worth the breath it takes to utter it. It shouldn't be said just to placate someone. And you really need to learn how to talk to a woman without offending her."

She picked up her fork. "Much less a woman indeed," she muttered, stabbing a piece of beef with more force than necessary.

The remainder of the meal passed in silence with the three of them each concentrating on the food in front of them, though Daniel watched Mr. Finch the entire time.

Olivia drank the last swallow of her wine and set the glass down. She wiped her lips and laid the cloth napkin beside her dish. "Thank you for the meal." She turned to the footman. "Have you finished?"

At his nod, she stood.

Mr. Finch rose. "You aren't leaving? We haven't discussed my favor."

"I don't think there ever was a favor to be asked. I'm not certain what you hoped to achieve this evening, but I'll not be a party to it any longer."

"I do have a favor to ask." Urgency colored his voice.

Olivia did her best to refrain from rolling her eyes. One thing that could be said about Mr. Finch was that he certainly was tenacious. "I don't think I'm inclined to do any favors for you."

She crossed the room, Daniel once again at her

side. She stopped at the door, her manners coming to the fore. "Thank you again for dinner."

"I want you to teach me how to read." The words burst from Mr. Finch like a bullet from a pistol. He stood with his hands clenched at his sides, a tide of red coloring his cheekbones.

"Teach you to—"

"Read," he interrupted before turning to the man standing beside her. "If you breathe one word about this, I'll kill you where you stand."

"He won't say a word to anyone." She moved to the table. "Do you truly not know how to read, or is this another ploy to detain me here for some reason of your own?"

"I do not," Mr. Finch uttered through gritted teeth.

"But you said you own a business, a gaming hell."

He dipped his head in acknowledgement. "Aye, I do. I'm quite accomplished at taking care of the money or spotting a person attempting to cheat, but Lazarus takes care of any contracts that are needed and deals with the shopkeepers for the food and such."

"But you said earlier that he doesn't know about your secret." Olivia sank into the chair she had vacated.

"He doesn't. I'm very adept at making it look like I can read. I've had years of practice, after all."

"Why do you want to learn now? Why me?"

Mr. Finch sat across from her. "I've wanted to learn for years but didn't know how to do it without the people who work for me finding out, much less the pigeons who come in to lose their money." He glanced at Daniel, who lounged by the door. "My business would be ruined, and any investment Lazarus has in it would be lost as well."

"But why me?"

"Lazarus told me how you often spent time teaching some of the soldiers and camp followers how to read when the battlefield was quiet."

"What else has he told you?" Had her greatest secret been shared without her consent or knowledge?

"Just that you helped him with Rachel, that you have the skills of a good doctor but without the schooling."

"I would have to disagree with him on that point. I received a great deal of schooling whether I wanted it or not on too many battlefields caring for too many young men who didn't deserve to die the way they did."

"I've offended you again," Mr. Finch said with a sigh. "You are a mighty prickly woman."

She tried not to smile at his words but couldn't keep her lips from curving upward. "I'm not offended. I just don't like the time I spent trying to save the men who died fighting the king's wars being belittled like it was no more than spending the afternoon doing needlework."

"I do apologize then, for that wasn't at all what I intended." He took a long swallow of wine and set the glass. "Will you teach me to read?" he asked in quiet voice.

She knew how much she longed to find a way to end her nightmares, her overwhelming fear of thunderstorms.

How could she turn away someone who wanted her help so badly when she had no honest reason to decline. She watched him fidget with the bread knife, his gaze riveted on it as though it held all the secrets of the world while he waited for her answer.

She took a deep breath and let it out slowly. "I will."

She just hoped this wouldn't become one more thing she regretted in an already long list of regrets.

Chapter Fifteen

Amanda rushed to Olivia's side as soon as she and Will entered the ballroom. "I'm so glad you came. Isn't Riverton the best husband to throw a ball in honour of my birthday?" As though noticing him for the first time, she turned and addressed Olivia's companion. "Mr. Prescott," she said, giving him only the politest of greetings. "Would you mind if I borrow Miss St. Germaine's company for a moment?"

"Not at all." Will took a step back.

Amanda threaded her arm through Olivia's and hurried her through the crowd to the ladies' retiring room. Once inside, she closed the door and took a quick glance around. "Have you taken leave of your senses?"

"I have no idea what you mean," Olivia said, though she knew exactly what her friend was talking about.

"Did I not tell you weeks ago consorting with a mere mister would do nothing to enhance your reputation?"

"I'm not concerned with my reputation among people who claim friendship when I'm present only to spread vicious gossip about me when I'm not."

"Perhaps you should be. My championing you as a friend will only buy so much tolerance. And being seen with Mr. Prescott will undo any good my name has done."

Olivia crossed to the mirror and checked her appearance. The deep emerald green gown brought out the reddish highlights in her brown hair. She tucked a wayward curl into place and sighed. She was tired of this conversation. She and Amanda had had it more times than she cared for, with the same results each time. "I don't see why."

"Have you not heard the rumours?"

"Would those rumours be spread by the same people who insist Hargrove has taken up with Glenville's wife when in fact she is his niece? If so, I doubt there's any more truth to the lies about Mr. Prescott as there was about Lord Hargrove."

"You know as well as I do, truth doesn't matter. Damage can be done by rumours alone. People are saying your Mr. Prescott and the criminal known as Lazarus are one and the same. Surely, you must care if he is a thief or worse."

Pretending a nonchalance she didn't feel, Olivia gave a one-shouldered shrug. "Of course I would care if it were true. Do you not think I would know if the gentleman I'm allowing to escort me to various entertainments were a criminal?"

"I'm not certain. Perhaps you wish for the attentions of a suitor, and any man who shows an interest is enough."

Stung by her friend's remarks, Olivia turned away from the mirror. "Much like you before you managed to trap Riverton into marriage by being found in his arms?" She didn't bother to keep the sarcasm from her voice.

Amanda's gaze iced over. "Heed my warning, Olivia. Cut ties with Prescott. Do not make me choose between you and my standing among the *Ton.*" She wrenched the door open and stalked out.

Olivia sighed and went in search of Will. She supposed she should tell him there would be no future invitations coming from the Rivertons. Perhaps his friend, Lord Hargrove, could provide them, although the elderly man hadn't been seen in company for some weeks.

She slowed as she saw him speaking with a couple. He met her gaze and gestured for her to come forward. She crossed to stand beside him.

He placed a hand on the small of her back, and though she knew it wasn't acceptable to allow him such familiarity, she stayed where she was.

"Olivia, may I introduce Miss Emma Tompkins?" He looked to the young woman standing opposite him. "Emma, this is Olivia St. Germaine."

"A pleasure to meet you," Miss Tompkins said, a smile as bright as a sunny day crossing her face. "I'm so very happy to see Lazar—Mr. Prescott has decided there is more to an existence than seeing to others."

"Thank you," Olivia said taking an instant liking to her. She had to admit Miss Tompkins's comment had aroused her curiosity. Perhaps she would have a chance to talk to her later.

Casting a reproachful look at Will, the young woman laid her hand on the arm of the gentleman beside her. "This is my betrothed, Mr. Blaine Hobson."

Feeling the sudden tension in the air between the two men, Olivia offered her hand to the tall dark-haired man in front of her. "Mr. Hobson. It's so very nice to meet you. I must say I was very taken by your poem, *Death Rides the Night*."

He waved away her compliment and bowed over her hand. "The pleasure is all mine, despite your companion."

Olivia raised her brows at the comment.

Emma gave her a rueful look. "I'm afraid Mr. Hobson and Mr. Prescott tolerate each other purely for my benefit." She smiled up at her betrothed. "The musicians have taken their places. Shall we cause a scandal and dance?" Mischief glowed in her eyes, and Olivia knew she wanted to further her acquaintance with the young woman.

"As you wish." Mr. Hobson nodded to Olivia and led his intended to join the others moving onto the dance floor.

"They seem quite nice," she said, watching them walk away.

"Emma is indeed a special woman."

Will's words were like a stab to the heart. Was the animosity between him and Mr. Hobson due to Will loving Emma himself? "How did you meet her?" she forced herself to ask.

"I came upon her one night trying to fight off footpads intent on relieving her of more than the meager coins she carried. I helped her escape them—"

"You saved her," Olivia interrupted.

He inclined his head in agreement. "From that moment on, I let it be known she was under my protection; that anyone hurting her would answer to me."

"Much as you have done with me," she said the words tonelessly. "How many women do you have under your 'protection'?"

"Emma, who with Hobson at her side, no longer

needs it and yourself." His gaze tracked the young blonde woman around the dance floor.

"She means a great deal to you," Olivia said. Her voice more subdued than she meant it to be. A sense of loss curled around her heart. How had she come to care for a man who clearly cared for another?

"Yes, she does. I failed Mary, and when I met Emma so desperately in need of help, I vowed I would not leave another woman to be used by society and cast aside."

"I see." Olivia watched as Miss Tompkins laughed up at something Mr. Hobson said. Did Will feel the claws of jealousy every time he saw the two of them together?

He moved in front of her, cutting off her vision of the dance floor. "Do you?" He stared at her as though trying to read her thoughts. "Emma is like a sister to me. You, however, mean a great deal more."

"There is no need to pay me false compliments. I know we are in truth nothing more than two people using each other to find our loved ones."

"Is that all we are?" he asked in a tone she'd never heard him use before. "I guess I shall have to convince you otherwise." He clasped her hand in his and led her toward the other dancers.

The evening passed too quickly as far as she was concerned. She had danced twice with Will, and though she knew she risked a scandal, she wished she could dance with him again. He had let her see a side of him he often kept hidden. He charmed her with anecdotes about various guests, had danced with Miss Tompkins while Olivia herself had partnered Mr. Hobson who was polite but reserved.

She watched Will and Miss Tompkins come toward her, his head bent to hers in a solicitous manner. Jealousy ate at her, but she pushed it aside. While she may have feelings for him, he seemed to have no genuine feelings for her other than toying with her affections. It seemed he felt it was his duty to care for any woman who had no one to care for her.

"Thank you for sending Rachel to me," Emma said as they drew close. "You were right. She learns quickly and shows quite a talent with the needle."

"I'm glad." Will's gaze tracked a liveried servant around the room. "If you ladies will excuse me." He bowed over their hands and turned away.

Olivia watched him pass close enough to the servant so to anyone watching, it looked as though he had accidentally bumped into the man, but she saw the slip of paper pass between them. Will pocketed the note under the pretext of adjusting his coat.

He stepped out onto the terrace. Olivia turned to his friend who seemed content to watch the dancers swirl around the floor. "Would you excuse me as well? I feel the need for a breath of fresh air."

"Oh, of course. I felt overwhelmed the first time I attended a ball with Mr. Hobson."

Olivia smiled her thanks and threaded her way around the room. Being seen on the arm of a man in trade, not to mention rumoured to be a criminal, kept most of the gossips at bay, and she was able to make her way to the French doors leading to the terrace without any delays. She pushed the door open and stepped out into the night air.

The hint of a breeze cooled her cheeks, and she felt the tension of the evening fade. Will stood in the shadows facing her. He frowned when he saw her but continued his conversation with a well-dressed gentleman she didn't recognize. Not wanting to interrupt, she stayed near the door and enjoyed the starlit sky.

She didn't want him to think she was trying to eavesdrop, but even if she wanted to, their low tones didn't carry on the night air. A moment later, the man moved down the stairs and disappeared into the garden.

"Why did you follow me?" Will asked as he came to stand beside her.

Olivia shrugged. She really didn't know why she had. "Curiosity, I guess."

He smiled and led her to the edge of the terrace. "Do you suppose I could entice you to take a walk in the gardens?"

"As much as I would like to accept your offer, I fear we are already courting scandal by being out here alone."

He lifted her gloved hand to his lips. "I feared as much." He pressed a kiss on the back of her hand and released her.

Wanting to hold onto the warmth of his kiss, she covered the hand with her other.

"Would you mind if I joined a game or two in the card room?"

Olivia grinned. "Wanting to fleece a pigeon or two, are you?"

"I see Harry's been doing more than watching out for you, but no. Sandhurst has been seen in London. I want to ask a few questions of his cronies who are present tonight to see if the duke has indeed returned. I've learned that a man who is intent on his cards will often say things he ordinarily wouldn't when he's not otherwise occupied."

"I see." She smothered a yawn.

"You're tired. We'll go."

"No." She made a staying motion. "This might lead you to Mary. Besides I promised Amanda I'd stay at least until after Riverton unveiled his birthday gift to her." Though after their earlier confrontation, she wasn't quite certain if Amanda would care if she were there or not. "You do what you need to and find me later."

"Thank you." He curled his fingers around hers.

"Olivia."

She jumped at the sound of her name, and Will's hand dropped away. "Lord Michael." She hated the way her voice sounded—as though she had gotten caught doing something illicit. She pressed her hand to chest. "You frightened me. I was just returning to the ballroom, would you escort me?" She didn't want to leave the two men alone. The last thing she needed was gossip being bandied about that they were fighting over her.

"I think not. I believe Mr. Prescott and I have an understanding to reach."

Will raised an eyebrow but didn't utter a word.

"Be polite," she whispered near his ear and headed for the door.

Turning the knob, she opened the glass panel and stepped inside, but not before glancing back over her shoulder for one last glimpse of him.

He smiled at her and felt his heart squeeze painfully. She had a way of looking at him that made him want impossible things. And when she smiled, he found her even more alluring. At this moment, he wanted nothing more than to pull her into his arms and show her how much she meant to him. But that was not to be. He turned to the pompous ass beside him. "You aren't going to make the mistake of threatening me, are you?"

"Miss St. Germaine has led a sheltered life and is unaccustomed to the attentions of someone like you."

"A sheltered life?" Will nearly laughed aloud. "Are we speaking of the same young woman? The Miss St. Germaine I know has seen more of the horrors that men do to each other in the name of war than any man in that room." He gestured to the ballroom.

"Yes, well. We don't speak of her time assisting her brother. It's unseemly."

"She did a lot more than 'assist' her brother. She faced the hell of battle and its aftermath and is still more of a lady than most women I've met."

His lordship's nose wrinkled as though he smelled a foul odor. "I can just imagine what sort of women you are acquainted with."

"I suggest you think long and hard before you utter another word."

"I did not come out here to debate the merits of the women in your life. I do not care who you consort with, but you will cease courting Olivia at once."

"And if I choose not to?"

"Then you might find yourself floating in the Thames right alongside all the other bodies you're rumoured to have dumped there."

"You shouldn't make threats you aren't capable or willing to carry out." Will grabbed his lordship by the cravat and slammed him against the brick wall, careful to keep them both out of sight.

"You see I have no such qualms about doing so." He wrapped Huntley's cravat around his hand, tightening the length of cloth around the marquess' neck. "I will continue to see Olivia, and she will continue to see me so long as she wishes to. If I hear even the slightest rumour of scandal attached to her name because of her association with me, you will wish you were floating in the Thames." He gave the material a twist and felt a sense of satisfaction as the other man's eyes began to bulge and his face turned red. "Do we understand each other?"

Huntley gave the barest nod of his head. Will released him and stepped away.

His lordship sagged against the ivy covered wall, gasping for breath.

"I suggest you remember this conversation, *my lord*, for I shall find it much easier to hunt you than you will to hunt me."

****

Will lifted his head, focusing on the sounds around him. "Did you hear that?"

"Hear what?" Lord Coddington shifted the cards in his hand and frowned.

Concentrating on filtering out the noise of the room, Will stared at the far wall.

"Pay attention, Prescott, or leave the game," Baron Sutton groused.

"I believe I'll sit this round out." Will set his cards on the table. The sound came again. "It seems a storm is coming. My horse becomes rather high-strung at the sound of thunder." He sent a silent apology to Olivia for saying she was a horse, but he was certain she wouldn't want any of the men at the table to know of her fear.

"Not thunder," Coddington said, still frowning at his cards. "Riverton arranged to have a fireworks display in honour of her ladyship's birthday."

"Fireworks?" Will stood up from the table. He was certain Olivia would be affected by the booming sounds of the fireworks. They were after all a form of explosive.

Coddington set his cards on the table with a sigh. "Yes, you know, showers of lights in the sky and god-awful bangs after each one."

"Where are they being held?" Will tried to keep the urgency from his voice.

"Back garden," Sutton snapped. "Now, do you mind if we get on with the game."

Will hurried from the room and down the hall to the ballroom. He scanned the guests, but there was no sign of Olivia. He pushed past a couple on their way out to the terrace with a muttered apology and ran down the stone stairs to the gardens. The crashing noise overhead drove him down the path to the right. Sparkling blue and green lights filled the night sky. Will started to run.

He reached the edges of the crowd and looked around. No sign of Olivia. He moved through the throng.

"Miss St. Germaine, have you seen her?" he asked Blaine and Emma when he ran into them.

"No—" Emma began, but he didn't wait to hear the rest. He raced through the people gathered there. He called Olivia's name, but she was nowhere to be found.

He stopped to look around. Perhaps she was inside the house. Yes, that made sense. She wouldn't be out here close to the source of noise that would seem so much like cannon fire. He made his way back the way he came. As he reached the edge of the crowd, he froze, every fear he'd ever had crystallizing in that single space in time. Olivia stood on the edge of a balcony three stories above the ground. The bright moon and the light from the fireworks display illuminated her so clearly, he had no doubts it was she.

He ran down the path, dodging other guests, but never slowing down. He felt ice cold and too hot all at once. He sprinted up the steps leading to the terrace and dashed inside. The faster he tried to run, the slower he seemed to move. Time stood still. Taking the stairs two at a time, he reached the third floor and turned to his left, opening every door, hoping he was headed in the right direction and thankful the fireworks had seemed to come to an end.

He came to an open door halfway down the hall. Pushing it open further, he stepped inside. The light breeze filtered into the room through a pair of sheer white drapes. He strode to the opening and sent up a silent prayer.

He stepped through the open French doors. Olivia stood on the edge of the balcony railing facing the night sky.

"Olivia," he called in a gentle voice so as not to frighten her.

"Can you not hear them, Phillip?"

Knowing she was lost to the past, he edged closer. "Hear them?"

"The wounded. Can you not hear them calling out to us, their cries like the moaning of the wind through the trees in the winter season?"

"I hear them." Will moved to where she stood. He wanted to reach out and grab her but was afraid it would frighten her into stepping off the small slab of stone.

"Does it not break your heart?"

"Aye, it does." He held his hand out to her. "Come, I shall need your help to see to them."

"I don't know if I can do it anymore," she whispered, never taking her gaze from the place only she could see. "Don't you understand, Phillip? Those we could not save haunt me. I cannot eat. I cannot sleep. Some days, I cannot even breathe. They are with me always, every hour of every day." Her voice broke, and she took a shaky breath. "Please do not make me lie to another man who will breathe his last and tell him all will be well."

Will hated her brother even more than he had before. Did Phillip not realize what he had done to her, what exposing her to war had done to her? "I am sorry, Olivia, but I must ask that you assist me this one last time."

Her shoulders slumped. She let out a sigh that seemed to come from the depths of her soul.

Afraid she would take a step forward, Will brushed her fingertips with his. "Take my hand and come back this way."

She began to move toward him. He grabbed her around the thighs and yanked her off the ledge. He lowered her feet to the ground and crushed her to him, thanking a God he'd long stopped believing in.

After a long moment, he wiped at the suspicious moisture in his eyes and ran his hands up and down her arms. He needed to touch her to ensure she was really all right. He pulled her close and cupped her face between his hands. She stared at him and in her gaze, he saw the pain of every soldier she had ever tried to help.

"Will?" Confusion clouded her eyes.

"Shhh. Everything is all right." He rubbed her back as she pressed her cheek to his chest.

"I had another episode, didn't I?"

"Yes." As much as he knew it would hurt her, he couldn't lie. She knew the answer to her question and lying would only make her feel more ashamed when she had no need to feel that way.

She burst into tears.

Every sob stabbed at his heart. Wanting to offer comfort, he whispered to her, trying to reassure them both that she was all right. He pressed gentle kisses to her hair and face, tasting her tears as they coursed down her cheeks. He tried to ease the shudders that racked her frame, that cut through the defenses he'd spent years building as though they were no more than a line of toy soldiers to be knocked over on a child's whim. He felt shattered inside and for the first time in his life, uncertain of what to do.

He rested his forehead against hers. "I need you to walk on your own until we get to the carriage, can you do that?" He wanted to carry her out of there in his arms, but as much as he didn't give a damn about causing a scandal, he knew she would.

"Yes," she said in an almost inaudible tone. She stepped back from him and closed her eyes. She inhaled a deep breath, held it, then released it and opened her eyes. There was no trace of emotion in her gaze. Her face was an expressionless mask. "Shall we go?" she asked in a calm voice that gave nothing away.

He placed a hand on the small of her back and led her into the room, down the hall, and out into the night where Fingers lounged against the side of the coach.

His expression must have given away what he was feeling because Fingers took one look at him and quickly opened the carriage door. Will helped Olivia inside. "To Miss St. Germaine's home with all speed," he said and pulled the door shut behind him.

Instead of taking the seat opposite her, he sat beside her and held her in his arms. She rested her head on his shoulder as the coach began to move. "I'm sorry you had to leave the ball on my account when you finally had the opportunity to find out where Sandhurst may be."

"Do not apologize. I learned all I was going to from Sutton and Coddington. And I don't think I could have stood to lose any more blunt to them. The way they play cards, it's a wonder they haven't been well and truly fleeced long ago."

"Did you learn anything of use to you?"

"Shall I have Fingers return to Riverton's with a note explaining our departure without thanking them for the evening? Perhaps saying you've taken ill?" he asked, ignoring her question.

"There's no need. I fear my friendship with Amanda has come to an end."

"Because of me." He knew he was the cause of contention between the two women.

"No, because of me. I will not be told who I can and cannot associate with. A true friend would be respectful of the friendships I have with others whether she liked them or not, not threaten to withhold her friendship because others aren't of her social class. Especially as I'm not even of her social class. I fear Amanda is only friends with people who can do something for her in some way."

"I'm sorry. What do you think you did for her?"

Olivia shrugged. "I'm not certain. Perhaps I was a way for her to show her benevolence to the rest of society—by taking a social outcast under her wing and befriending her." She hesitated for a moment. "Do *you* think I'm ill?"

Will knew what she was really asking. Did he think she belonged in Bedlam? "No more than anyone else I've met. In fact, I believe you are saner than most. If you weren't, you wouldn't be so affected by the experiences of your past." He pressed a kiss to the top of her head.

"Thank you," she whispered.

The carriage pulled to a stop, and Will opened the door before Fingers had a chance to do so. He stepped out and helped her down.

"Why are we here and not at the front of the house?" She looked around the lane behind the townhouse.

"I thought it best. Your association with me has already cost you your friendship with Lady Riverton. I don't wish to cause your reputation more harm by being seen entering your home at this late hour."

"I suppose you're right." Olivia sounded defeated.

He wished he could go back and change the night's events. If he could, he would never have left her side.

She opened the door to the servants' entrance. "Daniel and Bridget have the night off and are visiting relatives. Jennings will have retired long ago." She took a deep breath. "Would you come in for a while?" She looked down at her hands. "I fear I don't wish to be alone quite yet."

"I am always happy to spend time in your company."

She gave him a wan smile as though she didn't quite believe he wasn't humouring her. "Thank you."

He followed her through the house to what he knew to be her favorite room in the house—the library. A fire burned low in the grate, casting shadows around the darkened room. Olivia lit the branch of candles sitting on a table just off to the side of the door. While she was busy lighting various tapers throughout the room, he stirred the embers in the hearth, coaxing them into flame.

He turned to find her staring at him. She'd never looked more beautiful, and he could think of nothing more than stripping her gown from her and laying her down on the carpet. He felt himself harden and turned away under the pretext of tending to the fire.

He may want her more than he'd wanted any woman, but he wouldn't ruin her for another man. She deserved a marriage, children, and so much more than he could offer. Angry at himself for wanting her, he stabbed at the embers with more force than necessary.

"Why are you angry?"

"I'm not." He set the fireplace poker against the wall.

"You are. I can hear it in your voice, and I can see it in the way you are standing."

"I'm not angry," he snapped, upset that she could read him so well.

"Then why do you stand with your back to me?

You don't have to stay if you wish to be elsewhere."

Will grasped the edge of the mantel, the raised carvings biting into his fingers. "I'm standing here—" He turned to face her. "—because…to keep from touching you. I'm standing on the other side of the room because if I get too close to you, I'm going to kiss you, and I don't know if I'll be able to stop." He waited to see the fear his words would bring.

"What if I want the same thing?" she whispered.

He took a step forward, unable to believe he heard her correctly. "Are you certain? I don't want you to regret anything that may happen tonight."

"I'm very certain." She removed her pelisse and set it over the back of the divan.

His eyes gleamed like onyx, and he crossed the room in two strides. Olivia barely had time to draw a breath before he hauled her into his arms. She grabbed at his shoulders to keep her balance. He bent her over his arm and took her mouth with a kiss she had spent far too long dreaming of.

The hot press of his lips set her afire, burning away her reserve, her caution. Her sense of self-preservation turned to ash as she twined her arms around his neck and pressed closer. She knew it was wrong to allow him to hold her like this, to touch her like this, but he made her feel like she was someone who could be worth loving, a woman who was precious and beautiful, not the oddity she truly was. And for tonight, just for tonight, she wanted to be that woman.

He kissed his way down the side of her neck lingering there as he pulled free the ribbon threaded through her curls. She leaned her head back to give him better access.

The sudden touch of his mouth on the slopes of her breasts at her neckline caused her a moment's hesitation, but the graze of his teeth across her nipple made her gasp with pleasure and her fingers tangle in his hair.

"I'm used to taking what I want, and I have wanted to touch you like this since the night you first came to the warehouse," he murmured as he maneuvered her back against the sofa. He settled her against the soft cushions and followed her down, his hand tracing a path from her ankle ever upward.

His fingers slid over her calf in a light caress that left her shivering in their wake. The thought of where he might touch her next sent a rush of warmth between her legs.

He paused and lifted his head. "If we continue much longer, I may not be able to stop. Are you certain you want to do this?"

"I'm very certain," she said and began unfastening his waistcoat.

He placed his hands over hers, drawing them to a halt. "It can be painful for a woman the first time."

"It won't be my first time."

He stiffened. "It won't."

Afraid he would think her a wanton, though he had every right to do so considering how she was acting, she rushed into speech. "I was to marry. Lieutenant Elliot asked me to be his wife. We anticipated the marital bed. He was killed three days later."

"I'm sorry." Will looked at her, his expression unreadable.

Olivia felt him withdrawing from her even though he hadn't moved. "It was nearly four years ago," she said and with a boldness she didn't think possible, she pushed his frock coat from his shoulders. "I think I'd rather do something other than talk right now." A sense of satisfaction filled her when he removed his shirt and waistcoat with such haste, she heard the material tear.

He grinned and took her mouth in another soul-searing kiss. Knowing she wasn't a virgin, he allowed himself free rein to show his desire.

When his tongue slipped between her lips, she welcomed him completely, arching up against him, opening to the hungry assault of his mouth. She tasted as sweet as any piece of candy he'd ever had, and he wanted to devour her whole. Shifting her so she sat astride him, he pressed her against his arousal.

Will ran a hand down her back to the enticing curve of her buttocks. He squeezed the soft flesh, and she groaned against his lips. Trailing kisses down her neck, he bared her breasts and suckled first one then the other. He slipped his hand under her gown and stroked her leg, bringing it between his own. He pushed his thigh against her, thrusting it urgently between her legs.

"Will," she breathed, her head fell back onto her shoulders as her desire took over.

Hearing her call his name raised him to new heights of arousal. "Olivia." He fed her short quick kisses. "Do you remember I once told you I burn for you?"

"Yes," she panted as his fingers stroked her.

"Do you burn for me?"

"I do."

He touched her womanhood, and she cried out her release. Will unfastened his trousers and slipped inside her warmth. It was like being squeezed by a velvet glove. He closed his eyes and tried to keep from moving. If he didn't get under control, he'd be finished before he started.

Olivia shifted and he groaned. "Will, please."

Her words were all he needed. His hands gripped her waist, and he began to move, laying claim to her in a way he never could with words.

She moaned when he thrust up into her a bit, then a bit more, until he was moving like a madman. Faster and faster as tension coiled through him until he could hold back no longer. He groaned her name as he found his own release.

She collapsed against his chest, shudders racking her frame. He rested his head against her shoulder. She had just had intimate relations with a man on a sofa in the library…and she had never felt better in her life.

She slid her hands up his chest and cupped his jaw. She gave him one last lingering kiss then stood. She slid her arms back into the sleeves of her gown and adjusted the bodice. Looking up from fluffing her skirts, Olivia saw Will putting himself to rights.

He stood and without touching her, moved to the other side of the room. "Regrets already?" he asked in a mocking tone.

"What?" She felt out of her depth. Something had happened to change how he felt, but she didn't know what.

"You got what you needed, so now I'm to be dismissed? If I'm to be used like a whore, the least you could do is toss me a coin."

"What are you talking about?" A sudden chill chased over her skin.

"You couldn't get away from me quick enough

once we were finished."

"So I could show you to my chamber, so you could make love to me in a bed," Olivia snapped. "I may have led you to believe I am without modesty considering what we just did, but I have no desire to risk running into Jennings half clothed."

Will closed his eyes, and he sagged against the edge of a club chair. When he met her gaze, his were filled with remorse. "Olivia, I...I'm sorry I took something beautiful and ruined it because I let my past rule my tongue."

She stood in front of him and took her hand in his. "Perhaps you can make it up to me."

"How would I do that?"

She placed his hand on her breast. "By showing me how sorry you are."

He nuzzled her neck, his fingers caressing her satiny skin. "I think it may take me hours."

"I hope so." Her fingers entwined with his, she led him from the room.

Chapter Sixteen

Olivia fidgeted with the lacy edge of the drapery. Where was Mr. Finch? She glanced at the clock on the mantel and felt her temper begin to spark. He was twenty minutes late. And he had chosen to meet at the Brass Key saying it was neutral ground, whatever he meant by that. Mayhap she should have heeded her first instinct to turn down his request to teach him to read after all.

She gave Daniel and Bridget an apologetic smile. Neither one of them was happy with her at the moment. Both felt she should have nothing to do with Mr. Finch, but she found it hard to turn down someone who wanted so badly to learn to read and in that at least, he had seemed earnest. But considering his lateness, perhaps she hadn't read him as well as she thought she had. He owned a gaming hell after all. Weren't most successful gamblers better liars than most, able to fool others into believing what they wanted them to?

"We will wait a few more minutes. If Mr. Finch doesn't arrive, we shall leave."

"That be the most sensible thing ye said all morning," Bridget muttered, her arms folded across her chest as she leaned back in her chair.

Daniel hid a grin but at least held his tongue.

A knock at the door was preceded by its opening. Olivia turned away from the window, glad Mr. Finch had finally decided to make an appearance. But it wasn't he.

The proprietor, his bald pate shiny with sweat, stuck his head around the door. "You're certain I cannot bring you refreshments?"

"No, thank you." She didn't see the point of having refreshments if they would be leaving soon. "But thank you for your trouble," she added, knowing by occupying a private dining room, she was costing him money.

"Very well," he said, a frown creasing his forehead as he withdrew.

She drummed her fingertips against the mantel, her impatience growing. She and Bridget still had stops to make at the dressmaker's and the stationery shop, and she had hoped to be home in time for afternoon tea.

Deciding Mr. Finch's desire to learn to read had been a ruse after all, Olivia gathered her cloak and reticule. "I think we've wasted enough time." She withdrew a few pound notes to pay the proprietor for the use of the room and his patience.

Daniel stood just as Mr. Finch sauntered into the room, looking like he hadn't a care in the world. "Ah, Miss St. Germaine, you are looking as lovely as ever."

"You, sir, are late," she bit out, angry at being kept waiting without so much as an apology.

"Because you, madam, were determined to meet at an ungodly hour."

"Eleven o'clock is not an ungodly hour. I have been up for hours and am normally so."

Mr. Finch plopped down on the small divan pushed against the far wall. "You know what they say. 'Early to bed, early to rise—'"

"Makes a man healthy, wealthy and wise," Olivia interrupted, "which you seem to be none of."

"Wrong, it makes a man want to hang himself out of boredom."

Olivia barely managed to keep from rolling her eyes. "Shall we begin your lesson?" She took a seat at the linen covered table and began laying out small squares of vellum.

Mr. Finch pulled out the chair opposite and sat down. He frowned as he gazed at each square.

She touched the first piece of paper. "This is the letter A." She tapped her finger on the next sheet. "This is the letter B."

He sat back and scowled. "I'm not daft, I know my letters."

"You do?" She was surprised. Teaching him to read might be easier than she had expected if he already knew the alphabet.

He placed five of the squares in front of him, the letters F, I, N, C, and H. "This is my name."

"Correct." Olivia placed the letters O, L, V, and A in front of her, then reached over and took the sheet containing the letter I from him and placed it between the L and V. "What does this say?"

"I don't know," he snapped. "I can't read."

"Then how did you know the letters you picked out spell your name?"

"I learned that much myself. How do you think I would have managed to fool everyone so long if I couldn't spell my own name?"

Conceding he had a point, she pointed to the sheets in front of her. "This is my name, well it would be if we had two squares showing the letter I. The second one should go here." She pointed to the space between the V and A.

He folded his arms on the table. "So how did you and Lazarus come to meet?"

"If you are as good friends with Lazarus as you claim, I'm sure you already know." She pulled the pieces of paper from under his forearm.

"I do know Lazarus can't deny a damsel in distress. It's his one failing." Mr. Finch leaned closer. "So, tell me what trouble is Lazarus protecting you from?"

"The only trouble I'm having at the moment is your unwillingness to pay attention," Olivia retorted. She would be sharing no secrets with him.

"Do you know your hair is quite lovely? It is beautiful in the lamplight."

"Flattery will gain you nothing." She laid out the letters in his name. "Do you know what sound each of these makes?"

"Fingers tells me you tended to Lazarus after he was shot." He ignored her question. "How did you come to do that?"

"I'm sure I don't know what he is talking about," Olivia prevaricated. She wasn't certain how much Mr. Finch knew and how much he was guessing at, but she wasn't going to give him any information until she knew if he truly was a friend of Will's or not.

"Fingers doesn't lie." He rearranged the squares to spell his name once more. "I tried teaching him, told him it makes things easier when dealing with a woman." He winked at Bridget who turned a bright red. "But the lessons never took."

"These lessons won't take either if you don't pay attention." Olivia didn't appreciate the fact that he admitted to lying to women as a matter of course. Was he lying to her right now? Could he in fact read and was merely toying with her for reasons of his own?

"Lazarus tells me he's helping you search for your brother. Have you succeeded in locating him yet?"

"I did not come here to answer your idle questions," she said, losing patience. "Do you or do you not know the sounds these letters make?"

"Answer my question, and I'll answer yours."

"No, I have had no word from Sir Phillip and have no idea where he might be." Deciding to turn the tables, she raised her finger when he started to speak. "What do you know of Mr. Hammond?" Will had refused to discuss the man with her, and this might be her only chance to learn about him and why he and Will seemed to be enemies.

Mr. Finch sat back, his gaze wary. "Nothing."

From his shuttered expression, she was certain he knew something. "Nothing?" She let her disbelief drip from the word.

"Yes, absolutely nothing. It's a religious thing, you see."

"Religious?"

"Yes, I'm a devout coward."

"What does that have to do with Mr. Hammond?"

"We cowards know better than to have anything to do with or know anything about Hammond. It's much safer that way." He pointed to the letter C. "So, what sound does this make?"

Knowing he wasn't going to tell her anything more, she allowed the subject to drop and answered his question. They spent the next thirty minutes going over each letter and the sound it made and the sounds certain letters made when put together.

****

Olivia exited the stationer's shop. Will stood just outside the door. She came to an abrupt halt, causing Bridget to bump into her. She hadn't seen or heard from him in the three days since they'd spent the night of Amanda's birthday ball making love. When she had awoken the next morning, he was gone but had left a note saying he had another lead on Mary's whereabouts and would be in touch soon.

"Will." She smiled at him, feeling her cheeks grow warm and a well of happiness bubble to life.

"We need to talk. Where is your carriage?"

Olivia pointed to where Daniel stood two shops away.

Will took her package from her and handed it to Bridget. "You may return to your mistress' home in the coach. I will see Miss St. Germaine home."

"I can't be seen entering your coach without a maid or chaperone of some sort," Olivia protested.

He looked around. "Can you be seen in a public establishment?"

"I guess." She didn't know what was going on. Had Will found Mary? Had he finally found out where Phillip had gone? Why didn't he just say so? He must know he could speak freely in front of Bridget.

"Then it's settled. Bridget will return home with your footman, and I shall see you home after we've spoken." He ushered her toward a small shop wedged between a millinery and a jeweler's.

Olivia looked back at Bridget and shrugged. "Go," she mouthed. She didn't want the young maid standing outside waiting when she wasn't certain how long she was going to be.

As soon as she stepped inside, the delicious aromas of bread, cakes, and muffins caused her stomach to rumble. She pressed a hand to her midsection, hoping it wasn't loud enough for anyone to hear. It had been hours since she'd eaten breakfast that morning. He guided her to a small section where tables for two were set near the window.

He waited for her to take a seat, then dropped into the remaining chair, his eyes closing for a moment in what looked like relief. Olivia thought it strange, but maybe she misinterpreted his expression. Perhaps he was enjoying the heavenly smells as well.

She tried to take a shallow breath through her mouth hoping if she didn't smell the cakes and such, her stomach would cease its rumbling. Instead it seemed as if she could taste the sweet confections, and her hunger increased. Much too late for it to do any good, she realized she should have had something to eat before leaving to meet Mr. Finch for his first reading lesson.

She glanced at Will. He was speaking, but her attention strayed to the display of treats. She forced her gaze back to him and nodded, hoping she hadn't just agreed to something she would regret.

In an effort to concentrate on the conversation, she focused on the people seated behind him. A handsomely dressed gentleman sat facing her, his movements prissy as though he were afraid the simple act of eating might stain his bright yellow waistcoat.

Her gaze dropped to his hand. His fork stopped partway to his mouth as he responded to his companion's question. A golden yellow bite of muffin rich with plump raisins, or were they currants, clung lovingly to the tines of the fork. Olivia licked her lips, feeling saliva pool in her mouth.

Her hunger taking over, she checked the pocket of her cloak. Nothing but a bit of lint. As Will droned on, she rooted through her small reticule, knowing she'd spent all of the funds she'd brought with her at the stationer's. Hopefully a coin had gotten lost in the bottom. She didn't believe so but searched frantically.

"Are you listening to me?"

Olivia looked up from the depths of her reticule, trying to recall one word he'd said. Something about Sandhurst, but that was when they first sat down. Surely, he'd gone on to another topic since then.

"Well?" Will asked, a hint of impatience in his voice.

She bit her lip. Her stomach growled, reminding her of its empty state. She was consumed with hunger, and he was chastising her for not paying attention. No doubt, he carried a purse full of coins to buy any delicacy that caught his fancy.

Her gaze flitted back and forth between him and the tempting display of treats. She leaned forward and spoke in a low voice, "Would you purchase something for me to eat? I'm famished and haven't any money left."

He stiffened, his mouth compressing into a hard, tight line of anger.

"I've changed my mind," Olivia said, taking note of his expression. She gathered her cloak and reticule and stood. "I'd like to leave." She took a step back from the table.

His hand shot out, catching her by the wrist. "Sit

down." His voice was low and harsh, an unmistakable order.

Glaring at him, she tried to wrench her arm free.

"Sit. Down." The demand louder this time.

"Have you forgotten? I am not one of your minions to be ordered about as it pleases you." She pulled free.

"You will do as I say."

She raised her eyebrows in disbelief. She couldn't believe his arrogance, but then he was used to people bowing and scraping to do his bidding. He could have been a nobleman acting the way he was; after all, they always thought they had the right to treat others however they wished.

"I think not." She turned and headed for the door.

He was at her side in an instant, his hand closing around her arm. "Come sit down. I will buy you something to eat."

"I don't want anything. I'm not hungry anymore." As soon as she said the words, she realized it was true. Her hunger had evaporated under his highhanded treatment.

"Yes, you are."

"No. I'm not."

"You are making us the center of attention," he growled.

Olivia pushed his hand from her arm. "No, you are doing that all on your own. I want to leave."

He closed his eyes and took a deep breath, then met her gaze. She saw the anger banked there but didn't care. "Come and sit down, and we'll both have tea and cakes." He stared at her. "Please."

She gave a small nod and led the way back to the table. She didn't believe he wanted tea. It was his way of exerting control. She was certain what had happened to him when he was a child made him determined to control every situation.

He waited for her to sit, then took his own seat, signaling to the serving girl moving among the tables. Without asking what Olivia would like, he ordered a pot of tea and two scones with lemon icing.

Touched that he remembered how much she liked lemon scones, she felt herself softening toward him.

Their food arrived in a matter of minutes. Olivia picked up her fork and ran the tines though the icing, eager to taste the tart sweetness.

"What were you doing at the Brass Key earlier today?"

She ate a few bites before answering. "I met someone there. I was properly accompanied by Bridget." She didn't mention Daniel had been present as well.

Will pushed his plate aside. He hadn't been hungry before he ordered the treat, and he was even less so now. Why was she being so secretive? "Who did you meet?"

Olivia ignored his question and concentrated on eating the last bite of her scone.

A tiny drop of icing clinging to her bottom lip distracted him. He wanted to catch it with his tongue. Would she taste of lemons? The sudden image of her lying beneath him, the shiny mass of her hair spread over his pillow as she lifted her hips to meet his thrusts popped into his mind. He shifted in his seat.

"It's not important," Olivia finally answered drawing him back to the present. She wiped her mouth with her napkin, removing the icing that had tempted him so.

Her answer irked him. "Why can you not tell me? Why must you go out of your way to vex me?"

"Why can't you trust me the way you do your men? Do you make them account for their whereabouts at every moment of the day?"

"My men are loyal to me. I don't have to question them." His voice had risen with each word. He hated that she had the ability to make him lose his temper as no other. He took a gulp of tea in an effort to regain control.

"Have I ever done anything to make you think I am not loyal?"

"You lie to me." The words came out calm, cold, and just the way he wanted them to.

Olivia laid her hand against her chest. "I have never lied to you."

"You lied by not telling me you met with Finch at the Brass Key," he accused.

"If you already knew who I met, then why did you ask?" she snapped.

"To see if you had something to hide, which you must or you would have told me you met with him." He leaned forward, his voice a low hiss, "I will not share your favors with anyone. And especially not with Finch."

Olivia grabbed the teacup in front of her and threw it at him. Warm liquid dripped off his nose and chin, soaking into his shirtfront. The cup landed in his lap. He blinked in shock.

Pushing back her chair, Olivia shot to her feet, her gaze full of blue fire. "I thought you knew me, but you don't know me at all. Kindness costs nothing, *Lazarus,* yet there are times when you hoard it like gold."

She stormed from the shop. Will suddenly became aware of fifteen pairs of eyes all staring at him with various expressions of mirth.

Chapter Seventeen

Will ripped the cloth sack off his captive's head. "Hello, Your Grace."

The Duke of Sandhurst stared back at him, his left eye a dark purple and nearly swollen closed. Blood caked the corner of his mouth. His hands tied behind his back caused the bloodied tear in the shoulder of his coat to gape open.

"Fingers tells me you are ready to take me to my sister. Is this true?" Will leaned back against the leather seat of the coach. "Think long and hard before you answer."

Sandhurst gave a small, slow nod.

"Good. Where shall I tell him to take us?" Will felt a small measure of relief, but he wouldn't be truly at ease until he had seen Mary for himself.

"Surrey."

"I have been to Surrey. She's not there." He pressed his hand against the duke's shoulder.

The other man cried out and tried to slide away.

Will held him in place. "I'll not be trifled with any longer. You will take me to my sister, or you will simply disappear from London, never to be seen or heard of again." He pulled the duke forward until they were only inches apart. "Do you understand my meaning?"

"She's in Surrey, I tell you."

"Where?"

"Ashtead."

He thrust the man back against the seat and rapped on the roof of the coach. "To Ashtead in Surrey," he ordered, and they began to move.

Sandhurst shifted on the bench. "Do you think I fear you? Well, I do not."

Will raised an eyebrow. "You should." He pulled the ruby-encrusted dagger from inside his coat. "I suggest you hold your tongue the remainder of our journey else you're wont to lose it." He had no desire to listen to his grace's sniveling displays of false bravado.

Sandhurst heaved a sigh but said nothing more.

Will replaced the dagger and looked out the window at the passing scenery. Who would have guessed the mighty Duke of Sandhurst would have chosen St. Giles of all places to try and hide. The man blended in no better with the residents of the stews than Will himself did among the *Ton*. Having him taken and held until Will could get there had been as easy as promising a coin or two for the duke's capture.

As he gazed out the window, his thoughts turned to Olivia. He'd sent a bouquet of flowers with a note of apology within hours of their argument. He seemed to spend more time apologizing to her than anything else. Him, a man who swore he'd never regret or apologize to anyone ever. He wished he could have gone to tell her in person how sorry he was for insulting her, but word had come that the duke had been found, and he couldn't risk the man slipping away once more.

He'd never seen her so angry. But he had been so furious when Harry had reported seeing her with Finch at the Brass Key, not once but twice. Will had gone to

Finch who denied even knowing Olivia much less meeting with her on two separate occasions.

It pained him to lose Finch's friendship. They had survived living without a home as youths, had decided to pool their resources to open the gambling hell in an attempt to leave their criminal pasts behind. Had Finch been bamming him all along? Had his desire to be a legitimate businessman been all an act, part of some long range plan to take control of the docks? Had he and Hammond been in league with each other all along? Will rubbed his chin. No, he couldn't, wouldn't believe all he and Finch had been through together meant nothing. There had to be some other explanation. And as soon as he had Mary under his care, he would find out exactly what that explanation was.

The coach slowed and stopped. Will looked at his timepiece. The trip had taken less time than he thought.

"We be just outside of Ashtead. Where do I go from here?" Fingers called.

Will looked at Sandhurst waiting for him to speak.

The duke looked out the window as though to get his bearings. He directed them through town, ordering them to stop at a small church just on the other side of the village.

Will stepped out of the coach. The church, with its edifice of weathered gray stone, looked remote and forbidding. A small graveyard stood off to the side, the graves overgrown with grass and weeds seemed long forgotten. "She's here?"

Fingers climbed down from the driver's box and hauled Sandhurst out of the coach dropping him on his knees in the dirt. He yanked the man to his feet. "It don'na look like no clergyman's been here for a while.

How can Mary be here?"

"She's here," Sandhurst said, his voice low and sure.

"Then take us to her. No more dallying about." Will gave him a push toward the church.

The duke stumbled then gained his footing and veered off to the right toward the gate in the center of the fence surrounding the cemetery.

Will froze. She couldn't be in there. That would mean…No, Mary wasn't dead. He hadn't failed her that badly. "No, she's not there." He hadn't realized he spoke the words aloud until Sandhurst turned back, his expression filled with remorse.

"You killed her." Will lunged at the duke, his fists pummeling the other man, not giving him a chance to speak. He knocked Sandhurst to the ground, his hands closing around his neck, squeezing the life out of the bastard as he had done to Mary.

Fingers dragged him off Sandhurst. "Ye don'na know she's in there," he said as he ducked a blow.

"She is." Will knew it with such certainty, he could have attended the burial. He kicked the duke in the ribs as he tried to climb into a sitting position. "Tell him."

"Mary and I came here together," Sandhurst gasped. "I wanted to marry her, but she became ill."

"You wanted to marry her," Will scoffed. "You expect me to believe that. You are a duke. My sister was your niece's governess."

"I didn't care," Sandhurst shouted, showing anger for the first time. "I loved Mary. When she became ill, we decided to wait until she was well. But she never got better, she kept getting worse." He looked out over the graveyard as though trying to distance himself from what he was about to say. "She began coughing up blood. After that..." He paused then spoke in a low subdued tone. "...she was gone in a matter of days."

"You think I believe that drivel," Will snarled. "Stand up," he ordered.

Sandhurst struggled to his feet and stood facing him.

"I will tell you what happened, and then I'm going to kill you and leave you to rot in an unmarked pauper's grave just like you did my sister." Will pointed the pistol he held at the duke's heart.

"I did not kill Mary. And I didn't leave her in an unmarked grave. I've never forgotten about her," Sandhurst shouted. "I loved her." He shook his head and breathed in through his nose. "I truly loved Mary," he said in a calm voice. "Why do you think I haven't remarried when I have no heir? It's certainly not for lack of opportunity. Do you know how many marriage-minded mothers throw their daughters in my path at every turn?"

"It is rumoured you killed your wife. What would keep you from killing a lowly governess with no known family?" Will asked, refusing to acknowledge Sandhurst might be telling the truth.

"And you are rumoured to have blinded a man and much more. Are all of those tales about you true? I'd say not, or you'd have been in Newgate long ago. My wife and two-year-old daughter were killed, but not by my hand. We were in a carriage accident. I nearly died myself. Ask your friend the poet, Mr. Hobson. He came upon us soon after the accident." The duke looked Will in the eye, his gaze never wavering, and Will knew he spoke the truth.

He lowered the gun. He wanted to howl at the moon, tear Sandhurst limb from limb, but it would do nothing to bring Mary back. Guilt rolled over him. He had failed his sister when she needed him most. "Take him back to the nearest inn and leave him," he ordered before stalking away.

"I'll not tell anyone that you abducted me—"

Will turned and glared at Sandhurst, and the other man immediately shut up. In a matter of minutes, he had been freed from his bindings and helped none too gently into the coach. Fingers climbed into the driver's box and headed off.

Alone until Fingers returned, Will walked to the cemetery gate. His hand hesitated on the latch, afraid to see Mary's grave, but needing to nonetheless. He pushed it open, and the hinges screeched from disuse. The first thing he would do once he arrived back in London was arrange a proper burial even if he needed to employ a resurrection man to do it.

He walked along the overgrown path, noting the few cracked and worn markers. Up ahead, set off in the corner, the grass had been clipped, weeds pulled, and fresh flowers lay against a large stone marker. Will hurried forward. Mary's grave. He crouched beside the marker, his fingers tracing the beveled edge.

It was inscribed with three simple words that told Will Sandhurst had spoken the truth. "My Beloved Mary."

He traced the words with a finger. "I'm so sorry," he whispered. "I should have kept you with me. I could have taken care of you, but I thought keeping my distance until I could make a legitimate life for us was best. I was wrong." He wasn't sure how long he stayed like that, only moving to stand when he heard the gravel crunching as someone came up the path.

"I'm sorry for yer loss, Lazarus," Fingers said, his voice gruff. He stood a few feet away as though trying to give Will a measure of privacy.

"Thank you."

Fingers nodded. "I'll be waitin' at the coach." He turned and walked away.

"I'll be back soon," Will whispered and followed his factotum out of the graveyard. He swiped at the tear traveling down his cheek and entered the coach.

****

Will stood in the foyer of Olivia's home. Not sure why he was there, what had pushed him to seek her out after learning of Mary's death. But he felt the overwhelming need to see her, to be near her if nothing else. He needed the comfort of her presence.

"If you will follow me," Jennings said as he approached.

Will followed the butler into the back garden. Olivia was bent over a rose bush, pruning shears in hand.

"Did you find her?" She set the scissors aside and hurried over to him, removing her gardening gloves as she did so.

"In a manner of speaking." Now that he was here. He didn't know what to say.

"What does that mean?"

"I found her grave." He stumbled over the words. "She's dead."

Olivia stared at him for a moment, then asked in a quiet voice, "Is Sandhurst...?"

Will ran a hand down his face. It bothered him

more than it should that she knew he was capable of taking a man's life. "No, he lives. He said he wanted to take Mary to wife, that she became sick and never recovered." He hesitated for a moment. "Surprisingly enough, I believe him."

"I'm so very sorry." Olivia laid a hand on his arm. "I know how you must feel."

"You have no idea how I feel." Will paced away from her.

"Are you so certain of that? I have a wealth of regret for not being able to save those who I promised would survive their injuries on the battlefield. While I may not have been related to them, I felt their deaths keenly. Each and every one of them. I still do."

"Caring for a man whom you have no feeling for, not even that of friendship is not the same as failing to protect your sister," Will snapped. He did not want her kindness, her understanding. It only made him feel worse. "I'm sorry. I am not fit company today." He turned on his heel and headed around the side of the house, eager to be gone before he took his anger over his failure to protect his sister out on Olivia and said something he truly regretted.

"Will. Wait," Olivia called after him. "Please stay. We don't have to talk. We can just enjoy the silence of the garden."

He ignored her and headed for the coach, signaling for Patrick to leave. He needed to get away from her before he humiliated himself by allowing her to see the heart-breaking grief that threatened to overwhelm him at any moment. Now more than ever, he had to make things right for Olivia. He couldn't bear to fail anyone else, especially her.

Chapter Eighteen

Olivia sat on the rose satin divan and looked around. From the rich red of the carpet, to the burgundy drapery, to the beautiful furnishings, it was the most opulent room she had ever been in, even outshining Amanda and Riverton's drawing room which Olivia had always thought of as lavish. Too bad, such a room was in a whorehouse.

She sent a smile to the stunning woman who reclined on a divan near the window and tried not to let her nervousness show. The woman, who'd introduced herself as Belle, smiled back.

"Hammond should be here soon," Belle said. "I can't imagine what is keeping him." She gave a catlike smile. "Or should I say who is keeping him."

If she had hoped to offend Olivia by the innuendo, she failed. Instead Olivia decided it was time to stop being polite. "I do not know why I was brought here, nor do I know what happened to my companion." She stood. "I wish to leave."

"I wouldn't worry too much about old Harry. He's being kept occupied by one of my girls, and I'm certain he won't be complaining." Again the catlike smile curled Belle's lips.

"Be that as it may, I will be leaving." Olivia headed toward the door, surprised the other woman made no move to stop her. She opened the heavy oak door and came face-to-face with an ox of a man.

With broad shoulders and a barrel chest, he stood a good head taller than she. His hair was brushed back from a high forehead in a manner that seemed to highlight the scar running across his eye to end at the corner of his lips, pulling his mouth up into a permanent macabre grin.

Refusing to show her sudden fear, she crossed her arms over her chest as she'd seen Will do hundreds of times and tapped her foot. "Please move. I'm leaving."

The man guffawed as though she'd said the funniest thing he'd ever heard. He poked her in the chest with enough force to send her stumbling back a few steps. "Ye have spirit for one so small. Guess I'll be givin' ye a sportin' chance then."

"What does that mean?" She refused to be cowed by the man's show of strength.

"Have a seat, yer ladyship. Yer gonna tell me what I wanta know about Lazarus."

"I don't know anything about him," Olivia said and realized there was some truth to the lie. She didn't know a great deal about him. He had a great number of secrets, and he'd shared precious few with her.

"I'd say ye know a lot about him since you like to have him in yer bed." He gestured for her to sit.

Belle laughed. "I can just imagine what that must be like with the two of them, can't you, Hammond?" She turned to Olivia. "Do you lie there and count the linens in your head while he's rutting above you? Knowing Lazarus, I'm certain you don't get past the number ten, but then you probably find that a relief."

Olivia felt her face flame with mortification, but she stood her ground, her arms still crossed over her chest.

Hammond grabbed her by the arm, towed her across the room, and pushed her onto the divan. "Things'll be easier if'n ye lose yer high and mighty attitude." He sat across from her.

"I don't know anything about Lazarus," she repeated.

"You'll tell me why he's giving up territory he's been controlling fer years. What's he up to? There's people sayin' he's trying to climb out of the gutter he was born in. Are ye apart of that?"

"Why does it matter if any of that is true or not?" she countered.

Hammond sat back and rubbed a finger over his scarred lip. "You'd be better off if'n ye didn't ask why and answer me questions."

"I don't know the answers to your questions."

"Ye know in some places, death be just a normal event like night following the day." Sitting forward, Hammond rested his forearms on his knees. "Would ye be likin' to see some of those places?" He grabbed her arm and nearly pulled her off the divan. "'Cause yer goin' to if you don't answer my questions."

"I'll tell you what I know, but it isn't much." Olivia tried to keep her voice steady. She was frightened out of her wits, but she didn't want them to know it.

"Thought ye might." He sat back against the chair.

"Lazarus is helping me look for my brother. He's been missing for some time, and I am worried. In return, I'm using my friendships among the members of society to gain him entrée to various social events. He is searching for a nobleman. I don't know who, and I don't know why," she lied, trying to give just enough information to keep herself unharmed yet not betray Will any more than she had to.

Hammond stroked his scar as he stared at her, and Olivia had the distinct impression he was trying to decide if she had spoken the truth or not.

"How did ye meet?"

"He came to my home some weeks ago looking for my brother."

"Who be yer brother?"

"Sir Phillip St. Germaine." Olivia frowned. If he didn't know her brother's name then how did he know about her?"

"St. Germaine ain't missing." Hammond laughed and shook his head as though she was an imbecile for believing such a thing. "Just look in any opium den in London, and you'll find him in one of 'em." He tapped his lips. "Course he might be hidin' now that Finch be looking fer him."

"Mr. Finch?" Olivia felt as though she'd walked into the middle of a farce where she was the main character and didn't know what was happening. "Why would Mr. Finch be looking for Phillip?" It dawned on her what Hammond had said earlier. "And what would he be doing in an opium den?"

Hammond laughed and turned to Belle who had moved closer. "She really is a naïve one, ain't she?"

His laugh came to an abrupt halt when the door to the parlour opened. Will stood on the threshold, his gaze bouncing between the three of them before landing on Hammond. Olivia felt her fear drain away.

She should have known Will would come for her. He'd always been there when she needed him, even when she didn't know she needed him. She could so very easily fall in love with him. *You are in love with him*, a voice inside her said, and she knew it was true.

Olivia stood.

Hammond looked up at her and back at Will. "Have ye come to rescue the fair maiden from the dragon?" he mocked.

"Actually, I didn't know she was here," Will said, barely sparing her a glance.

"Well, mayhap ye should sit and join us. We was just discussing her brother since ye be helping her find him and all." Hammond gave her a sly look. "Have ye had any luck?"

Will sauntered across the room to stand by the fireplace. "I haven't bothered looking. Finch will find him soon enough unless he kills himself first."

"Wi—Lazarus?" Olivia stared at him in confusion.

"Come now, Miss St. Germaine, you don't expect us to believe you didn't know your sainted brother was an opium addict?" he sneered.

"No, I don't believe it. Phillip would never use opium. He was against anything with addictive properties." Olivia didn't understand what was happening. "He hated using even laudanum on the battlefield unless absolutely necessary."

"Because he wanted to ensure he had a supply for himself. How many men do you think suffered needlessly because of your brother? How many men died in agony while your brother worked on them without the benefit of any type of pain relief? What kind of man would do that to another?"

Will's questions lashed at her like a whip. His voice was calmer than she'd ever heard it, but his words bit deep. She covered her ears with her hands. "Stop saying such terrible things. I don't know why you're doing this, but I won't listen to your lies."

He pulled her hands away from her head. "It's time you faced the truth."

Belle sat on the edge of Hammond's chair, a fascinated expression on her face. His expression gave nothing away, but his gaze was calculating.

Angry at being humiliated in front of them, Olivia spun away from Will. "Do you mean to tell me you knew where Phillip was all this time?"

"Well, in one opium den or another." He made a careless gesture with his hand.

"You used me." Olivia stared at the man she thought she loved.

"You gave me the perfect opportunity when you came looking for me. How could I not? Your connections with the Rivertons gained me far more access to the *Ton* than Hargrove ever could."

"But you helped me through the storms, and after Patrick—"

"I had to keep you thinking how wonderful I was. How else to get into your bed?" He lounged on the divan as though he was discussing nothing more important than the weather. "I wanted you. That wasn't a lie. And I had you." He sent a grin in Hammond's direction. "More than once."

Olivia hitched in a breath. He couldn't have hurt her more if he had struck her with his fist.

He looked at her over his steepled fingers. "You were…convenient." His voice was low and cold, freezing her to her very soul. "And not very good." He winked at Belle. "Which is why I'm here. I've come to visit one of your lovelies."

"Since I'm in such a good mood, I'll let you take your pick." Belle stood and held out her hand to him.

Will rose and let her lead him across the room. Olivia could only stand by and watch. She felt as though she were caught in an unending nightmare. After her years on the battlefield, she had always thought she was adept at reading men and what they were really after. How could she have been played for such a fool?

He stopped at the door and turned back, his eyes coal dark and expressionless. "In the future, I suggest you remember this—If you play in the dirt, you are going to get your skirts dirty. I'm sure Huntley is still willing to crawl into your bed even if you are soiled."

She stared at him, fighting to keep any emotion from showing on her face. He turned and left the room, Belle on his arm. Bile rose up the back of her throat. Olivia fought the waves of nausea and rubbed her arms. She'd never felt so used, so dirty in her life.

"I guess ye were tellin' the truth," Hammond said as he rose. "Ye really didn't know anythin' about Lazarus." He strode from the room, leaving her alone.

Chapter Nineteen

Olivia sat at the table her chin resting in her hand and stared out the window. Five days after that horrible afternoon when she'd seen the true side of Lazarus and she still felt so ashamed. She didn't think of him as Will any longer. She doubted the man she knew as Will ever existed.

"And then Prinny walked down Bond Street in his unmentionables."

She turned to her companion. "What did you just say?"

Mr. Finch grinned at her. "I knew you weren't paying attention when you didn't correct me at every other word when I was trying to read this thing." He pushed the children's book aside.

"I'm sorry. I fear I'm not very good company today." She gave him a half-hearted smile. "But you are making very good progress after only three lessons."

"Why don't I teach you something?"

Olivia recoiled. "I've learned enough lessons lately, thank you."

"I'm sorry for what Lazarus did to you." Mr. Finch reached out to touch her but curled his fingers into his hand instead. "He's a fool."

"Thank you for telling me the truth when I asked. I *will* pay you back the money Phillip stole from you."

He put a finger under her chin and lifted her face to

look at him. "And I told you, I'll not take your blunt. You are already paying me back in a much more meaningful way. You are giving me freedom by teaching me to read."

Olivia moved away from his touch and pulled the book back between them. She turned the page only to have a pair of dice drop onto the book.

"How about we take a break, and I teach you how to play Hazard? Unless you already know how?"

"No, I don't, and I'm really in no mood to play games." She set the dice aside.

"Then that is the perfect time to play. Nothing puts a body in a good mood like winning money." He picked up the dice and set them in front of her. "You can be the caster. You must call a main which is any number between five and nine and place your bet on the table, which I have to cover. I can then make a bet of my own if I wish. If you throw the number you called, you win the money on the table."

She moved the cubes back in front of him. "I am not gambling with you."

He looked around the room, then hopped up from his chair and began collecting various curios from around the room. He brought everything back to the table and pushed half of the items toward Olivia. "In place of blunt," he said by way of explanation.

"You certainly are determined," she said, feeling the corners of her mouth quirk upward.

"No more than you when I am trying to distract you from that blasted book."

"Which is what you are trying to do now."

He smiled at her. "Exactly. Now call a number between five and nine."

Olivia tried to scowl at him but couldn't quite manage it. "Eight."

"Now place your bet."

She pushed the small ivory music box forward.

"I shall match your bet with my vase." He pushed a tall thin crystal vase next to the music box. "Now roll the dice."

Olivia shook the cubes in her hand and dropped them onto the table.

"Eight. You won." He pushed the items toward her.

They played on with him explaining various rules as the game continued. Olivia still wasn't quite sure what the difference between a "chance" and a "main" were, but she found herself so caught up in trying to understand the rules, she was able to forget about her heartache for a short time.

She clapped her hands as she won the very last trinket from Mr. Finch's side of the table.

"You really are quite lovely. Did you know your eyes sparkle like sapphires when you laugh?" He gazed at her, his expression serious. "I see why Lazarus is so taken with you. You make a man forget what he really is. Make him believe he can be more than he is."

Feeling uncomfortable at his sudden compliments, Olivia pushed at his shoulder in a playful manner. "Ha. You just want a chance to win back my vase."

"Of course," he said, taking her lead. "I shall be right back." He strode from the room.

She couldn't figure out what he was up to when he returned with a handful of spoons.

He retook his seat and set the silver on the table. "It'll take the rest of the afternoon for you to win all of these."

Olivia laughed. "I think the next time we play, you have to bring your own belongings to wager with."

A commotion sounded out in the hall, and Mr. Finch stood. Olivia heard Jennings yelp, followed by a crash just as a man stepped into the doorway.

Will stood there taking in the two of them looking so comfortable with each other. Finch swore there was nothing between the two of them, but it was obvious he lied. Jealousy pushed him forward. "I told you to stay away from her."

"Go to hell," Finch bit out, stepping in front of Olivia as though he needed to protect her from him. Him of all people.

"She's mine. She will always be mine." Will lashed out, punching his former friend in the jaw.

Finch staggered back but didn't raise a hand to defend himself. "I'll not fight you."

"Good." Will landed another punch to the side of his head, and Finch fell to his knees.

"Stop it." Olivia crouched beside him, her hands held above them in protective gesture. "Stop it."

Will froze, his chest heaving as his anger fled in the face of her fear.

"Why are you forcing your way into my home?" she demanded as she helped Finch to his feet. "You've said everything I would ever want to hear."

Her servants must have gathered behind him because her gaze went somewhere over her shoulder, and she gave a small shake of her head. He heard the sound of retreating footsteps.

"I've come to explain," he said, knowing in trying to protect her from the likes of Hammond he had to give her up.

"And what would you explain?" she snapped. "How much I meant to you?"

"Obviously not very much if you are already keeping company with another man," he snarled. Already jealous at finding her laughing with Finch, his own temper flared back to life.

"I guess we were both mistaken then."

"Olivia." Finch laid a hand on her arm.

The sight of him touching her made Will see red. "Remove your hand from her, or you'll lose it," he growled.

"Why?" she demanded. She moved closer. "I thought you didn't care about me. For me. Yet, you act the jealous suitor. Did you lie before?" she asked, an unspoken plea in her voice.

He remained silent. He wanted to tell her the truth, but it would only put her in danger if Hammond thought he could use her against him. No, she was better off hating him.

The hope in her gaze dulled and disappeared. Tears welled in her eyes and spilled over. "I will have you know I am not crying because of you." She dashed a hand across her cheek, pushed by him, and ran from the room.

Of that he was certain; he doubted anyone had shed a tear over him in his entire life. But he wished it were different. He had never wanted anyone to cry over him until he met Olivia. He wanted her to love him, not the man he was trying to be, but the man he was right now. He wanted to spend his nights with her lying soft and warm beside him. He wanted her to tell him about her day and he doing the same. He wanted them to share their secrets together. He wanted so much more, but he'd learned that that kind of life would never be his. Mary's death only proved he failed those he wanted to protect the most.

And if he had to hurt Olivia's feelings to keep her safe, he would, over and over again. It was the only thing he could do to keep Hammond from using her against him.

"You are the biggest horse's ass I have ever met." Finch leaned against the table. "And if you hurt Olivia again, you'll answer to me."

"You do know how I feel about idle threats."

"It's not a threat. You broke her heart, humiliated her, and now you think you have the right to tell her who she can associate with?"

"Not with you. I told you before to stay away from her." Will grabbed Finch by the collar and slammed his upper body against the table. "Stay away from her. Do you understand me?"

He told himself it was to protect Olivia. Jealousy had nothing to do with it. He knew what kind of man Finch was. He would never settle down with one woman, and Will wasn't going to stand by and watch him break Olivia's heart. Hadn't he just done that?

"I can't," Finch said, his voice muffled by the table linen.

"Why not?"

"She's teaching me to read." He angled his head to look Will in the eye.

"What?"

"She's teaching me how to read."

Stunned, Will released him and stepped away.

Finch stood, straightened his waistcoat, and shot his cuffs. "I asked her not to tell you."

"Why didn't you tell me? We've been friends since we were lads?" Will couldn't believe he'd never known. Finch had hidden his secret well. He looked at the man with a new-found respect.

"I didn't want you to think I couldn't handle my end of our business dealings."

He nodded and turned to go. "Promise me you will take care of her."

"You really do love her, don't you, Lazarus?"

"She's like magic," Will whispered, unable to turn around and face his friend. "She makes me believe anything is possible. That I can leave my past behind, become a better man. A man she deserves."

"How can a man as smart as you are, surviving the childhood you did, be so damn stupid?" Finch asked, disgust dripping from every word. "She cares for you, don't you know that?"

Will spun around. "It doesn't matter. How I feel for her, or she for me doesn't matter. If Hammond finds out, he'll use her against me." He closed his eyes against the tide of anguish rolling over him. "He'll hurt her to get to me. I can't risk that. I failed Mary. I won't have Olivia suffer because of the life I've led. I rather have her hate me."

"Then I suggest you find a way to take care of Hammond so he's no longer a threat."

****

"You have a visitor." Jennings held out the silver salver, a gold embossed card in its center.

Olivia knew without picking the calling card up who it belonged to. She set aside the letter she'd spent the last three hours trying to compose with a sigh. "Please show her in."

"Very well." Jennings withdrew only to return seconds later. "Lady Riverton," he announced.

"Thank you, Jennings." Olivia stood, not at all certain why Amanda had come. After their conversation at her birthday ball, she was the last person Olivia expected to come calling.

Amanda swept into the room looking quite fashionable in a pale blue gown and glanced around as though she expected to find someone else present.

"Shall I ask Bridget to bring us tea?" Olivia asked, gesturing for Amanda to take a seat.

"No. I've had more tea and biscuits than I can stand today." She patted her flat stomach. "I don't want people saying Riverton's wife has gotten fat." She sat on the edge of her chair and arranged her skirts so they fell over her shoes. She looked at Olivia through her lashes. "I've spent the morning making excuses for your early departure from my birthday ball. Some people said they saw you standing on the edge of the balcony railing."

Realizing Amanda hadn't come out of concern but to gather gossip to spread, Olivia gave her a puzzled look and took a seat opposite her. "How strange. You know I dislike heights, so it's rather absurd to believe I would be standing on a balcony ledge."

"Yes, that's what I told them." Lady Riverton sounded disappointed.

"I'm sorry you felt you needed to explain my departure the other evening. I was taken with a headache and didn't want to ruin your celebration." Olivia leaned forward as though to impart something important.

Amanda leaned toward her, anticipation lighting

her eyes.

"To be honest, I didn't think anyone would notice. Most of your guests suffer my company only because of you."

Lady Riverton let out a deflated sigh and sat back. "Are you still keeping company with Mr. Prescott?" she asked under the guise of adjusting her skirts.

Every single night when I shut my eyes Olivia wanted to answer but knew better. Deciding she wasn't going to be manipulated by Amanda any longer, she gave the other woman a hard stare. "No one has the right to decide who makes us happy. Who we can be happy with. If you've come to give me another ultimatum, you've wasted your time."

"So you are still spending time with him."

"No, I'm not. And not because you told me I must choose between your friendship and him."

"Do you love him?"

Agitated by the question, Olivia rose and moved toward the bell pull. "I think I shall have Bridget bring tea after all."

Amanda stood in front of her, halting her progress around the room. "Olivia, do you love him?"

"Yes, yes. Is that what you want to hear? It doesn't matter, so why make me say it? Are you that eager for gossip to share with your friends?"

A wounded look on her face, Amanda took a step back. "I would never do that. I know you don't believe it, but I do value our friendship." She resumed her seat. "Do you know there are times I am quite jealous of you," she said in a soft voice.

"Jealous of me?" Olivia could hardly believe it. "Why? You are a darling of London society. People clamour for invitations to your entertainments. You're married to an earl. A very wealthy earl, I might add. You want for nothing."

"I want for a great deal," Amanda whispered, running a finger across the arm of the chair. "I want to be married to a man who loves me, not tolerates me because I trapped him into marriage, not someone who pretends to care when we are being watched and ignores me when we are alone." She took a shaky breath. "I want to be able to share things with him...the good things...the bad things...I want him to tell me about his day, to be able to tell him about mine." She lifted her head and looked at Olivia. "I want what you seem to have with Mr. Prescott."

Olivia laid a hand over Amanda's. "I had no idea you were so unhappy. But I fear you are seeing something between Mr. Prescott and myself that doesn't exist."

"Are you certain?" Amanda's voice took on a pleading quality. "He seems to enjoy your company, to enjoy just being in the same room with you."

"It was a sham. He needed access to the *Ton,* and by pretending an interest in me, he got what he needed."

"I'm sorry he used you that way. But it was better you found out before it was too late."

It was already far too late, but Olivia didn't bother correcting her.

"Will you forgive me for being so cruel to you at times?" Amanda asked, tears in her eyes. "I don't think I can bear to lose the one true friend I have."

"I forgive you." Olivia hugged the younger woman. "Just remember I will still not allow you to manipulate me."

Amanda leaned back and grinned. "I wouldn't dream of it."

Knowing her friend couldn't help but try to do so in the future, Olivia burst out laughing.

Chapter Twenty

Olivia frowned and stepped out into the hall for the second time in ten minutes. Mr. Finch was late. He hadn't been late for any of their lessons after that first time. Of course, she had agreed to hold them in the late afternoon which probably made all the difference.

Was it possible he wasn't coming? She hadn't seen or heard from him since Lazarus had interrupted their last lesson nearly a week ago. She should have stayed in the room after Lazarus had attacked him, but she couldn't do it. She couldn't stand there and pretend indifference after she had humiliated herself by all but begging him to say he cared for her. She had laid her soul bare, and he hadn't cared, hadn't even had the decency to ask for forgiveness. He'd been so calculating in his pursuit of her and just as callous when he'd told her she had been "convenient." He couldn't have hurt her more than if he'd stabbed her in the heart.

She hugged her arms to herself against the sudden ache in her chest and turned back to the library. She'd send a note to Mr. Finch's establishment and asked if he intended to keep their appointment.

The door knocker sounded two hard knocks, followed by a strange noise. She moved further into the hall as Jennings headed toward the door. If that was Mr. Finch on her doorstep, he was going to get an earful. She had better things to do than sit around and wait for him to arrive. *Or worry over him.*

Jennings opened the door, and Mr. Finch fell against him. The butler caught him but sagged under the weight. He sent Olivia a frightened look and held up a bloody hand.

"Get him inside." She flew down the hall. "Close the door and lock it."

Laying the injured man on the floor, Jennings quickly latched the door.

She dropped to her knees beside her student. He'd taken a beating; blood seemed to be everywhere but mostly on his shirtfront where two crimson stains continued to grow. "Who did this to you?"

"Lazarus," Mr. Finch said as he struggled to sit up.

"Will did this to you?" Olivia recoiled in shock.

He grabbed the front of her gown and pulled her to him. "Get Lazarus."

"We will," she soothed, easing him back to the floor.

"Send for him," he said, his voice an urgent whisper. "Yer not safe." His eyes rolled back in his head, and his hand fell limp against his chest.

"Daniel," Olivia yelled, checking Mr. Finch's breathing.

The footman came running.

"Find Lazarus. Hurry. Tell him to come. Tell him we need him. Tell him Mr. Finch has been attacked."

"I'll use the private lane and cross over Lady Bagley's property in case the house is being watched." Without waiting for a response, Daniel spun on his heel and ran toward the servants' entrance.

"Help me move him to the patient room," Olivia ordered as she grasped Mr. Finch's arms. "Jennings," she commanded when the butler hadn't moved.

He grabbed Mr. Finch's legs, and between the two of them, they managed to maneuver him into the small examining room and onto the cot. Olivia quickly washed her hands never taking her gaze from the unconscious man before her. Who could have done this to him? And why? But those were questions to be pondered later.

"Go get Bridget and lock yourselves in one of your rooms." At Jennings' sound of protest, "I don't know what's happening, but I won't have you or Bridget hurt because of something I may have brought to our home because of my association with Mr. Finch...or Lazarus."

Olivia ripped Mr. Finch's shirt open and ceased breathing for a moment. Multiple stab wounds marred his chest and shoulders. "Go," she ordered when she realized Jennings still stood in the room.

"I may be old, Miss Olivia, but I am not a coward. I will not hide in my room to leave you to face whatever may happen." He gestured to the man before her. "And it looks as though you'll need help caring for your friend. I'll fetch Bridget, but I *will* be back to assist you."

Olivia glanced up for a quick second, watching Jennings leave the room. While he was right, she did need help, she wished he would have done as she bid.

The two servants hurried into the room and quickly set to work. Bridget handed Olivia the implements she needed while Jennings set about cutting away Mr. Finch's clothes so Olivia could better examine him for other injuries.

Olivia tied the last stitch in the laceration nearest

his heart. She had probed the opening and saw no blood welling up from the region of his heart, but it caused her to worry he could bleed internally. Thankfully, most of the wounds didn't seem very deep, though the gash across his palm did cause her concern.

She began wiping the blood from his nose when she heard the main door to the house close. She handed the cloth to Bridget and put a finger to her lips signaling them to remain silent. Slipping from the room, she closed the door behind her with a quiet click.

Footsteps echoed down the hall, and she moved forward, trying to see who was in the house without being seen. She edged closer to the stairs. Her shoulders slumped with relief as she spied the man coming toward her.

"Phillip." She crossed the open space to meet him. Everything would be all right now. Her brother was home and would protect them until Lazarus arrived and learned why Mr. Finch was attacked.

Phillip looked her up and down. "Still pretending to be me, I see," he mocked.

Not sure what he meant, she hesitated then realized her clothes were bloodstained from attending to Mr. Finch. "A friend was hurt. I was trying to help."

Grabbing her arm, Phillip nearly pulled her off her feet. "You're helping him? Did you give him laudanum?" He shook her hard. "My laudanum. Did you give him my laudanum?"

"What are you talking about? We haven't had any laudanum in weeks." Olivia wrenched her arm free and moved away from him.

She looked at her brother, really looked at him. His hair flopped over his forehead and hung in greasy hanks to his shoulders. While naturally thin, he'd lost more weight, leaving his skin tightly stretched over his cheekbones. There was a gray pallor to his skin. His clothes looked as though he'd slept in them for weeks, and he reeked of body odor and something she didn't recognize. "What happened to you? Where have you been?"

"Who are you to question me?" he roared. "I let you live in my house, eat my food, and you dare to question what I do?"

"I'm just concerned." Something was wrong. Phillip had always been meticulous about his appearance even on the battlefield.

"I suggest you concern yourself with finding some laudanum." He advanced on her.

"I told you, there isn't any."

"Don't lie to me." He struck her across the face.

Olivia fell to her knees from the force of the blow, her hand clutching her cheek. She stared up at him in bewilderment. He had never raised a hand to her. He wasn't himself. Had Lazarus been telling the truth? Had Phillip been addicted to laudanum all this time, and she never knew it?

She struggled to her feet.

"Get the laudanum."

"Please listen to me." Olivia held out a hand to him.

He slapped it away and grabbed her by the neck, slamming her into the wall. "You." He slammed her against the wall again. "Will." And again. "Get." And again. "Me." And again. "Laudanum."

He released her, and Olivia slid down the wooden paneling to land in a heap on the floor. She fought to stay conscious. She had to protect Jennings and Bridget.

She looked up at her brother. He gazed down at her, hatred twisting his features.

"Get up," he ordered.

She put her hands on the floor and pulled her knees under her, willing her legs to hold her once she gained her feet. A vicious blow struck her in the ribs. Olivia cried out as pain exploded along her side.

"I said get up." Phillip grabbed her by the back of her gown. The sound of material tearing filled the air as he tried to lift her to her feet.

Gathering whatever strength she had, she kicked out at him, catching him along the side of the knee. His leg folded beneath him, and he fell to the floor.

"You'll pay for that, you little bitch," he snarled.

Olivia scooted away from him and pushed to her feet. She ran to the door.

His hand closed around her ankle, and she crashed to the floor, leaving her stunned. It took everything she had to roll onto her back. She had to move, tried to move, but she couldn't make her limbs cooperate.

Phillip put his hands around her neck and squeezed. Olivia tried bucking him off, her legs kicking the floor in an attempt to gain leverage.

He kept squeezing.

Unable to breathe, she clawed at his hands. She could feel her strength draining away. Her hands fluttered against his grasp before falling uselessly to her sides.

The sound of a gunshot filled the air. Phillip's body jerked, and he fell on top of her. Olivia pushed at him and rolled a few inches away, gasping for breath. She turned her head and looked at him. His eyes stared at her, but there was no life left in them. Blood streamed from his open mouth to pool on the floor.

She scrambled to her feet and halted in mid-movement, her hand clutched against her throat.

Patrick stood in front of her, a pistol in his hand.

"Are you all right?" He moved toward her but kept a measure of distance between.

Looking from the gun to Phillip to Patrick, she made the connection and nodded.

Will raced into the room and with a howl of rage, launched himself at Patrick. The two men fell to the floor with a crash. Will landed blow after blow while the younger man tried to ward them off.

Olivia rushed across the room. "Will, stop." She wrapped her hands in the collar of his coat and tried to pull him off Patrick. "Stop. He saved me. Will, please."

Her words finally penetrating, he pushed himself off the youth and rose. "He saved you?"

She nodded. "Phillip, he was…" She touched her neck. "You were right. He was addicted to laudanum."

"Opium," Patrick corrected. "Finch paid the men who run the opium dens to deny St. Germaine access. When he couldn't get any more opium, he became desperate. It was why he came here looking for laudanum."

"How do you know this?" Olivia asked.

"I overheard Finch telling Lazarus what he planned ta flush St. Germaine out. I thought it best to keep an eye on the dens and see what happened."

"I see you are learning what I've been trying to tell you all along. Knowledge is the true power." Will offered Patrick his hand. "Thank you for being there when Olivia needed help."

The young man blushed and looked at her, sorrow in his gaze. "I'm sorry for what I done to you before. And I'm sorry for killing yer brother."

"You didn't truly kill him," Olivia said in a soft voice. "I think the brother I knew died a very long time ago."

Patrick gave her a sad smile of thanks and left the room.

Will touched her swollen cheek with a gentle fingertip. "Are you certain you are unhurt?"

"I will be fine. The blood is from Mr. Finch. I think Phillip may have been the one who attacked him."

"How is he?"

"He's lost a great deal of blood, but I think he will recover."

"Good." Will drew her into his arms, needing to feel her heartbeat against his.

"Will," she sighed his name against his chest.

"Lazarus."

Will looked over Olivia's head to the man in the doorway, two constables standing behind him. "Durant."

"Mr. Durant? How?" Olivia turned.

"I sent Harry to fetch him when Daniel found me. I wasn't certain what was happening. I wasn't sure if you would need the Watch."

The Runner came into the room. "Who would have believed that—Lazarus sending for the law." His gaze shifted from Phillip's body to Will. "I see I wasn't mistaken in my thinkin' the constables would be necessary."

"My...my brother, he attacked Mr. Finch. I was caring for him when Phillip arrived. He demanded laudanum, but there is none. He became enraged. He…" Olivia faltered, her hand touching her cheek then her throat.

"He attacked her." Will stepped into the breach. "He was strangling her. I—"

"I shot him. Lazarus left a pistol with me in case any of his associates tried to hurt Miss Olivia."

Will stared at Jennings in shock. The butler was lying through his teeth. Why was he covering for Patrick, for him?

Durant looked like he wasn't quite convinced Jennings told the truth. He glanced between the two men. Will couldn't let Olivia's servant be taken into custody for killing her brother. He took a step forward, determined to tell the Runner the truth, whatever the outcome.

The butler caught his eye and gave a slight shake of his head. "I'm speaking the truth. Do you think I would confess to killing a man when I didn't? Especially if that man was Miss Olivia's brother?"

"I suppose not," Durant said grudgingly. He waved the two constables forward. "Remove the body." He turned to Olivia. "You'll have to make the necessary arrangements for burial."

"Yes. I will as soon as possible." She averted her gaze as the two law officers carried her brother from the room.

"Lazarus." Durant gave him a nod of farewell and left the room.

Will breathed a sigh of relief. He'd been certain the Bow Street Runner would have used St. Germaine's death as a means to have him taken to Newgate.

Olivia stood in the doorway, watching the men

leave.

He came up behind her and led her down the hall to the library, giving the servants the chance to clean up the blood without her being present. Unable to help himself, he wrapped his arms around her, reassuring himself that she truly was all right.

He couldn't believe he almost lost her. He'd nearly thrown away any chance he had at happiness in order to keep her safe from Hammond, and she almost died at the hands of her brother.

He tipped her mouth to his and gave her a soft gentle kiss that grew in intensity. She met him eagerly, her arms twining around his neck. He gave her one last kiss.

Lifting his head, he held her close. "I don't know what I would have done if anything had happened to you." He rested his hands on her shoulders. "I thought I knew everything I needed to and then I met you. Since then I've learned it's not what you have in life, but who you have in it. I've learned you can do something in an instant that will give you a lifetime of heartache. I've learned these things because of you. But most importantly, I've learned the circumstances of my upbringing may have influenced who I am, but I am responsible for the man I've become. And I want to be a better man. You make me want to be a better man. I know I have no right but…" He reached into his pocket and pulled out a small gift box. He took her hand and placed it in the center of her palm.

Olivia hesitated then lifted the lid. Nestled in a bed of white satin, sat two geese fashioned out of gold, their wings spread as though they were in mid-flight. She lifted the brooch out of the box and gave him a quizzical look.

Will took the pin from her. "Did you know geese mate for life?" He fastened it to her dress. "Will you be mine for the rest of our lives?"

"I don't understand." Olivia backed away from him. "You said you didn't care about me. You said I was convenient."

"I didn't want Hammond to know how much you mean to me. I was afraid he'd hurt you to get to me. I had to say those things, pretend to come to Belle's for one of her girls, to make him believe you weren't important. I swear I did not touch one of her girls." The look of uncertainty in her eyes pushed him forward. "I'm so sorry. Sorry for the things I did that hurt you. I'm sorry for the things I said, and I'm sorry for the things I haven't said."

"What haven't you said?" Skepticism colored her voice.

"I should have told you long ago, but I was…afraid."

"The great Lazarus?" she scoffed. "What could you possibly be frightened of?"

"I'm afraid of a great deal—Losing you. Not having you in my life. Loving you.

"You love me?" she asked, shock and awe filling her gaze.

He took her hands in his. "I have loved you from the moment you didn't turn away from me once you knew who and what I was. You came into my life like an unexpected gift. One I didn't even know I needed until it was given to me."

She smiled, happiness lighting her face. "I believe those are the best kinds of gifts." She sobered. "What about Hammond? What's to keep him from striking out at you through me?"

"He and I have come to a mutually beneficial agreement. He will take control of the docks, the smuggling operations, and the rest on the condition he doesn't strike out at anyone associated with me. I will still keep the warehouse and continue to use the docks to offload the ships I have contracts with to sell their cargo. I was just leaving a meeting with him when Daniel found me and told me you needed me."

"How can you be certain he will keep his word?"

"I've given Hammond what he's wanted for years. The docks. He knows I can take them back in an instant. And with him taking over the smuggling operations and such, I now have the power to send him to gaol. One word about what truly goes on there in Durant's ear, and Hammond will be lucky if he ever takes a breath outside of Newgate again. He knows not to cross me."

Will clasped his hands around her waist and leaned back to look down at her. "So you will marry me? Despite my past?"

"Yes." Olivia laughed. "Yes. I will marry you."

"Thank God. I'd hate to think I nearly died for nothing."

Will turned to see Finch propped up in the doorway, Daniel on one side, and Jennings on the other. Happiness bubbled up inside him and laughter spilled out.

Perhaps a life on the right side of the law wouldn't be so bad after all. And with Olivia by his side, he could finally be the person he always wanted to be.

A word about the author...

When Katherine started talking to her friends about the characters in her head as though they were real people, she decided it was time to start putting all those people populating her mind along with their exploits down on paper. Friends have gotten used to Katherine's imaginary friends but still often ask, "Wait, is this a real person?" whenever she mentions someone they don't know.

Katherine lives in upstate NY with her family but threatens to move South at the beginning of every winter season.

Contact and friend Katherine on Facebook by searching for **Katherine Grey, author** or visit her blog at http://katherinegrey.blogspot.com.